SOVEREIGN SACRIFICE

AIR AWAKENS: VORTEX CHRONICLES

BOOK FOUR

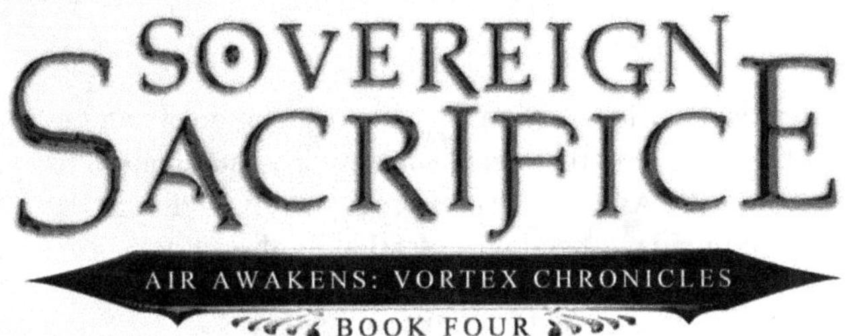

SOVEREIGN SACRIFICE

AIR AWAKENS: VORTEX CHRONICLES

BOOK FOUR

ELISE KOVA

Silver Wing Press

Published by Silver Wing Press
Copyright © 2019 by Elise Kova

Cover Artwork by Livia Prima
Editing by Rebecca Faith Editorial

eISBN: 978-1-949694-13-0
ISBN (paperback): 978-1-949694-14-7
ISBN (hardcover): 978-1-949694-15-4

Books in the Air Awakens Universe

AIR AWAKENS SERIES
Air Awakens
Fire Falling
Earth's End
Water's Wrath
Crystal Crowned

GOLDEN GUARD TRILOGY
The Crown's Dog
The Prince's Rogue
The Farmer's War

VORTEX CHRONICLES
Vortex Visions
Chosen Champion
Failed Future
Sovereign Sacrifice
Crystal Caged

A TRIAL OF SORCERERS
A Trial of Sorcerers

Also by Elise Kova

LOOM SAGA
The Alchemists of Loom
The Dragons of Nova
The Rebels of Gold

MARRIED TO MAGIC
A Deal with the Elf King

See all books and learn more at:
http://www.EliseKova.com

*to the hundred and eleven
who have my eternal gratitude*

CONTENTS

THE
MAIN CONTINENT
VANGAR
GRAYSTO
SOLARIN
"THE CAPITAL"
RIVEND
MOSANT
THE GREAT IMPERIAL WAY
TIX
OPARIUM
THE
SOUTH
LYNDUM
PACA
LEOUL
SHAN
THE FINSHAR
DELTA
HASTAN
THE
EAST
CYVEN

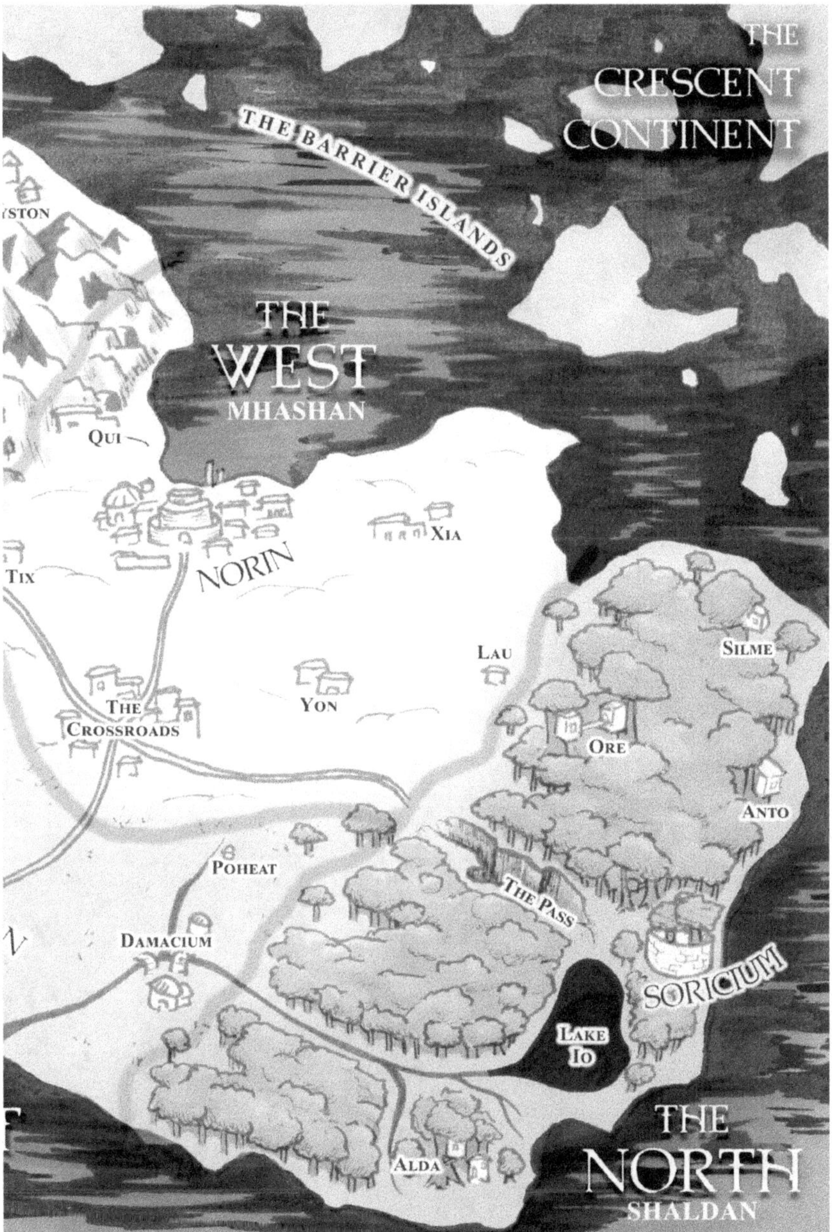

THE CRESCENT CONTINENT
THE BARRIER ISLANDS
THE WEST
MHASHAN
YSTON
QUI
XIA
TIX
NORIN
LAU
SILME
YON
THE CROSSROADS
ORE
ANTO
POHEAT
THE PASS
DAMACIUM
SORICIUM
LAKE IO
ALDA
THE NORTH
SHALDAN

N
DOLARIAN
DARK ISLE
BEAUTY'S BEND
TEETER ISLE
LITTLE BROTHER BAY
NORIN
MONLAN
GREATER ATOLL
SHATTERED INLET
VARGA
TWILIGHT FOREST
BELLAST
MAROON ATOLL
TORIS
DANT
MALLON
DIAMOND SANDS ISLES
THE SHATTERED ISLES
RISEN
MERU
WARICH
FARTH
ISLE OF FROST
LUTH
HOKOH
CASTAWAY ISLE

PROLOGUE

FIERA EASED HERSELF AWAY from the smoldering remnants of the fire she'd been using to peer along the Mother's red lines of fate to catch glimpses of the future. She sat back on her heels, hands on her thighs, and stared out the wide, open window that overlooked her dying city. She had been charged with the sole duty of protecting them… and she had failed.

"At least it will finally be over," she said thoughtfully. The words made her vision real.

For nearly ten long years, the Solaris Empire, led by Tiberus Solaris, had laid siege to Norin. Mhashan would not fall easily. Fiera had used the sword to see to that. And her father would never surrender; the blood of the greatest king to ever live, King Jadar, flowed through his veins and hers. They had a family name to honor, though their ideas about how exactly to do so couldn't have been more different.

She pushed herself away from the small fire pit, standing. Her scrying room was attached to one of her sitting rooms, accessible through a curtain. Fiera made her way across her chambers and into her closet. She'd need her finest to deliver this message. If they were to fall, they would fall with the same dignity they'd lived and fought with.

Dressed in deep crimson splashed with accents of bright silver, a decorative pauldron over one shoulder with chain mail draping off, Fiera stepped into the halls of the castle.

Things were quiet. But they usually were these days. Hunger was beginning to scrape the very bottom of every citizen's stomach. Most of the castle staff had been dismissed long ago with the command to conserve their energy. Fiera knew at least half of them were dead now.

Only an extremely loyal few remained at their posts.

Heading down a wide staircase, Fiera stepped into a side hallway accessible through a narrow door on the side of the stairs. When she was a girl, this hall had been filled with the sweet scents of perfume and fine soaps, imported from the Crossroads. Now, it was merely damp. Humidity beaded on the walls from the heated washing tubs. Sweet-smelling soaps had run out long ago; now, the best they could do to clean their clothes was boil them.

A middle-aged man tended the steaming tubs. Magic radiated off of him, sparking throughout the room as he kept each of the large, wooden basins bubbling hot. He went from tub to tub, stirring the contents.

"Hanc."

"Your highness." The man released the over-sized spoon he'd been holding and dipped low into a bow. When Fiera was young, an elderly woman would threaten to crack her knuckles with the too-large spoons if she was caught snatching soap shavings for her personal use. Fiera didn't know where the woman was now; she'd vanished like all of Hanc's other helpers. "What can I do for you?"

"I need you to collect all the bedsheets in the castle and begin stitching them together." Luckily, the tubs were filled with colored garments. That meant he should have plenty of white sheets at his disposal. "It doesn't matter if they're clean and the stitches do not need to be tidy—merely sturdy." He stared at her, clearly working to process the odd request. "I need you to do this with haste, as many as you can. Do you understand?"

"Yes, your highness," Hanc said slowly. Then, timidly, "Any particular way they should be stitched together?"

"Not really. So long as they are white—or close enough to white—and the banner you make is large, it should be enough."

"I shall do so when I finish this wash and—"

"You shall do so now," Fiera interrupted firmly. "There is precious little time. Remember, you need to do as many as your hands can bear in the coming hours and only stop when the time comes to use what you have produced." Hanc gave a small nod. Fiera wished she could tell him more, but it was better not to. They all needed to keep their faith in these final hours. Ignorance while doing so was the best she could give them. Fiera went to leave, but paused in the doorway. "One more thing."

"Yes?"

"Tell no one of this task save my brother. But wait to go to him until the time is right. Perform your duty as discretely as possible. Start with the sheets not on beds to avoid suspicion, then those in vacant rooms. Use my quarters if you need a place to work." Fiera doubted she would spend much time in them in the hours to come.

"How will I know the time is right?"

"Trust me when I say that you will." It would be obvious what he was making when the time came for it—if it wasn't obvious already. "Work with speed, Hanc."

"Yes, your highness."

Fiera left him and started back up the stairs. Her hands worried the familiar stone banisters as she wound up to the royal council rooms. A war council was convened at all times of the day, it seemed, though the discussions had dulled the longer the siege dragged on.

When she stepped into the stately room, the men and women who had been lounging in velvet tufted chairs stood instantly.

"Your highness." They bowed rigidly, hands at their sides.

"Captain." Zira, Fiera's head knight and right hand, saluted.

"Report on the city's status," Fiera commanded.

"Grain stores have been entirely depleted outside the castle," Denja reported, adjusting the scarf around her head. She had once been a councilor of commerce, and a good one at that. But the war had robbed her of much purpose other than rationing. Perhaps, in the days to come, her skills with negotiation could be put to use again. "We're relying entirely on the sea now." Her eyes were now on Twintle.

"In the waters we dare to sail, fishing has been scarce... Though, the fishermen claim that with the season's shift, new fish should come to the area. There's still the reserve of dried fish at my warehouse at the docks," Twintle, councilor for maritime, picked up Denja's report.

"No breaches reported by the guard along the outer wall. No movements of the Imperial army since half their forces retreated two weeks ago," Zira added.

It was a standard report Fiera had been receiving for years now. The only variant was that each time she heard it, there was less and less to say. Most had thought she was far too young to be placed at the head of the Knights of Jadar five years ago when it happened at her seventeenth birthday. But war changed girls into women, and softness into steel.

"Any report of Imperial ships at sea?"

Twintle shook his head. "Not since our last effort to drive them away."

"The pirate Adela?"

"No sightings," Twintle said, with no small amount of relief.

Fiera nodded, relieved as well. They had enough to worry about. Adela could go terrorize the brutish and uneducated masses on the Crescent Continent.

"Open the grain stores of the castle to the soldiers. Denja, anything you can dredge up from the bottom of barrels in the castle or city is to be turned out. Ask the nobles again to search their larders—by surprise this time. Let's see if we can't find anything hidden away in their cabinets. All combatants have first claim. Let the people eat after our military, and then a curfew is in order. All non-combatants are to remain indoors."

"If I open my warehouse—" Lord Twintle began from the other end of the table.

"You will quickly run out. Yes, I realize." Fiera rapped her knuckles against the table twice; a ring in the shape of a silver phoenix rung out loudly. "This ends in the coming days. Feed our troops, give them strength."

"You had a vision." Ophain, her brother and eldest sibling, said softly from the head of the table opposite her. He still had not risen to greet her.

The man was a shade of his former self. Fiera remembered him towering over her with broad shoulders and a noteworthy amount of muscle ever since she was a girl. But he had been one of the first in their family to begin refusing food to help it last longer, and his perpetual fast had taken a toll.

"The Mother has blessed me with the sight," Fiera affirmed. "This ends. So if you agree with my will, brother, see it done."

All eyes shifted to Ophain. Officially, he was the head of the council as the crown prince. But Fiera was the head of the Knights of Jadar, the soldiers of the West, and that made her nearly his equal.

"I will see it done."

"Then I will be the one to tell Father," she said to him and turned to Zira. "After, I will address the people. Send criers for a royal announcement now and meet me in the armory."

"Yes, your highness." Zira bowed low, hovering there as Fiera left the room.

She rotated the heavy silver ring around her ring finger, worrying away at the smooth silver. *It would end.* She had told them the truth in that. Fiera paused, staring out a window lining the hallway. She imagined a city burning, ransacked by their enemies.

Was it wrong not to tell even her most trusted advisers *how* it would end?

Pushing the thoughts from her mind, Fiera continued on to her father's chambers. More and more often, she found him on his wide balcony. The sheer curtains that drifted in the open archways of his room obscured his form.

"Do I hear the soft footsteps of my youngest child?"

Nothing about her was still soft. "Yes, Father."

"Approach, girl."

Fiera did as she was bid. Even as the head of the Knights of Jadar, she was still a girl to her father, and no amount of cunning deeds or ruthless bloodshed would change that.

"What have you come to trouble me with?" Even as he spoke, silver crown heavy on his brow, King Rocham gazed out over the city. Fiera wondered if he, too, could imagine it burning.

"We are making preparations for the end." That brought his attention to her. Rocham's dark eyes set against leathered skin scrutinized Fiera, and she let no weakness show. "The Mother has gifted me with a vision."

"Finally," he murmured. "Well, tell me."

"This will all end soon."

"How does it end?"

"We will lose." This was the one man whom telling could make a difference—though Fiera doubted it would. She knew how deep her father's pride ran.

Rocham settled back once again to admire his kingdom, likely one of the last times he would see it in the bright afternoon sun. Soon they would be looking from this balcony at just another stretch of the Solaris Empire. The history and name of Mhashan would be wiped from the maps and reduced to "the West."

That was, assuming they still had their heads attached to their shoulders when Tiberus Solaris ruled.

"Then we shall die fighting." Her father stood and Fiera's heart sank. "As is our way."

"As the head of the Knights of Jadar, I must remind you our forces are tired and weak. If—"

"I was the one who gave you that title. It does not give you the ability to question me," he cautioned.

Fiera continued despite. "If we fight, the losses will be even greater than they otherwise have to be. Let us at least attempt peaceful negotiations."

"I tried to negotiate with the monster Solaris ten years ago. He is a power-hungry child who cannot be reasoned with."

"Father—"

"And if we are to lose," the King continued, not hearing her. "then I will die killing the bastard."

Were it not for her years of training, she would have shouted at him. Her hands would ball into fists and she would tremble with rage. But Fiera was a weapon. She'd been hammered, sharpened, and forged from birth.

Her brother would rule. Her older sisters were royal prizes— trophies to be married off as it fit the crown. Thus, her father had not needed her to be genteel. He'd needed her to be a soldier, a tool that could take the shape of whatever the kingdom required.

And that was what she had become.

"You will not kill him. With the size of the Imperial army, you will not even come close to him," Fiera said, level, as the king started into his quarters. "But perhaps we can—"

"I will take no more of your treasonous talk. The time for negotiations has long since ended. If Norin is to fall, then I shall burn it to the ground myself before I let Solaris sit on my throne." Fire sparked to life in the air over her father's shoulders.

Fiera merely stared at him, willing her face to remain passive. Not a single emotion would betray her by floating to the surface. She had weighted them all, burning them deep within the flames of her gut.

"And as the head of the Knights of Jadar, you will heed my orders. Go and ready the soldiers. Prepare them to take one last stand for King and country. Prepare them to die."

"Yes, sir." Fiera gave a bow and strode from the room, not one crack in her stony mask.

She strode down the hall and down a flight of stairs. The royal quarters were toward the top of the castle. Down and to one side were the council chambers, comprised of meeting rooms and offices. Down and to the other were the barracks, training grounds, and armory. Two strong pillars of the Ci'Dan family had lifted them centuries ago to royalty: diplomacy and combat.

Fiera strode between racks of swords in one of the oldest armories to the very back right corner, where an unassuming second door, bolted with a heavy lock, waited. At the door's side was a black-haired woman, eyes shining in the light of the mote of fire hovering over Fiera's shoulder.

"The criers have been sent. I gave them my horse to do it with," Zira reported, pushing away from the wall. "Ophain is carrying out the rest of your orders."

"To the letter?"

"To the letter."

"Good." Fiera tugged at a chain around her neck. The lock on the door had only one key—the one she was never without. Through the door was a narrow hallway, illuminated by an inferno at its end.

The wall of fire filled the stone passage, perpetually burning, just in case anyone dared try to break into this most sacred chamber. With a soft sigh, Fiera relaxed her flames. With it, the slow sap on her power vanished.

Maintaining the flame, day and night, was a leech on her. But a worthy one. For behind the wall of flame, a silver scabbard hung on a wall, embellished with rubies as large as a trout's eyes that picked up the faint blue glow emitted by the pommel.

"Zira, I fear this may be our last battle together," Fiera began as she reached for the sword. "The Mother told me little of our fates following the end of this war."

"If it is the Mother's will that I die this day, I do so with the honor of serving you," Zira said with ease. The woman was one of the greatest mercenaries ever to come out of the Nameless Company. She knew the face of death as early and as well as her own mother's. "May I make a request of you, princess?"

"Anything, you know it is yours."

"I know we spoke of my defending your family. However, if it is possible that this is our last battle together, I would like to stand by your side."

Fiera's hand ran lightly along the scabbard of the Sword of Jadar. The room was empty, save for the lone sword and a narrow table below. It made the weapon seem all the more powerful.

Yet the sword's strength was wavering. When the war started, her father told her where it had been hidden—slumbering, waiting to defend Mhashan—since the age of Jadar. Fiera had been the one to take the sword, learn what she could, and harness the latent powers of the crystal it was crafted from. Doing so had dulled the sword's energy and nearly killed her.

But the walls surrounding Mhashan had held for ten years.

"Then by my side you shall be. See to it that my brothers and sisters are protected by the best in your stead. Entrust the key to the old escape route to my brother, if need be."

"What about your father?" Zira missed nothing.

"The king can defend himself," Fiera said, deathly quiet. Her father had his chance to live for the people and refused. So she would let him die with his mistakes; his fate was on his shoulders alone. "Do not waste the loyalty of good men on him." Fiera pried her gaze away from the weapon to look Zira in the eye. The woman had been with her now for four years and, from the start, they seemed to have a bond that transcended words.

Fiera felt fate keenly. She knew its pull, just as she knew when someone's red lines were knotted to hers. She might not always understand the purpose right away, but the Mother revealed all in time.

"Understood," Zira said with a small bow.

Without a moment's more hesitation, Fiera lifted the Sword of Jadar and strapped it to her wide belt. It was cumbersome. But so were the trappings of leadership. She had born worse burdens and still walked.

Zira at her side, they left the castle together. A score of Knights joined them in the royal stables—right at the end of the long drawbridge that connected the castle to the city across a wide, dry moat. Fiera doubted her father would even raise the drawbridge. He'd convinced himself he was ready for this fight, ready to meet his end.

She, however, was not ready to meet hers. Someone needed to defend the people of Mhashan, even after they became citizens of the Solaris Empire. She held the sword that could do just that.

Fiera sought a life of service, not glory in death.

At the end of the drawbridge, their group of Knights met with another already there, filling in the gaps. They all wore red armbands bearing the seal of the Phoenix of the West, a sword clutched in its talons, emblazoned in silver. A crate had been carried out for her to stand on.

There were no cheers or fanfare as she stood atop the humble wooden box, looking out over those assembled. Fiera took a slow breath and clutched the leather-wrapped pommel of the sword. She tried to draw power from it—whatever power was left—so she could find the strength to do what must be done.

"People of the West, this siege has gone on for nearly ten long years," Fiera began, her voice echoing off the buildings that lined the square. "But I am Fiera, Princess of Mhashan, youngest daughter to King Rocham, and head of the Knights of Jadar, and I have received a vision from the Mother above. The end is near, and we must be ready for it."

“I CANNOT TELL YOU what the final outcome will be—the goddess did not bless me with this knowledge.”

Vi watched Fiera speak from among the crowd. She was still shaking, but no longer from the remnants of the goddess's power surging through her as she was thrown through time and space. Now, she shook because of the face she stared at.

Fiera was dead.

The woman standing before her, speaking before her, had long been a corpse in the world Vi knew. It should be all the proof she needed that the goddess had, truly, remade a new world. But Vi's mind couldn't comprehend it. Her head ached just trying to.

“But I can tell you that it will end soon,” the princess continued to the blank-eyed, defeated masses. “We are feeding our soldiers and Knights with the last of the food stores, so they might better protect you. Whatever is left will go to women and children first, then all others.

“A curfew has been set on the city for civilians. Everyone is to be in their homes between the hours of one in the afternoon, until eleven in the morning."

She could hear and understand the language of old Mhashan—Vi realized—a language she'd only studied a handful of times with her tutors and had been very far from mastering mere hours ago. She was able to comprehend it without effort.

Hours ago? Or had it been days? Or years? How long had she been with the goddess? How long had it been since Taavin—

Her mind stalled, hand instinctively going to the watch around her neck. *Taavin.* Her last memories of the man were clouded with hurt and confusion, punctuated by a fire that burned so brightly it consumed him.

"That's only two hours we can be about," someone murmured from Vi's side.

"This isn't a curfew—it's more like house arrest," someone else said, oblivious to her panic. They were all oblivious to her. Not one person had the slightest idea that a traveler from a distant time was among them.

"If you do not have a timepiece, or can't otherwise accurately tell time by the sun, you are encouraged to err on the side of caution and remain indoors," Fiera continued, ignoring the growing murmurs rippling through the crowd. When she spoke, the people stilled, as though transfixed. Fiera had a magnetic quality Vi could feel influencing her, even through her relative panic. "This is for your protection. The only people that should be in the streets are soldiers."

Dawning recognition washed over Vi: Fiera was trying to prevent citizens from getting caught in the crossfire.

"You have one hour to collect what food and supplies you can before we all settle in for this long night." Fiera drew a sword and Vi nearly let out an involuntary shout of surprise. Her hands flew to her mouth, suppressing a strangled gasp as the princess lifted the shimmering weapon above her head. "Flame burn eternal!"

"And guide us through the night," the citizens around her chanted, going stiff with arms at their sides in a sort of Western salute.

Vi didn't say anything. She didn't mirror the salute. Her sole focus was on the crystal sword Fiera had lofted over her head.

A sword that should've been long destroyed, held by a woman who should've been long dead.

The princess left with her host of Knights. The rest of the castle guard walked through the crowd, encouraging people to disperse.

She turned on her heel and pulled up the hood of the tunic she was wearing. It kept the heat of the afternoon sun off her brow, and it kept her from making eye contact with anyone. Vi stayed with the masses until they mostly disappeared and she was alone once more in an all-too-quiet street.

A door caught her eye. It was unassuming, wooden, nearly identical to most others. But this one she remembered. Vi walked over slowly, running her hand along the wood. For some reason, this door stuck in her mind, vivid with the ghost of a white X that had been painted on it when she'd last been in Norin.

"No White Death," she whispered.

"Excuse me, can I help you?" Vi jumped, looking over her shoulder at a young woman who stood behind her. She couldn't be older than fifteen and carried a mostly empty basket—save for two tiny jars of what Vi recognized as spices and a hunk of dry fish meat. The young woman's eyes widened. "P-princess?"

"No, I'm—" Vi didn't get a chance to finish before the woman was on the ground, head bowed.

"Princess, you grace our humble doorstep. May I invite you in? What service can we give you?"

"I'm not the princess." Vi knelt down, pulling back her hood. Fiera's hair ran down her shoulder blades, where Vi's stopped just past her shoulders. The hair alone wasn't enough, as the woman studied Vi's face. It took longer than Vi would've expected for her to finally admit that she wasn't the princess. But then again, a commoner like her likely had only ever seen Fiera from a distance.

"But... you look just like her."

"I know, many have told me." Vi reached out, grabbed the

woman's basket, and returned it to her. Every moment felt as though she was underwater, moving against the current.

I'm not the princess. She wasn't the princess this woman was thinking of. She wasn't Fiera. But she also wasn't a princess at all… not anymore.

The crown princess, Vi Solaris, was gone.

"What do you need, then?" The young woman took the basket, clutching it protectively, as though Vi had been trying to steal it rather than return it.

"I'm a bit lost." That was the best way to put it, though it was a drastic understatement.

"Lost? What area of town are you from?"

Vi's mind retrieved a map of Norin easily from the depths of her cartographic knowledge. She could pick anywhere and make it believable. But she wasn't from anywhere here, and picking somewhere at random wouldn't help her. She needed a quiet place to get her thoughts in order, not an easy way out of this encounter.

"I don't remember," Vi lied, rubbing her head for emphasis. She stood. "I woke up in a stable. And I don't remember anything before then." It was easy to inject the words with the slightest bit of panic and terror. She had more than enough of each to go around. "I don't know where to go and I don't know how to find out."

The young woman shifted, tucking a section of bangs behind her ear. "We don't have anything to give you."

"May I just sit on your doorstep, then?" Vi asked. "Your second floor juts out slightly and gives some shade from the afternoon sun."

"Fine." The young woman pushed past her. "Just don't think of trying to come in." She slammed the door shut behind her, and Vi was alone.

She crouched down and sat on the stoop. Her hands worried the watch at her neck as her brain tried to organize her thoughts.

An hour must've passed, for guards began to sweep through the city, telling the few stragglers on the streets that the curfew had come into effect and it was time to go inside. Just as Vi was about to use her Lightspinning to make herself invisible, a guard started her way and she cursed her luck. She couldn't blink out of existence now.

"You, it's time to go inside," the man commanded gruffly. Vi was focused on the red strip of fabric that circled his bicep. The symbol of the Knights of Jadar instantly unnerved her. But at this point in history, the group had yet to splinter and turn on her family. "Did you hear me? Go inside."

"I don't have anywhere to go."

"Get inside," the man repeated, pointing to the door.

"This isn't my home."

"Then go back to your home."

A bitter, raspy laugh escaped her lips. "If only. I don't have a home."

"Please, I don't want any trouble." The man sighed and glanced over at his fellow soldiers. They had already moved on. "If you truly don't have a home, there are shelters not far from the castle. I don't care where you end up. But I can't leave you out here. Anyone who's not a soldier or a Knight must be indoors, royal orders."

Soldier or a Knight. She could fight. The thought hovered in her mind for a long second. Vi opened her mouth before closing it again slowly. Would she fight against her grandfather?

On one side of this war was her grandmother, on the other her grandfather. Her heritage versus her Empire. Though it wasn't even *her* Empire anymore. Vi let out a groan and held her head.

"What's wrong with you?"

The door at Vi's right opened suddenly, the young woman from earlier in its frame. "She's with us—I mean, she's not. But we'll take her in."

"What?" Vi wasn't sure if she said the word in her surprise or just thought it loudly.

"Come on, inside with you." The woman grabbed her arm, helping Vi up.

"See to it that none of you are caught out past curfew," the

Knight cautioned with a pointed look at Vi before starting along.

"We'll follow orders," the young woman called back. Without another word, Vi was ushered inside a tiny foyer connected to a narrow stair. There were no other doors and the top landing was dark enough that Vi couldn't make out much. The woman locked the door and leaned against it with a sigh.

"Thank you," Vi said softly.

"Don't thank me, thank Granny. She was the one who said I couldn't leave another woman out there to fend for herself." She looked Vi up and down and added with a mutter, "Though you seem perfectly capable."

"I still appreciate it." Vi didn't comment on her capacity to defend herself.

"Well, show that appreciation by not making us regret it." The young woman ran a hand through her short-cut hair. "The name is Lucina, by the way."

"Nice to meet you, Lucina."

"Do you remember your name? Or is that gone too?"

"It's gone too." Vi didn't know what compelled her to hide her name. No one knew of Vi Solaris in this world. Her name, however unconventional it was, would mean nothing.

Yet that was precisely the reason why she didn't want to share it. Her name was precious—the only thing that was truly hers that she still carried. Even the watch around her neck was different than the one she had received from Fritz. Her mother's watch had been destroyed, the replacement from Taavin now hanging in its place.

Call out to me. Some of his final words thrummed across her thoughts like fingers dancing on the strings of a harp. *When you are settled, call out to me.*

"Well, I'll need some sort of name. Can't just say, 'Hey, no-name girl,' whenever I need you."

"How about Yullia?"

"Yullia it is." Lucina ascended the stairs. "Granny is sleeping, so don't wake her." Her voice had fallen to a hush. "Granny sleeps in the living area on the first floor. I have a room on the second floor. You can take dad's old room."

Before Vi could inquire further, Lucina pressed a finger to her lips as they emerged onto a landing area that was utilized as a living space. There was a kitchen, a sitting area with distinctly low-profile, Western furniture, and a cot in the corner where an ancient woman snored. Lucina headed up a ladder in the corner to the floor above. Vi followed as silently as possible.

"You'll be in here." Lucina opened the door immediately to the right at the top of the ladder.

"Your father won't need it?"

"Dad's dead."

"I'm sorry," Vi said. But her tenderness seemed to confuse the young woman. "Did… I say something wrong?"

"Half of this city is dying or dead. It's weird to hear sympathies and I don't want them." Lucina shrugged and hastily changed the topic. "Remember, we don't have anything for you. All you're getting is a bed. If I even catch you looking at our food—" She drew a kitchen knife from her belt "—I won't hesitate to kill. No one would notice or care about another body."

Vi lifted a hand, placed her fingers against the flat of the blade, and pushed it away. "I'm not going to give you reason to fear me," she said firmly, locking eyes with Lucina. "I mean you no harm."

"Well…" Lucina hadn't been expecting Vi to take the threat in stride. She tucked the weapon back in her belt. "See that you don't."

The young woman started for the ladder and descended quickly. Vi made a point to close her door loudly enough that Lucina would hear it—but hopefully not too loudly that it disturbed the sleeping old woman whom she had to thank for this hospitality.

The room was small. A bed, a chest at its foot. A narrow window, barely large enough to let light in, faced the blank wall of another building.

Vi sat heavily on the bed, sinking her face into her hands, her elbows on her knees. An ache ran so deeply within her that she didn't know where it stemmed from, or what hurt most. Physically, her body felt fine. No, great. Not even the scars from Ulvarth's shackles marred her wrists. Yet her joints seemed to protest every movement, as if they carried an invisible weight.

Quiet had never been so loud.

"What is going on?" she whispered to no one. A hand dropped to the watch around her neck. Magic pulsed under her fingertips.

This watch—no, not *this* one… but a watch nearly identical to it had connected her with Taavin. It had begun this whole relentless series of events that had chewed her up and now spit her out in a place she had no business being.

"Curse you," she muttered, burying her face in her hands again. She didn't know who she was cursing. The goddess, Taavin, fate itself? All of them, *curse all of them*, for all she cared. "You told me to summon you? Summon a dead man?" Vi laughed, a sound that was crazy to her own ears. "Fine, Taavin. I'll honor your mad, last wish. *Narro hath hoolo.*"

The words sparked in her mind, bright and true. Meaning poured from them into glowing lines of yellow light that spun from her like ropes of fire. They connected to form familiar glyphs.

From those glyphs came the outline of a man—a man she thought she'd killed with her own hands. A man whose brilliant green eyes could not be dulled by the sands of time no matter how many times they were turned over.

"T-Taavin?"

2

Ｈ̲Ｅ ＳＴＡＲＥＤ ＡＴ ＨＥＲ for a long minute before looking around the room, much as he always had whenever she'd summoned him. As though this interaction was perfectly normal and planned.

As though she hadn't *killed him* hours before.

The facts compounded on the surreal nature of her current state, making it feel as though she watched him from outside of her body. Their roles were reversed. She was the specter, and he was the real person.

Because nothing about her world could possibly be real right now.

"I see you've found some quiet corner to hide in." He breathed a sigh of relief. "Where are you this time? I don't recognize this place."

"I don't recognize any of this." Vi was on her feet, working to keep her voice quiet. The building was sturdy and seemed well-built. But Lucina and her grandmother would definitely hear if panic got the better of her and she began to shout. Vi took a staggering step closer to him. "Taavin… where are you? What's going on? Are you all right?"

Her hands reached for him as she drew closer. Closer to the man she had killed. Closer to the man who had held and hurt her. Nearly close enough to touch, to reassure herself that this wasn't a psychotic break.

Taavin's fingers wrapped around hers. They weren't as solid as she remembered. Was this identical to how she'd first spoken to him in Shaldan? He'd seemed so real then, as though he'd been standing in the room with her. Now, the ghost of magic wriggled around his body. It created a barrier she couldn't seem to cross.

He uncurled one hand and pointed his index finger at the watch over her chest. "I'm here."

"The watch?" Vi looked down at the faintly shimmering glyphs that hovered over the token. "Yes, I remember it connects me to you, but where are *you*?"

Pain flashed through his familiar emerald eyes. Taavin opened his mouth, then closed it, as if unable to find the words. His finger had yet to move. "I'm *here*."

"In the watch?" Vi dared to ask. Taavin nodded. "But… how?"

"The watch was the key to it all." She remembered him saying as much in Risen. "In it were my memories… all of them. In it, the Champion's future is ensured and preserved. In it, my consciousness now lives, so I may guide you."

"I don't understand." She wanted to. Vi repeated his words mentally, but she couldn't siphon out the deeper meaning clearly hidden beneath them.

"One moment." Taavin gave her hand a light squeeze and, without further warning, stepped away. He stretched out his arms before him and curled his open palms, as though holding an invisible book. His lips moved with low whispering tones; it must have been some kind of Lightspinning, but Vi couldn't make out a single word. She suspected that even if she could, she wouldn't have understood them.

This was a magic the goddess had given only to him.

The glyphs above her watch spun faster. Like a spigot, magic poured from the necklace into symbols that hovered between Taavin's arms. He watched them carefully as they piled, one atop the next, shifting and changing. The green of his eyes faded to the same pale blue as his magic, glowing brightly in the dark room.

Finally, Taavin lowered his arms, the light between them vanishing into the still air.

"All right, I think I've cobbled together the swiftest explanation that will make it easiest for you to understand," he began. "You met Yargen, correct?"

"Yes."

"What did she tell you?"

Vi sighed and closed her eyes, thinking back to her interaction with the goddess. She remembered pain, then life, then Queen Lumeria—who hadn't actually been Queen Lumeria, but Yargen masquerading as the sovereign.

"She told me… That she was restarting the world," Vi paraphrased. "Returning me to a time before her power had been turned against itself, and destroyed."

"Exactly. You know what time you're in, yes?"

"Norin fell in three hundred twenty-two." Vi raised a hand to her forehead and shook her head. "Just saying that aloud is madness."

"Yet you know it to be true. You can feel it in your marrow, just as you can feel Yargen's power. This will all be easier if you don't try to fight the truths before you."

"Don't tell me what I can and can't feel," Vi snapped. She was a rope fraying at all sides. "I'm sorry, I didn't mean to be curt," Vi said hastily. "It's a lot to process is all. I was just thrown back in time and now I'm talking with someone akin to a ghost. Not to say I'm not happy to see you, but…" She trailed off in the wake of Taavin's tired smile.

"I understand. You're not alone in feeling jarred by all this. From my perspective, I just died for the ninety-third time and it gets no easier."

"Ninety… third?" Vi repeated. He seemed determined to look anywhere but at her.

"This point in time is the furthest at which Yargen can remake the world with the limited power she had," he continued, determined to ignore her probing stare. "So it is where our work must begin. Your job is twofold. Foremost, your goal is to ensure the birth of a new Champion and another attempt, should you fail. While doing so, you must collect the crystal weapons in order to consolidate Yargen's power once more and prevent Raspian from ever being set free."

"So I am to change the past?"

"There is no past—not the past you knew, at least," he said gravely. "The only time that exists is the one in which Yargen exists. The world you and I knew, the world we were born into, is no more. She lives in this world now, in you."

"But this world exists along the same lines of fate… so it appears identical," Vi said, remembering more of what the goddess had told her. She sank heavily onto the bed behind her. "My mother, father, brother?"

"They do not exist, yet." He was silent for a long moment, then added softly and apologetically, "And the Aldrik, Vhalla, and Romulin who will exist, will not be the ones you knew."

She looked down at her hands. They were trembling again. Her whole body shook. Vi felt painfully cold, like no matter what she did, she'd never be able to warm up again. "I wanted to save them."

"Preventing the Crystal Caverns from being tampered with is how you will save them."

"No, the family I loved is gone—you just said so." Vi tilted her head up to the man as if pleading with him could change the terrible fate she found herself in. "The world was in danger, so I did everything I was told; I did everything to stop it from ending. I did it all to save my family."

"And this is how we will stop it so your family is never in danger again."

"The world—my family—merely ended at the hands of a

different tyrant!" Vi was on her feet again, pacing. Her magic crackled, stronger than ever before, ready to collect in her palms and burn the whole broken world and all its pieces. "Raspian didn't end the world, so Yargen did? So we could try to fix a new version of it? How does that make any sense?"

"The timeline we were on was a failed future. It made sense to abandon it."

"The timeline." Her hands shook harder. "Don't call it a 'timeline' as though it's just dates and facts in a book. There were *people*, Taavin. Hundreds of thousands of people. A whole world of them. My family was in that world… and they're all gone now." Vi didn't remember approaching him, but her fists knotted in the simple tunic he wore—the same garment he'd had on when she'd found him in his room that fateful night. A night that might as well have been a thousand years ago. "Yargen killed them all."

"Yargen is life. Vi, don't think of it as them dying." His hands wrapped around hers again. His tone was soothing. "As it stands now, they never existed in the first place. But fate can see them born again in this world—a world you will save. You saw it yourself, the end of the world."

For a brief second, her eyes were as haunted as his, as visions of her falling before a dark god flashed across her mind.

"If we had remained in that world, Vi," he continued, "the cycle of light and dark would've ended. Raspian and Yargen would've battled again. But since she was weak and didn't have all her power, he would've killed her for good. There would've been no eventual return of the goddess, no great war, no subsequent age of light. Darkness and death would've ruled forever. It was the end."

"You're saying no matter what… the life of everyone in that world was forfeit? Every beautiful, hidden corner, every person, all would've been destroyed?" Her voice quivered alongside her hands. She had been born into a dying world and she was the only person to survive it.

Vi felt profoundly unworthy of each breath she took.

"Yes."

"I thought, as Champion, I could save it. Save… them."

"You were chosen for this world, where you stand now. It was the last Vi's failure that doomed the world you knew." A ghost drifted around his words, one that seemed to cloud his vision whenever his eyes settled on her.

Ninety-three times. His earlier words stuck in her mind.

"How many times have we had this conversation?" Vi whispered.

"What?"

"How many times have you explained all this to me?"

"I don't know what you're asking." The lie was so obvious Vi had to bite back bitter laughter.

"Yes you do. I know you too well, Taavin; I see behind any mask you try to wear." She swallowed, her throat drier than the Waste. "This isn't the first time I've asked, is it?" Taavin pursed his lips together and narrowed his eyes. "How many times, Taavin?" she reiterated. And then, just to twist the dagger, added, "How many times have you died by my hand? Has the world been rebuilt? How many times have we tried and failed to stop Raspian? How many *other Vis* failed?"

She didn't know why she was asking. She'd already figured out the answer.

"Ninety-three."

Somehow, hearing it from his lips was worse than she expected.

Vi's fingers slowly uncurled from the man's garb. She smoothed out the wrinkles thoughtfully, almost gently. The motion was a stark contrast to the torrent of anger brewing within her. Abruptly, she went to the narrow window. It was her only source of fresh air and she desperately needed to take a breath.

"Ninety-three times," she finally repeated quietly. The world had been destroyed, rebuilt, destroyed again, over and over, ninety-three times. It was incomprehensible to her.

Mortal minds weren't made for this.

Vi stared at the stone wall outside of the window, willing the wind to blow, to feel some movement in the air. But everything was stagnant, making a hot day only hotter.

"What makes you think we can do this now?" Vi asked without looking at him.

"Nothing." That drew her eyes back. Taavin elaborated without further prompting. "I don't know if we will be successful this time, or the next, or the time after. But I have faith eventually we will. I have to, otherwise we are trapped in this torturous vortex forever, always spinning, down and down."

They were cursed. She'd known it on Meru. He'd confirmed it now.

"How long have you known this was our fate?"

"Only when you used the word *thrumsana*. It unlocked the stored memories from my past selves in the watch, returning them to me. Then, I knew what must be done to finish the turn and start anew."

Vi narrowed her eyes slightly. She vividly remembered the power that had been unleashed when she used that word. Just as vividly, she remembered learning not long before that Taavin had betrayed Vi and her father to the Swords of Light. That wound had yet to be mended, and now Vi wondered if they'd ever have the chance. Did she have any right to still be angry with him for a father that no longer existed?

The thought made her throat close up.

He had betrayed her. She had killed him. Perhaps it was better to destroy the hurt of those transgressions with the world she'd known.

Mother above, her head ached.

"What do we do now?" Vi forced herself to ask.

"We need to be careful going forward." Taavin crossed to her side. "Very careful, for a number of years. Until you ensure Vhalla receives the watch, the birth of a new Vi—a new Champion—isn't guaranteed. Which means if you die… it ends for good."

"It *will* end for good." *Ninety-three times.* That was ninety-two too many. "We will end it, this time." Vi turned to him.

Taavin placed his hand at the small of her back, staring down with worried eyes. He wasn't as warm, she realized. Little things kept adding up that made his presence here torture. He wasn't really with her any longer. *Not really.*

"I told you once: I look back, you look forward. This is the curse you always felt, but never fully knew. You're forced to see the end of the world encroaching, and you feel an obligation to try, futilely thus far, to prevent it. Whereas I…" He swallowed hard. "I remember the past. I exist to watch and be a living record of your every action. To serve as your aide in finding what will succeed by ensuring you don't repeat what failed. I remember every time you've fallen and every hurt you've endured. And the only thing that enables me to carry on is the knowledge that someday, I will see you again."

Or some version of me, Vi wanted to say, but couldn't. The truth, even though they both knew it, was too cruel to speak aloud. If what he was saying was true, every Vi was a unique person that lived, fought, and ultimately perished underneath the wheel of time.

"So you must be careful, until Vhalla Solaris gives birth to a Vi Solaris in this age." Vi gave a small nod. She was too tired to fight. Taavin must've sensed as much. "You should get some rest. Norin will fall soon, and you'll want to be nimble to try to get close to Fiera and the sword when it does."

Vi grabbed his bicep before he could pull away. Her grip tightened, trying to press through the thin barrier of magic that kept him from her. "I want you to stay," she whispered. Pain flashed across his face.

"I wish I could. But you know how this works." He leaned forward, planting a gentle kiss on her forehead. "Now, rest."

With that, he vanished; the glyphs above her watch dimmed and faded, and the room seemed darker and lonelier than ever before.

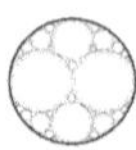

An explosion woke her.

Vi was on her feet in an instant as shock waves rattled the city.

She heard shouts, and the clash of steel on steel. Her heart raced as she stared at the door.

Vi took a step forward, and one back, then two forward. *Keep yourself safe*, Taavin had said. Another rumble shook the city, and she was off. Running, Vi threw open the door and was down the ladder in a breath, steps ahead of Lucina.

"Yullia!" Lucina called after her, following close behind. "Where are you—"

"Lucina. Lucina!" The young woman's grandmother was upright in her cot, calling out to her granddaughter. Vi paused at the top of the stairs, watching as her wrinkled hand reached out, grabbing at the air, milky eyes unseeing.

"Granny, I'm here." Lucina rushed over to her kin, sitting on the edge of the bed as another shock wave rattled the city. The two huddled together tightly, holding each other.

"Lucina." Vi summoned the girl's attention with her name. "I'm going out. You'll want to lock the door behind me."

"Out? Yullia, there's a *war* going on out there."

"I know, and I have every intention of fighting in it. Lock the door behind me." Vi didn't know if that was entirely true. She still wasn't sure if she could pick a side in this war—not when both sides were her family. Or at least… once upon a time, they had been family. Though the waters were murky, Vi couldn't help wanting to jump in with both feet. Sink or swim.

She sprinted down the stairs, unbolted the door, and stepped out into the dusty street.

When she heard the bolt engage behind her, she started off in the direction of an orange haze. The fires of battle were already burning the city; what was once the greatest kingdom in the history of the Dark Isle would fall before the sun rose.

VI RAN TOWARD THE carnage along the main street of Norin. Doubt nipped at her heels as she fell into step with men and women carrying various weapons—everything from forged steel to fishing spears. Her beacon was an orange haze glowing off smoke rising in the horizon. If Vi kept solely focused on that, maybe she wouldn't question too much what, in the Mother's name, she was doing.

She pushed against the masses who were fleeing as fast as they could in the opposite direction. Women carried wailing children tightly in their arms; those large enough to walk were half-dragged along the dusty ground.

At first, most of the people fleeing seemed unscathed, but the further she ran, the more Vi saw wounded and dying.

A man staggered through the street, soldiers and civilians alike parting to run around him. His clothes had been nearly burnt off; charred ribbons clung to blistered and reddened skin. He stared with a pleading expression and a gaping mouth that couldn't seem to find the right words to beg for help.

Suppressing her instinct to gag at the putrid scent of burnt flesh and hair, Vi stopped right before the man, not daring to touch him on his reddened and bubbled side.

"Come this way." His eyes swung to her when he realized someone was speaking to him. Someone had actually heard his soundless cries. "I can heal you," Vi said softly. Somehow, little more than a whisper felt loud when the man's crazed gaze was on her. It was louder than the sounds of fighting in the distance, or the crackle of flames that blazed at the far end of the main street. "Will you come with me?"

He made a choked noise, barely bobbing his head.

Vi took his left hand—the one that hadn't been burned in whatever blaze he had been caught in. She led him out of the street, making sure no one bumped or jostled him in the process.

"This won't hurt," she whispered. She wasn't good at *halleth*, but surely, anything was better than the pain he found himself in. Vi murmured under her breath, "*Halleth ruta toff.*"

She kept the glyph tiny and tightly wound right underneath her palm, holding it above the man's burnt forearm in such a way that he would see nothing more than a faint glow. Vi focused only on mending his forearm, ignoring the rising sounds of battle and the countless others in just as bad a state as this man. *Grow, mend, heal,* she willed to the flesh through her magic. When his forearm was no longer blistered and red, Vi moved on.

Section by section, she mended the worst of the burns. She tried to focus on what seemed the most life threatening, but Vi was no cleric. Her healing was clumsy, scarred and knotted, just as Taavin had said it was when she washed up on the beaches of Meru. But it was better than dead. It had to be better than dead, she insisted to herself.

Vi lowered her hand, having finished with the side of the man's face. His eyes were on her, much more focused than before. He swallowed once before rasping, "Thank you, your highness."

He thought she was Fiera, just as Lucina had. Vi pursed her lips into a thin smile.

"You're welcome." Vi didn't see the point in correcting him. No one was likely to believe him even if he remembered the details of their encounter come dawn. "Can you tell me what's happening? Do you remember?"

He gave a nod. The scar tissue of his neck seemed to pull, causing him to wince slightly. "The wall finally fell. The Imperialists blasted through. They're in the city."

Vi looked in the direction she'd been heading. The fires burned brighter now, almost like an angry dawn on the horizon. She had read about the fall of Norin, but it wasn't a breach in the wall that had brought the noble city to its knees after ten long years—it was by an attack on the sea.

The fighting at the wall was a distraction to give the ships carrying the bulk of the Imperial army time to enter the port.

But what should she do with that information? If she did something, could she see Norin fall faster and potentially spare more from this man's fate?

A hand closed around her watch and Vi briefly thought of summoning Taavin. But if she did, he'd know she'd run into the fray, putting herself in danger. Perhaps putting the future of the entire world in danger with her. *Ninety-three times*. She'd hurt him enough for one day.

"Thank you for the information." Vi stepped away, leaving the man to hover, clearly still dazed. She'd done all she could for him. "Head for the northwest corner of the city. Avoid the port and the outer wall at all costs."

Vi ran upstream through a river of people. Then, all at once, there was no one left for her to push against. She found herself among burning rubble, the crackle of magic blazing through the sky.

Men and women littered the ground around her. Some were burned to husks. Others still oozed crimson into the cracks of the road. Vi stared at the carnage, at those soldiers still fighting in the distance, flames glinting off their plate armor.

She had seen death, up close. But she had never seen war. Standing before it now, Vi felt frozen in place. She wondered if she should feel terrified, if she should weep.

There weren't any feelings though. It was as if any single emotion was insufficient, and so they all left her. Everything was numb. She was presented with the embodiment of *juth calt*: the world had been shattered.

Without warning, a tiny jolt of magic broke the stasis Vi was unwittingly trapped in. Her heart began to race. The bodies around her were more than just corpses; they suddenly became men and women, people with lives, daughters and sons. Vi fought against the swelling sickness that threatened to overcome her.

Another crack of magic—one Vi would recognize anywhere.

When she turned, a wall of flame blocked her vision. The fire roared with unnatural power, connecting one blazing building to the next. It was no doubt a dividing line. The break in the wall must be on the other side and someone very, very powerful was trying to contain the flow of soldiers within.

Yet even a heavy curtain of fire couldn't hide the pull of something greater—a god-like magic. Determined and drawn by an invisible tether, Vi marched forward toward the fire, allowing her own spark to swell within her.

You feel it in your marrow. Taavin's words echoed inside her.

"Yes," Vi whispered to no one. He had been speaking about the truth of her situation. But Vi felt something far greater in her bones. Within her was a power that recognized and sought out its own— the power of a goddess.

You will be free of the bonds of time because my magic is in you, Yargen had said.

Raising a hand, Vi used her magic to bore a hole through the flames that barred her path. It was surprisingly easy, given how impressive the fire was. Whatever Firebearer made it was weaker than Vi expected, for she gained control of the inferno as though it had been her own power all along.

A tunnel opened up before her and Vi charged through, quickly releasing her hold on the fire. On the other side, more carnage waited.

The chorus of battle she'd heard echo over the crackle of the blazes throughout the city was now reaching its crescendo. The large wall surrounding the city had been blown in, reducing nearby buildings to rubble. Debris scattered inward, men and women fighting around large chunks of stone. Those with crimson armbands and red plumes seemed to have the upper hand, pushing back the silver-plated soldiers in short capes of Solaris blue and white.

The same jolt of magic pulsed through her, stronger and closer this time. Vi's eyes were drawn to a far corner, where a woman was locked in the heat of battle with a group of three. She wielded a sword that glowed with a blue haze; power crackled off of it as she alternated between swinging it and casting balls of fire off her free hand.

Vi watched in awe as Fiera Ci'Dan made quick work of three soldiers. She wondered if Fiera had even the slightest idea of how much the weapon was influencing her power.

"Push them back!" Fiera screamed to the soldiers fighting their way up the mound of debris where the wall once stood. "Don't let them through! Show them the strength of Mhashan." Fiera began running and Vi picked up her feet as well.

Their paths intersected near the center of the battlefield. Without missing a step, Fiera shifted her weight, bringing the sword across her body in a swing at Vi. Vi reacted instantly, dodging backward. Fiera held the sword out, keeping her at length, and met Vi's eyes for the first time.

They stared at each other, panting, unmoving. Energy crackled underneath Vi's skin—something more than her own power or Yargen's. Vi knew it as the hair-raising sensation of fate playing its hand.

"Your face is... You..." Fiera struggled for words between heavy breaths.

"There's no time to explain. But I am not your enemy."

"*Who are you?*" Fiera said, as she looked Vi up and down, lowering the sword.

"I'm a traveler, and I've come a long way to tell you…" Vi trailed off. To tell her what? That she needed the sword? That she was the granddaughter of another Fiera from another world? Vi had been acting on instinct, pulled along by her gut, and now she wasn't sure if it had landed her in a good spot.

"To tell me what?" Fiera pressed, with an expression that told Vi she'd seen right through her uncertainty. Another explosion rocked the city. Magic sloshed off the blade in her hand and Fiera cursed and turned, frantically scanning the wall. "Guards in the First Legion, go through the opening, find where they're trying to breach the city a second time!" Men and women pushed farther up the rubble and Fiera started in their direction. Vi gripped her forearm, and Fiera's eyes darted between the clearly offending touch and Vi's face. "Unhand me."

"It's a distraction," Vi blurted. "Tiberus Solaris is coming from the sea."

"What? There's no—"

"They split their forces, weeks ago, I think." Vi struggled to remember her history. The fall of Mhashan had seemed like ancient history when she'd studied it with Martis. Now she was searching her brain for every last detail she could recall. "He's coming from the sea."

Fiera's attention volleyed between Vi and the soldiers. She let out a string of curses before settling her gaze on Vi once more.

"Tell me why I should believe you." The princess lifted her sword. Oddly, it didn't feel threatening. It felt like a challenge.

"Because I know what fate has designed." It was the only explanation Vi could think of, and she knew it wasn't a very good one. Yet somehow, it was enough.

Fiera sheathed her sword, turning to the carnage. "Schnurr!" she shouted. A man who looked far too young to be on the battlefield came rushing over. "See to the troops here. I do not want the Imperials to take one more step into our city."

"Yes, your highness." The man gave a salute.

"Honor guard, to me!" Fiera commanded. Three men and two women ran over as Schnurr ran back into the fray. "We're going to the docks."

They all saluted. Not one questioned her. Not one uttered a word of dissent. These men and women were ready to follow their leader to the ends of the earth or the ends of their lives—whichever came first.

Vi wondered briefly if she'd ever commanded such loyalty from anyone.

"You're sure?" Fiera turned to her once more. Vi nodded. "Onward, then!" Fiera swept out her arm and cut a tunnel into the flame, much as Vi had.

The princess and soldiers took two steps ahead as Vi stared in awe.

The magic had almost felt like hers… It had almost felt like hers in the same way Vi would know her father's magic from anywhere. She might be from another version of the world, but something still connected her with the woman who would become the grandmother to a new Vi.

The group plunged through the tunnel of flame. Without stopping, Fiera continued along the street. Their pace was a jog, which felt agonizingly slow to Vi. But she was in a simple tunic and trousers. The rest of them wore an array of plate and scale mail. She used the pace as an excuse to take sidelong looks at the princess.

The woman had a sharp nose and angular eyes set atop cheekbones even stronger than Vi's own. Her hair had fallen free of whatever tie it had been in and was now knotting down her back. She was real, breathing, *alive*. But if the events of this world were transpiring along the same time frame as they had in Vi's world… she wouldn't be alive for more than a year.

Or would she?

In Vi's world, Fiera had died in childbirth—no, her father had corrected that. She'd died protecting a crystal sword. Now Vi desperately wished he'd told her all the details. Though perhaps they didn't matter.

Perhaps nothing from her world mattered now.

Her stomach knotted as they continued down the main street, turning off at the intersection Vi had walked with Jayme months ago. The docks weren't far when cannon fire rattled the glass of the windows around them. All seven dropped, hands covering their heads as cannonballs ripped through the city.

"What was—" one of the soldiers began.

"The wall was a distraction," Vi said, standing. "The Emperor is flanking you, coming from the sea."

"You call the usurper *Emperor*?" The long-haired woman drew a dagger, placing it at Vi's throat. "And just how do you know all this?"

"I—" Vi wasn't prepared to explain, and luckily Fiera didn't make her.

"I trust her," Fiera interjected, rising to her feet as well. The woman holding the blade at Vi's neck didn't move. "I said I trust her. Put down your weapon."

"What if she's a spy? She speaks like an Imperialist. No red-blooded Westerner would call that destroyer of kingdoms 'Emperor.' She looks like she could get away with masquerading as you, even. What if they sent her to take us from the wall? What if the ship is the distraction meant to pull you away?"

"If she's a spy, we kill her at the docks and return." The other woman with hair cut so short it barely reached her ears rested her hand on her comrade's shoulder. "Listen to our leader. We only have a few minutes before those cannons are reloaded."

Ultimately, the woman with the dagger at Vi's throat did as Fiera commanded, and they were off once more. Vi rubbed her neck as she ran and remembered Taavin's words—if she died now, it was over.

But no, it was only over if she *failed*. If she succeeded in this world and stopped Yargen's power from being turned on itself, then it didn't matter if a new Vi was born. Because there would be no more destruction and rebirth.

Vi's mind was silenced as they rounded the corner and caught their first glimpse of the great port of Norin. Fires blazed in the ocean from ships that were sinking beneath its inky waters. Three large warships with massive battering rams had invaded the port, leaving debris in their wake. Each ship bore a white sail emblazoned with a golden sun.

The ships had already dropped anchor; two were using makeshift gangplanks to allow a near-endless stream of soldiers into the city. Half of the Imperial army had been crammed into those bloated hulls, and now they were encroaching on the castle of Norin, on the civilians that surrounded it, and on the troops battling at the wall from behind.

"Mother above," one of Fiera's men uttered in shock.

Cannon fire rang out, and they all dropped once more as shrapnel and cannon balls ripped through the paltry collection of Western soldiers and buildings alike on the docks. Vi continued to stare, watching them fall. For the second time since she'd entered this version of the world, she felt as though she was watching everything from outside of her body—a history book come to life in the darkest of ways.

"Traveler." Vi hadn't realized they'd ended up side by side until she glanced over and found the princess at her shoulder. "Is Tiberus Solaris on that vessel?" Vi nodded, hoping her grandfather made the same choice in this world as he had in her own. "Then we press onward." Fiera sprang to her feet. "Quickly now!"

Vi, Fiera's five Knights, and the woman herself came to a stop at the center of the docks, right before the main vessel that had been unleashing an artillery assault.

Fiera drew her sword and shouted, "Tiberus, face me!"

The world seemed to hold its breath. Even the soldiers that had been marching down the gangplanks of the other two ships paused as Fiera's voice reverberated off rock and sea. Vi prayed this world was unfolding like her own, that she hadn't started out by lying to Fiera.

"I know you're there. Come out and duel me like the honorable man you claim to be. I am the sword arm of the King of Mhashan. You will not conquer us until you have conquered me!"

"You have been heard, princess." A deep voice filled the air.

Standing at the bow of the ship before them was a man clad in golden armor, trimmed in silver polished so brightly it shone white in the pale moonlight. His hair was the same hue as his armor and his face was clean-shaven, almost roguish—Vi had only ever seen portraits of her grandfather and he looked nothing like the young man standing before them now. She searched his face, seeking out some familial resemblance. But the only thing her father had inherited from Tiberus was the pallor of his skin. Fiera's features had won out in every other way.

Fiera pointed her sword directly at Tiberus. Raw magic sparked from it, falling to the ground like dying fireworks. "And do you accept my challenge?"

"I will accept your surrender," the Emperor said haughtily, in a tone Vi recognized from her own father.

"You must earn it first."

"You've lost this war."

"He's as arrogant as they say," the long-haired honor guard muttered.

A sailor ran up to the Emperor, whispering something in his ear. As they exchanged words none of them could hear, Fiera remained poised, waiting. Her arm didn't so much as quiver despite holding out the long sword.

"You may have your duel, princess. With whatever time is left," Tiberus said ominously before disappearing from sight. Soon enough a rowboat worked its way from the side of the boat to the docks.

"Your highness—"

"I told you before, this ends tonight." Fiera glanced over her shoulder at them before turning to the castle.

Vi took a step forward. Something in Fiera's eyes compelled her. She had an understanding no one else did, save Vi herself.

"You know," Vi whispered softly. Saying nothing, Fiera gave a small nod.

"As do you?"

It was Vi's turn to nod. "Fighting the Emperor won't change anything."

"I realize." Fiera shifted her attention to the rowboat that pulled up alongside the docks. "But the longer I can distract him, the more lives I can spare in the city. If I can be the outlet for his rage, act as the embodiment of my family, then he might spare my siblings."

It was a noble goal. Vi would've admired it more if it wasn't leading toward her grandfather and grandmother dueling. Bringing Fiera here had been a terrible decision.

Taavin had said she was here to change fate.

What if she changed it in the wrong way?

Three soldiers quickly disembarked, followed by Tiberus, then two more soldiers. Were it not for Vi, they would've been evenly matched. In a way they still were. Vi wasn't about to fight for or against either side if it came to blows.

"Sheathe your sword and I'll spare your life." Tiberus wasn't very tall, Vi realized. Yet he spoke with authority that towered above them all.

In reply, Fiera hoisted her weapon, pointing it directly toward the Emperor.

Vi inched backward, her heart racing. Had Fiera and Tiberus traded blows in her time? She swiftly ran through her options for diffusing the situation. If one of them was killed now, would she—rather, the new Vi—even be born?

"Let it be death, then." Tiberus drew his weapon.

"Wai—" Vi never had a chance to finish.

Horns blasted through the city in a low, sad song. She didn't recognize the melody, but it had everyone else holding their breath. Fiera turned to the castle.

From the tallest tower, a makeshift banner was unfurled. It wasn't much, but it would surely be seen from anywhere in the city: the white flag of surrender was draped across the castle of

Norin.

Like that, Mhashan fell.

"Zerian did it…" Tiberus murmured, turning back to them. "Kneel before your Emperor and you shall know my mercy."

Fiera's knuckles went white, but ultimately, she sheathed her sword. Vi watched as the princess fell to one knee.

"Your highness, do not kneel before—"

"We have lost," Fiera said back to them.

Tiberus turned to Vi next and she hastily dropped to her knee, bowing her head.

"Kneel," the Emperor demanded to the rest of the soldiers.

One man and the two women did as they were bid. But the other two remained on their feet.

"We will never kneel before Imperial swine."

"Kneel or die," Tiberus reiterated. "I am ready to give this city mercy, but do not test me."

"We are the Knights of Jadar—"

"And your commander orders you to kneel," Fiera snapped.

"Our commander would never bend her knee before a Southerner," one of the men seethed.

"The war is over," Vi said. "You see the banner." They all ignored her.

"Kill them," the Emperor ordered.

"No." Fiera was on her feet in a moment, blocking the Imperial knights. Swords were drawn from all angles, each pointing at someone different. "They are my responsibility." Fiera leveled her gaze at Tiberus. For his part, he had very little reaction.

Vi watched closely, seeing her father in both of them—seeing herself. She had given little thought to the blood that was spilled before her birth to build the Empire she would rule. She'd learned of it, but she hadn't comprehended the sacrifices or all the tough choices her family had made along the way to build what was known in her age as the greatest Empire the Dark Isle had ever seen.

"Go on, then," Tiberus said. It sounded like a challenge.

Fiera put her back to the Emperor and his soldiers in an incredible display of faith. "Kneel before our new Emperor."

"How dare you—"

"I said kneel!" Fiera shouted. "Mhashan has lost enough in the last ten years. We shall lose no more to foolish pride."

"I will die for my pride."

"Die, then." Fiera swung her sword in a wide arc. She didn't so much as flinch. In one movement, the princess struck down her once-loyal guards by slicing them both at the neck with deadly precision.

Vi watched as the corpses fell. With one swing of her sword, Fiera struck a bloody line in the ground that marked where Mhashan ended, and the rule of Solaris began.

4

VI STARED AT THE wide eyes of the men who had refused to kneel. Now, they were nothing more than two more bodies on the cobblestone streets of Norin.

"You, princess—"

"Fiera," the woman finished for the Emperor. There was an almost defiant air about her. "Princess Fiera."

"Fiera." The Emperor paused. Vi wondered if she was the only one who caught the brief expression of thoughtful surprise. "You were just a slip of a girl when last I saw you."

"It has been ten long years."

"Thank your father for that." Tiberus sheathed his sword, no more pleased than she was. "Speaking of, let us head to the castle. Perhaps now he will be more inclined to discuss the annexation of the West."

"My father is dead."

Vi tried to catch the eyes of the other three soldiers to see if they should stand as well, but an unspoken conversation was unfolding among them. Vi remained where she was.

"How do you—"

"Know?" Fiera wiped the blood from the crystal blade nonchalantly, incredibly calm given all that had transpired. "I know because I know my father, and he would've never surrendered this city to you. He would be a king of rubble before a servant to a foreign crown." She sheathed the weapon and Vi shifted her weight over her knee. She couldn't attempt to take the blade at this moment. Her best chance was to continue letting things play out and look for an opportunity. "I know because I have seen this future in the flames."

"Unfortunate you couldn't have seen a path to victory earlier," Tiberus said arrogantly.

Fiera didn't rise to the bait. "Your victory was the goddess's will."

Tiberus, for his part, didn't seem the slightest bit unnerved by the proclamation. He didn't so much as nod to address that he'd heard the incredible statement. But Vi could see in his eyes that he was filing away that particular tidbit for later.

She'd read that her grandfather had claimed it had been his divine right to unite the continent. Now Vi wondered if that idea had originated from him, or Fiera.

"Come, all of you. We start for the castle," the Emperor declared.

Soldiers fell into step around them and more were gained along the way as they trudged through the empty city roads. It seemed Imperial soldiers were patrolling around every corner of Norin, putting down the last fighters still loyal to the West. Tiberus's ploy to invade by sea had paid off.

Vi allowed herself to be shepherded along. Taavin had said to get close to the sword and Fiera. This likely wasn't what he'd had in mind, but the result was the same, which surely counted for something.

They walked in silence all the way to the large city square opposite the castle. Here, crowds of Western soldiers had been gathered. They were penned in by rings of Imperial troops that brandished weapons at them as though they were livestock.

"You three, with the rest of them," Tiberus commanded. Then, to Fiera, "You're with me."

"But—" Vi's objection was cut off by another.

"Princess, don't go with him," the long-haired woman in the group objected. "He will slaughter you with the rest of the blood of Jadar. Run now with the blade and—"

"Get in line with the rest of your lot," one of the Imperial soldiers growled, pointing his sword at them and motioning to the masses of surrendered Western soldiers.

"Princess!"

"Come on." Vi grabbed the woman's elbow as Fiera and Tiberus started along the castle's lowered drawbridge. "We have to trust that she knows what she's doing."

"And who are you to say that?" The woman jerked away. "You're not one of us," she said to the Imperial guards. "She's not one of us!"

"She looks like one of you. Now get in line."

"This is the will of the head of the Knights of Jadar," the short-haired woman to Vi's right said, giving the other woman a firm shove toward the opening in the line of Imperial soldiers. "Obey your commander."

"She's not our commander, not anymore," the man grumbled under his breath. "She murders the Knights she's sworn to lead. She kneels before foreign kings. She shames the Knights of—"

"Stay your blasphemous tongue." The short-haired woman just kept pushing.

The opening in the line of Imperial soldiers closed behind them and Vi found herself among a mass of Westerners, packed shoulder to shoulder with barely enough room to move around. This city square was large, but it was quickly filling to capacity. Half the people were coated in soot and blood. Vi took a deep breath, scanning the eyes of the Imperial soldiers brandishing swords in their direction.

Those swords were once intended to protect her. Her stomach

knotted as her brain tried to readjust her instinct. Nothing was right. Not even her skin seemed to fit in the same way it once did.

"Are you all right?"

"What?" Vi brought her attention to the short-haired woman at her left. The other woman from Fiera's guard, who had threatened Vi at dagger point, was still whispering in hushed tones with the man.

"You're not one of us." She gave Vi a once-over. "You're certainly not a Knight of Jadar… and you don't look like a soldier."

"I'm neither," Vi affirmed.

"Fiera didn't know you. Though she clearly trusted you." The woman's eyes were drawn back to the princess, now nothing more than a distant speck at the end of the drawbridge. "If you're a civilian, you should try to get out now while you still have the chance. There's no comfort to be had in Norin, but civilians will fare better than soldiers in the days to come."

"Do you think they'll believe I'm not a soldier?"

"Fiera could speak for you."

"She has more important things to worry about." Staying close to the remaining Knights of Jadar might be her best chance of getting back to the princess—and the sword.

"You're a true Westerner, sacrificing your wellbeing for her. Trying to help lead us to victory."

Vi snorted. "I'm not a Westerner."

"But your features are Western—so Western, you could've convinced me you're a lost sister to the princess." Vi stopped a snort of laughter at that. "And you speak our tongue so well."

"I don't know my parentage," Vi lied, staring at Fiera and the Emperor until they disappeared from sight into the castle. "And the language I picked up in my travels. I don't really have a home."

Especially not anymore. She was alone. The only person she had in this world was the man who had stolen her heart and betrayed her—right before she murdered him.

Yargen had an interesting sense of humor.

"Well, if you don't have a home, do you have a name? I'm Zira."

"Yullia."

"While it was under unpleasant circumstances, it is an honor to meet you, Yullia. I believe the goddess sent you for our princess tonight, to fight for her and this land. Fiera is keen to the will of the Mother; that must've led her to trust you."

"You have no idea…" Vi murmured.

"Listen up!" An Imperial major stood at the foot of the drawbridge, right where Vi had witnessed Fiera give her last speech hours ago, and boomed over the masses. His pronunciation of Western words was poor and Vi suspected it made his decree even more grating to the ears of those assembled. "You are to be split at random and will be taken to manor houses that have been converted to shelters where you will be held until further notice. Do not resist and the Emperor will see fit to let you live."

"I wonder how long that kindness will last," the long-haired Knight mused.

"I'd rather be dead than take kindness from that man," the other Knight grumbled.

"Quiet, Luke. If you were determined to die, you should've stood at the docks," Zira said.

Luke continued muttering to the long-haired woman, though it was too quiet for Vi to hear.

Not that she was paying much attention anyway. Her thoughts were back in time. According to the history she knew, the Emperor spared the majority of Mhashan's forces…

But only after he'd made a display of killing off the generals, and quelled the resultant outrage.

The war had ended. But the fighting wouldn't stop for weeks.

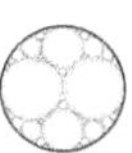

Martial law was enacted in the city—at least, that's what they were told by whispering servants who were allowed in and out of the manor house once each day to feed the soldiers held inside.

"Here." Zira startled Vi from her thoughts by thrusting a hunk of bread about the size of Vi's palm in her face. "Eat it before someone kills you for it."

"Is this… fresh?" Vi grabbed for the food eagerly, taking a bite so large she was forced to chew with her mouth open. The bread was soft, crust hard, free of mold or weevils, and still had that distinct aroma of fresh-baked deliciousness—a scent she hadn't smelled in the two weeks since she was imprisoned with the rest of the soldiers. "How did you—"

"The girls say that provisions have arrived from the East. It seems the Emperor has starved us enough and now wishes to win us over by filling our bellies."

Luke started a familiar litany of muttering. "If he thinks the West will bend before him for a few loaves of bread—"

"He's absolutely right," Vi interrupted, swallowing hard to get the rest of the too-large bite down. She needed water, but there was none to spare in the manor. Everything was rationed tightly; they were given just enough to be kept alive. So Vi bit the tip of her tongue until saliva coated her mouth—a trick Zira taught her. "The people have been defeated, shown the Emperor's power, made to feel desperate, and now, when he shows them kindness, they will be all too eager to accept it. It's hard to think straight when hunger is gnawing at you."

She had been learning as much the hard way these past two weeks. In the process, Vi was finding a new, dark appreciation for Taavin's time spent under Ulvarth. How readily she'd judged him for his actions back in the Twilight Forest. Part of her still did. Even during the longest nights of hunger pangs, Vi still didn't think she'd condemn a group of people to slaughter.

But she was only two weeks in. And he'd spent years in such a state. She twisted the watch at her neck, longing to summon the man once more but not having a scrap of privacy to do it with.

"*The Emperor*. You still speak like one of them."

"Well I'm in here with you, Luke." Vi took another bite of bread. "So either I'm not one of them, or I'm really stupid for not getting myself out before now."

"None of us are getting out of here alive," Kahrin sighed, her long black hair hiding her face. She was a far cry from the woman who threatened Vi when they first met. "They've taken all the generals, and half of the Knights of Jadar… We're next."

"We're not dead yet, so eat." Zira sat on the other side of the wide windowsill where Vi was perched. The other two remained in their spots on the floor. It was a corner of the room they shared with ten other random soldiers—men and women whose names Vi hadn't bothered to learn. "The princess will need us."

"The princess is dead."

"Shut your mouth," Zira growled.

"Do you really think the Emperor will be satisfied with just King Rocham's head? No, he'll want more royal blood to spill in a glorious display of power. And who better than the youngest child, the woman who led our army against him?"

"Fiera isn't dead," Zira insisted in the face of Kahrin's determination.

"If she was alive, she would've come for you of all people by now. You were always her pet."

"She's not dead." Vi tore off another chunk of bread, chewing it over and staring out the window.

"What do you know, *traveler*?" Kahrin spat. Her tone made plain that she had yet to relinquish her theory that Vi was a spy.

"More than you ever will."

"How dare you—"

"Enough," Zira snapped. "You three are exhausting me."

They all ate their remaining scraps of bread in relative silence. Luke mumbled something about the food sitting heavy in his stomach and making him sleepy, "likely drugged by Imperialist swine." Kahrin must've decided she was bored of being ignored, because when Vi looked over her shoulder next, she was gone.

"Do you know she's alive?" Zira asked softly, her voice hushed.

Vi gave a small nod that felt like a lie. What did she know? Precious little. The ability to gaze along the Mother's lines of fate was one thing, but she hadn't had a vision since entering the remade world. It was like she was trying to navigate a new city using ancient maps. She'd been biding her time, waiting, seeing how things played out. Tiberus and Fiera nearly exchanging blows on the docks had ignited a fear Vi hadn't expected. What if she messed something up? What if, in trying to improve the future they were now heading toward, she somehow made it worse?

She needed to speak with Taavin again.

"You have the sight too, don't you? Like she does?"

"I do."

"I heard what you said to her, at the docks…" Zira looked back to the window. "She told me of her vision before the battle. She knew we would lose. She knew her father would die."

"And yet she fought for Mhashan anyway." The meager piece of bread was gone all too swiftly, and Vi's stomach was grumbling even louder than before. But ignoring angry stomachs had become something they were all quite good at.

"Yes, she fought for Mhashan… but not to win. She wanted to save the people—to prevent as many as possible from dying. I don't understand the dance of royals, but I must believe that these deaths we hear of, however gruesome they might be, are still part of her plan. Fiera was always good at minimizing losses."

"The hard part of having royal blood is deciding how you spread the suffering. Who will bear the burden—many, or a few? Who? And how do you choose? Do you spread it as thin as possible, or is it better to absolve some and force others to pick up the weight entirely?"

"Are you certain you're not a bastard of King Rocham?" Zira chuckled at Vi's expression. "You speak like a royal."

"I've spent my share of time around them, I guess you could say."

"In your travels?"

"In my travels."

Booted feet came to a stop at the entrance of the room. There were no more doors in the manor; they had all been ripped off when the Imperial soldiers evicted the house's noble residents and declared it the new containment shelter for the former army of Mhashan.

"She's there. Zira Westwind is there." Kahrin pointed at them and spoke to the Imperial soldiers on either side of her. "The one with the shorter hair."

"Westwind…" Vi repeated softly. The name was familiar to her in a way she hadn't been expecting. "Your name is Westwind?"

Zira didn't have a chance to answer as soldiers approached. "Come," a broad-shouldered man barked in Mhashanese. Zira stood without protest.

"Where are you taking her?" Vi asked, jumping from the windowsill. The man ignored her and she repeated herself, forcing her tongue to make the sounds of the common language she'd spoken all her life, "Where are you taking her?"

The two soldiers stopped, gaping at her in surprise. They weren't the only ones; the soldiers of Mhashan wore expressions of curiosity at her deft outburst.

"That is none of your concern," one of the men finally said, before they dragged Zira out of sight.

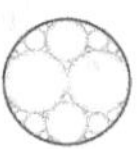

There was no word of Zira, and none from Kahrin or Luke either. After Vi's outburst in common, they began to shy away from her—prior suspicions of her being some kind of Southern spy reignited. Without Zira, Vi didn't have the energy or inclination to refute them.

Three days passed, and Vi became bolder about wandering the manor. She was growing tired of being cooped up, tired of waiting. Perhaps it would be better if she could remember more of the immediate details following the fall of Mhashan, but her studies—

or her memories of them—were lacking. She needed the counsel of the man who was tasked with looking back for her. But every room she entered was filled with people.

"How is it outside?" she asked one of the girls passing out hunks of bread. It had tasted so good three days ago, but had since grown stale. "Any progress?"

"Some." Vi stepped off to the side, leaning against the wall next to her. "There's rumors they might be lifting the martial law soon."

"Rumors don't hold water. Did they kill Zira?"

"I don't know who Zira is, but the killings in the square have ended."

That much was good, at least. The Emperor must be feeling more confident in his control of Mhashan. The next step would be—

"Criers today announced that tomorrow, there will be a ball held for Mhashan's court."

"A ball?" Vi repeated. After weeks of ruling with blood and an iron fist, there was to be a party?

"I think it's odd, having a party so close to so much bloodshed. But who understands royals? The ball is to follow some kind of announcement in the square opposite the castle."

An engagement announcement. The Emperor would secure his hold in the West with a marriage. Vi finished off her bread with one more large bite, thanked the girl, and left. If there was a ball, the castle would be open; he'd want as many nobles as possible to attend.

Vi waited for nightfall. She'd staked her claim in the corner of one of the rooms—crowded enough that no one would notice one person missing, empty enough that she could have the dark corner of what was once a closet to herself.

"*Durroe watt ivin,*" Vi whispered, standing and sliding into the skin of one of the Imperial soldiers she'd been watching for weeks. The brief flash of light didn't seem to wake any of those sleeping.

Carefully tiptoeing from the room, Vi stepped into the hall and walked with confidence. Magic was hot under her hand and the illusion blurred the edge of her vision. But it was far easier than the first time she had attempted a similar deceit—escaping out of the fortress of Soricium as Jayme.

"Lolan, don't you usually take the mornings?" one of the guards asked as she approached the exit.

"Usually. I'm covering half a rotation," Vi said softly, with the same Southern accent Ginger would use. Vi had picked this particular guard for her masquerade because she'd never raised her voice above a whisper. "Excuse me."

Keeping her head down, Vi stepped out into the street. The guards at the door said nothing more. They believed the illusion completely.

Vi took a breath of fresh air. Freedom filled her lungs.

She started down the street toward where she knew the Le'Dan's shop would be.

5

S
HE KEPT THE ILLUSION of Lolan's skin most of the way
through the city. Vi passed three other Imperial soldiers who
each gave her a bob of their heads before continuing on their
patrols. It wasn't until she reached the opulent area of town where
the Le'Dan shop stood proud that Vi stepped back into a side alley,
crouched, and finally let go of the magic running thin against her
palm.

Letting her eyes adjust to the darkness, Vi remained low,
waiting. The city had been quiet for weeks, which meant the patrols
were becoming more scarce. Even without them, the citizens stayed
hidden away. Tiberus had conditioned them all now, whether they
realized it or not.

After the next patrol passed, she eased out of her stance and
looked to the building across the road. The first floor was a shop; a
window above. Perhaps a loft for some kind of security or shopkeep
to sleep in? Vi had no doubt that the Le'Dans would keep their
goods heavily guarded, especially now, when the people around

those valuable goods were hungry and desperate.

She hastily crossed the street and came to a stop at the door.

"*Durroe sallvas tempre,*" Vi whispered, willing the magic to spin outward and encompass both her and the door. "*Juth calt.*" The inside mechanics of the lock built in to the door shattered with a *pop*, and Vi eased herself quietly inside. Her magic hid the jingling of the bell overhead.

Vi willed the glyph for concealing her sound to hover across the entire store. She stepped behind the counters and pulled back the fabric covering the cases. Jewels shone like colored stars in the faintly glowing light of her magic.

"No… not one of these." Vi replaced the cover, turning away from the cases. She didn't need showpieces designed to accentuate the Le'Dan family's skill. No, she needed something smaller, something no one would notice was missing, *hopefully*, until tomorrow night at the earliest.

Vi rummaged through the drawers behind the counters. There were all manner of jeweler's tools in the first four. She stepped lightly to the back of the room and kept her magic strong. With a glance, Vi checked the street. No sign of soldiers yet.

"Something, something…" Vi murmured to herself, trusting her magic to keep her thoughts from anyone who might be slumbering upstairs. In the back of the room, tucked between two towers of drawers, was a thin case. Vi opened it and her eyes settled on rows of pieces tagged with names, dates, and amounts. Some were marked as paid, some weren't.

She settled on a statement ring with a Western ruby the size of a quail's egg propped up by two silver phoenixes on either side. Underneath the ruby, the jeweler had emblazoned the Le'Dan family crest.

"Marla Le'Dan," Vi read the name off the tag before pocketing the piece. She didn't know who Marla was, and Vi knew most of the names of the important Le'Dans throughout history. Which meant this woman was perfect—Marla was someone people might recognize by name, but likely wouldn't know personally. And if the

Le'Dans hadn't found a way to get her ring to her yet, Vi suspected Marla was outside of the city.

The rest of the night unfolded with the same ease as breaking into the Le'Dan shop.

Vi made her way through Norin, slipping into the skins of various Imperial soldiers when necessary. She visited a dressmaker, furrier, and cobbler, relieving each of the pieces she'd need to enable the next phase of her plan.

Each of the stores was flush with goods covered in a thin layer of dust. Clearly, no one had been shopping for months, especially not in the more expensive areas of town. It made it easy for Vi to collect all her necessary supplies before dawn, giving her enough time to slip into an abandoned house just as morning broke.

She knew she should sleep, but her first moment of privacy had Vi extending her hand, reaching for one man.

"*Narro hath hoolo.*" Three simple words, and he stood before her.

"Vi," he said with immense relief. Taavin's arms wrapped around her, pulling her to him. Vi buried her face in his shoulder, pressing as close as she could, willing his embrace to feel as sturdy as she'd once known it to be. "It's been three weeks. Don't worry me like this."

"I'm all right." She shifted enough to look him in the eye. "See?"

"You're skin and bones… and in dire need of a bath."

She couldn't disagree. But rather than linger on that topic, Vi asked instead, "How do you know how long it's been?"

"From within the watch, I might not know what you're doing, but I have a sense of how much time is passing. My consciousness is stored there, so when I'm not in this world, it feels almost like twilight sleep—not really awake, but not fully asleep either." Taavin released one arm, running his finger across her forehead as if to brush away stray hairs. The ghostly touch was feather-light, and the strands that had escaped her braids barely moved. "What's happened?"

"I found Fiera," Vi began delicately. "Though, in doing so, I ended up getting myself captured."

"*Captured?*"

"I'm fine," Vi insisted once more.

"What did you do?"

"It doesn't matter. What matters is—"

"It does matter," he interrupted firmly. "I exist to chronicle time and keep record of your actions. I can't do that if you don't tell me them *exactly*. Our best hope for figuring out what will save this world is ruling out what won't."

With a palm on his chest, Vi pushed him away lightly. She folded her arms to guard herself—to try to hold in the truth. He was already worried enough. Vi walked over to the boarded window of the parlor where they stood. She could feel his gaze as keenly as the beams of sunlight that streamed through the cracks in the boards.

"I went out to find Fiera the night Mhashan fell."

"You went out?"

"Yes, into the fray." Vi could tell from his tone he was putting the events together.

"You went out into the field of battle knowing that if you died, this world is doomed?" Taavin stomped over, though the floor didn't so much as creak—his footsteps held no real weight. "What were you thinking?"

"I had to see it," she said without looking at him. Her eyes saw that night, replaying its events. "I had to see it with my own eyes. It made all of this real." She finally locked eyes with him. "Besides, didn't you say the first thing I must do is get the sword?"

"Yes, but—"

"Well, I have a plan to do that now."

"Is it just as reckless as your last plan?" Taavin frowned.

"I'm not sure if I should tell you. You might just scold me for it."

"Yes, I'm going to scold you for risking your life when the fate of our world hangs in the balance." Taavin gripped her hand, the touch a pale shadow of the intensity in his eyes. "*Think* about it, Vi. One mistake and the best that can happen is this world is headed for another future of death. The worst? An age of darkness from which there is no escape—death of all things, the atrophy of our world, a perpetual midnight without stars."

She squeezed his hand back just as tightly, looking up at his emerald eyes. "And if I do nothing, we are equally stuck in this loop, which is its own form of torture. I must act if I am to end this."

"But do so cautiously," he insisted. "Just telling someone the truth about yourself could tip the scales and change fate in a way none of us expect."

Sighing softly, Vi turned away, feeling her brow relax. He wasn't wrong. There was still so much about her predicament that she didn't understand. But she knew that doing nothing wasn't the solution either.

"Let me tell you what it is I plan to do next," she said finally. "You have the memories of all my failures; perhaps you can help poke holes in my orchestrations to give me the best chance for success."

She heard him breathe a sigh of relief.

"That, I can do."

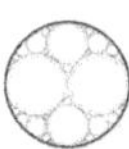

The last time Vi had laid eyes on the square at the drawbridge of the castle of Norin, it had been filled with the winners and losers of a ten-year war. Soldiers had held their heads in triumph and defeat. Now, it was filled with common folk and nobles alike. But the only soldiers were those in Imperial plate, bearing signets of the Solaris Empire.

Her layers of skirts swayed with her hips and flowed around her heeled shoes. Over her shoulders was a shrug; the ruddy feathers that adorned it reminded her of Fallor. In a dark way, it felt as though she was wearing the skins of an evil she'd vanquished.

Vi had managed a wash and found a mirror that enabled her to put a strategic plait in her hair. She'd woven the braids in a fashion her mother would wear for Imperial events. Most everyone else wore their hair down and loose, some swept theirs up with a simple braid wrapped through it. But none had quite the same intricate knots as Vi, and her style drew more than one look.

"Hear ye, hear ye." A man stepped up onto a stage positioned at the foot of the drawbridge. Knights fanned out before him, swords drawn with their points driven into the earth. "It is my honor to bestow on you your first Imperial announcement."

"*Honor*," a man snorted from somewhere behind Vi.

"In six months' time, your Emperor, ordained by the Mother herself to unite this continent, will be wed to the one much loved by the sun and much loved by your land." The ruffles at the crier's neck bounced up and down as he spoke. Each heaving breath carried his voice further than the last. "The Emperor Tiberus Solaris announces his betrothal to Lady Fiera Ci'Dan!"

Horns blasted and soldiers threw confetti into the sky over a confused crowd. Whispers collected to form a sound loud enough to be heard over the bellowing instruments. Frightened, concerned, and angry eyes sought each other out in turn. The commoners were less likely to keep their opinions to themselves.

"She would marry him?"

"The unbendable Fiera?"

"She was the leader of the Knights. Now she's nothing but an Imperial whore," the male voice from earlier muttered darkly.

At that, Vi glanced over her shoulders. But she couldn't see who behind her might have spoken. Was it the angry-looking commoner? One of the nobles behind him? Someone further back?

Vi looked forward once more, trying to push the remark out of her mind. She'd heard mention that Fiera's engagement to the Emperor Solaris had not been taken well. And why would it have been? Having seen the fall of Mhashan with her own eyes, she understood why the people were upset. Vi turned her gaze to the ground, wondering how much blood from the Emperor's killings had flowed right where she stood.

Still, the horns continued their celebratory trill, as though the people were as excited as the shimmering bits of paper happily floating through the air.

"Now, now!" Everything quieted as the crier raised his hands once more. "Members of the court, we invite you to join the Emperor in his first soiree in this land, to celebrate this most glorious union. Those who are not of noble birth, fear not, for you shall also enjoy minstrels and food."

"We do not want minstrels. We want our king—King Ophain!" a man shouted. "We do not want Tiberus's blood-soaked charity. We want our free—"

The declaration was cut short with a crunch and gurgle that echoed louder in her ears than the horns had. Vi couldn't see who had been shouting, but she knew he would never shout again.

Silence fell heavy atop simmering resentment.

"Now, please, enter the castle, Western court. Enjoy and be merry, all!" the crier finished, as though the outburst had never existed.

The mass split into two groups—nobles marching forward along the bridge, slowly filing into two lines, and commoners who were held back by the guards surrounding the crier's stage. Vi rolled her shoulders and adjusted the long, feathered coat that covered them.

With every step, she retreated further into her mask; by the time she arrived at the Imperial soldiers holding scrolls of names, she was no longer the woman who had been wasting away in a prison or a cat burglar stealing garments. She was Vi Solaris, crown princess to an Empire lost.

"Name," the soldier demanded.

"Marla Le'Dan." Vi worked to add a thick Western accent over the name.

"Marla… Le'Dan." The soldier checked his scrolls and then leaned over, murmuring something to the woman behind him. He turned back to Vi. "I don't seem to have your name."

"Excuse me? I am of the Le'Dan family. How can you not have

my name? Do you know who my family even is, *Southerner*?"

"I don't have your name on the lis—"

"Then find another list," Vi insisted. "Or perhaps this should be proof enough." She held out her right hand, the ruby catching not only the soldier's eye but the eyes of the other Western nobles around her.

The soldier looked back to the woman he'd deferred to before. She stepped forward and inspected Vi's ring. "Let her though."

"Thank you." Vi gave a huff she hoped conveyed that the transgression against her noble person would not be forgotten.

She fell into step with the stream of people passing through the glistening royal stables that flanked the wide entry, toward the grand doors of the castle. Vi glanced over her shoulder; the Imperial soldiers were already focused on the next people. No one around her seemed to be paying her any attention.

Vi made her way to the edge of the crowd and stepped back into the shadow of one of the stables before slipping behind a low wall unseen.

Hurriedly, she shrugged off her coat and pulled pins from her braids, allowing them to fall into a much simpler style. She ripped at the flowing skirt she wore over a clinging dress, casting it aside with the coat and incinerating it with a burst of magic. She yanked the ring from her finger, tucking it into a hidden pocket of her dress as she slipped back into the crowd without anyone so much as giving her a glance.

Smoothing over her dress once more, sufficiently satisfied with her altered appearance, Vi stepped into the great hall of the Western castle.

Her feet came to a stop as Vi let out a soft gasp. It was more magnificent than she could've imagined. The architect's sketches and blueprints Elecia had sent hadn't done the castle justice. Columns supported wooden rafters that soared high enough for gigantic iron chandeliers to hang unimpeded. At the far end of the room was the throne area—a place Vi could barely see over the heads of those gathered.

Stained glass along the upper walls picked up the glow of a thousand tiny flames, burning magically in the chandeliers and otherwise empty glass bulbs throughout the room. Vi took a step, placing her hand lightly on a column. This was her family's home. She ached at the thought and part of her—the part that shared blood with the Ci'Dan family—wanted to weep for all they'd lost despite all she herself had gained.

"There you are," a male voice said from behind her. "I knew you said you were thinking of getting a feel for the attitude of the crowds, princess, but I didn't think this was what you had in mind."

Vi startled, realizing he was speaking to her. Even from behind, he'd mistaken her for Fiera.

The man was a Westerner, through and through. He had short-cropped black hair and muscular shoulders that framed a barrel chest. His clothing was twice as fine as the average person's. But what made his identity as plain as the nose on his face was the thick chain around his neck—cast in gold and weighted by a diamond that could make even a Solaris blush.

Vi was face to face with Richard Ci'Dan.

"You'll never believe what's happened. I came down early myself because I was told my cousin Marla was here. Foolish Imperials, they know nothing, or they'd know Marla is—"

"I think you have the wrong person," Vi said softly.

Richard stopped himself mid-sentence and stared at her. He blinked several times, tilting his head, before taking a step forward to get a better look. He searched her face with a gaze as tender as it was knowing before that same expression became distant and inquisitive.

"You're *her*, aren't you?" he said finally.

"And just who do you think I am?"

"The traveler the princess foretold."

“SHE FORETOLD… ME?” Vi leveraged all her royal training to keep her surprise in check.

"She did. She said a traveler would come who wore her face."

Vi wore a knowing smile. Fiera's actions were gaining clarity. "Yes, I have come from very far to meet her."

"Sorry to say you don't have any hope of a private meeting. A public audience, perhaps tonight. But no one has been able to get to her, not even one of her oldest and dearest friends." He sighed heavily and looked toward the empty thrones at the far end of the room. "She's been kept sequestered under lock and key with that wretched man."

Vi took a small step toward Richard, looking toward the thrones as well. She said nothing, and the silence greased his tongue.

"I shudder to think of what he's done to her—what he's threatened her with—to bring about this union."

"Perhaps he loves her?" Vi suggested.

"Loves her?" Richard balked. "The man loves one thing: war. He's long been married to death itself. He doesn't love, he conquers."

"Have you met him?" Vi had always been told that, above all else, Tiberus had been over the sun for Fiera Ci'Dan. That while he had stolen her land, she had stolen his heart.

"No. Just how much socializing have you been able to do recently?" Richard's eyebrows arched. "Forgive my tone, and that I've yet to learn your name, Lady…"

"Yullia."

"Lady Yullia." Richard took her hand and brought it to his lips. "An honor to meet you."

"And you as well."

"You have an uncommon name. Might I ask where—"

Two doors at the far end of the hall opened and interrupted Richard before he could finish. A hush fell over those gathered. They turned collectively to the group of three standing in the doorway.

"Ophain, Lord of the West!" a crier announced as the man in front stepped forward along a white runner. "Sisters to the Lord of the West, Lady Tina and Lady Lilo." Two women stepped out, walking side by side.

"Lord of the West," Richard murmured at Vi's side. "He should be *king*."

Vi remained silent, watching the procession. Ophain was heartbreakingly similar in features to her father, save the hooked nose and slightly longer hair that he wore tied at the nape of his neck. Tina, the older sister, was spindly and elegant. Lilo was stouter and, despite all that had transpired, wore a serene smile on her face.

Perhaps she was smiling because she'd somehow avoided engagement to the man who had conquered their homeland. Both women making their way down the long runner to the dais were older than Fiera, and both were currently un-betrothed. They would've been the more expected choices.

"My friends, my noble kin," Ophain began as he reached the top of the dais. There were only two chairs behind him, Vi noticed, and he sat in neither. "I realize this celebration has come under… unconventional circumstances."

"That's a way to put it," Richard mumbled. He wasn't the only one.

"However, it is just that—a *celebration*," Ophain emphasized. "My darling sister, the youngest and I think we can all agree the strongest among us—" Lilo gave a nod from Ophain's left "—has been chosen as our future Empress. She is a woman whose hands were only for the sword and now, they will help hold up the Empire."

Any other proclamation, under almost any other circumstances, would have been met with cheers. But those gathered were silent. Slowly, a few people clapped—mostly the Southerners in attendance—and then a few more. A depressing showing for a crowd that dressed for a party but felt as though they were attending a funeral.

"Thus, it is my honor to present the Emperor Tiberus Solaris and future Empress Fiera Ci'Dan!" Ophain motioned to the back of the room, where the doors were still open wide.

Two figures emerged from the darkness and into the light of the hall. The Emperor wore the sun crown—a golden circlet with fiery sunbeams stretching up from its base. His crisp, white, double-breasted jacket and tailored trousers were a clear attempt to distance himself from the more flowing styles of the South.

Fiera walked in stark contrast beside him. Her crown was a simple silver band across her brow. She wore a tightly tailored, crimson dress with a split all the way up to her hip. Underneath were black leggings and boots that appeared to have the dust of training fields still on them. Silver pauldrons adorned her shoulders and a sword Vi would recognize anywhere was strapped to her hip.

The only thing connecting them were their hands. Tiberus escorted her with his elbow out, palm parallel to the floor. Fiera's hand rested atop.

They didn't look like they were walking into a party in their honor. They looked as though they were walking to war. Yet the effect seemed to work on the crowd, for as they passed men and women alike dropped to one knee and bowed their heads.

Vi was no exception, though she was one of the last to kneel, waiting long enough that Fiera's attention came to her and her alone. Vi held the woman's eyes until her knee met the floor. Fiera turned forward quickly, keeping her reaction to Vi's presence concealed.

"My newest and well-loved subjects," the Emperor started when they reached the dais. Fiera's siblings had stepped back to stand behind the thrones. "It is my honor to stand before you today. Not just as your ruler, but as your future kin."

Vi glanced over to Richard. His jaw was clenched tight, veins bulging in his neck. The man looked like he wanted to scream more and more with each passing second.

"It is my most sincere hope that you all will join us in celebration, now and over the next six months, as we prepare to join in union in the Cathedral of the Mother."

The room remained silent. The Emperor stared out at the crowd for another long moment before he stepped back and assumed his seat in the gilded throne tufted in blue velvet. Fiera, however, remained.

She swung her gaze across the room, a hand resting on the hilt of her crystal sword.

"Lords and Ladies of Mhashan," she began in Mhashanese. The Emperor didn't have much of a reaction, which told Vi that Tiberus was confident in what she was going to say. "I was your princess. More than that—I was your sworn protector. My father appointed me the head of the Knights of Jadar so that I may keep you all safe.

"I still hold that duty dear to my heart. I know you might not always understand how, but I fight for you. I will continue to fight for you until my dying breath. However, fate guides us to unexpected places. I no longer defend you on the field, but from a throne—a throne where I know I will find happiness. I am happy. Join me in that, my kin. Eternal flame."

Fiera finished with the common Western colloquialism—*fiarum evantes*. The term was both greeting and farewell, meant to inspire good will.

"Guide us through the night." *Kotun un nox,* Vi said aloud, when no one else would.

Others picked up the sentiment, echoing her. The words rippled through the crowd. One by one, they uttered the expression as a form of solidarity with their once princess and now future empress.

Fiera sat on her throne. As soon as she was settled, minstrels playing harps and lutes picked up a merry tune set to the fast beat of a drum. It was jarring to the very clearly uncomfortable atmosphere. But someone had planned for this, and servants passed wine around on trays. The nobles eagerly grabbed for the goblets, searching for anything to quench the awkward feeling that hung in the air.

Richard took one more long look at Fiera and Tiberus before turning, starting eagerly toward a servant passing drinks. Vi took a hasty step, falling into place at his side.

"I need a drink," he muttered. "Something stronger than the stuff they're serving here… but this is a start." He lifted a goblet off a tray but Vi refused it when he offered. She fussed with the skirt of her gown instead.

"Have faith, Richard Le'Dan. The South isn't all bad," Vi encouraged lightly with a pat on his chest. Lucky for her, he too wore a military-style jacket with pockets over both pectorals—one of which now held the ring Vi had lifted from the Le'Dan store. Taavin had cautioned her not to keep it beyond tonight. This was a much better solution than casting it in some dark corner. "You might even learn to like it someday."

Before he could retort, she walked away, her mission with him finished. One by one, men and women were lining up to pay respects to the Emperor. Vi stepped into the line and waited her turn.

"Emperor Tiberus Solaris," she said in Southern Common when it was her turn. "Lady Fiera Ci'Dan." Vi switched deftly to Mhashanese to address the princess. "It is my honor to come before you both and wish you well." Vi dropped to a knee.

"And what family do you hail from?" Tiberus asked. All of the other nobles had made it a point to very clearly state who they were when they swore their allegiance. Someone in the shadows was no doubt keeping a tally of which families weren't here.

"I have no family, your grace." Some murmurs. Vi could see movement from the corners of her eyes and wondered if the guards were already coming for her now that she'd identified herself as the person who did not belong among all the members of the Western court. "But I do come bearing an engagement gift."

"A gift?" Fiera asked, eyes locked with Vi's and filled with awareness. The question stopped short the guards who had just about surrounded Vi. The room was silent once more.

"Fiera Ci'Dan, you will bear a son." Vi pitched her voice as ominously and with as much gravity as possible. "He will have your flames, and sit on the throne of his father."

A small smile worked its way onto Fiera's lips as a guard approached, whispering in the Emperor's ear. Tiberus looked at Vi with renewed focus.

Vi opened her mouth to speak again, but was interrupted.

"Kind words, indeed," the Emperor said lightly. "A shame you felt the need to lie to say them. You are under arrest for masquerading as a member of the house Le'Dan. Guards, please take her to the dungeons. We shall sort out what to do with her later."

Vi stood, offering her elbows to the guards who were already reaching for them. She didn't struggle or try to get away. Instead, she walked like a princess, all the way out of the party and into the depths of Norin's castle.

They locked her in a cell without fanfare and promptly left. Vi waited for their footsteps to disappear down the hall. Fiera knew she was here.

If she waited, the princess would eventually find a way to get to her. But Richard's claim that Fiera was being kept under tight watch lingered—highlighting the advice Taavin had given her.

The party will be depressing for Fiera. She'll retreat to her rose garden.

"*Durroe sallvas tempre. Juth calt.*" Vi did away with the lock on the cell in the same manner as she had broken into the storefronts.

She went down the long hall that lined this wing of cells, magic gathered under her fingers. The one other prisoner was lying on his cot, back to her, and didn't stir as she passed—her footsteps completely silenced by her magic. One end of the hall stretched deeper into the dungeons; the other, where she'd entered from, was hazy with light. Vi glanced around the corner to find the guard on duty slumped in his chair, much as he had been when she'd entered.

Vi closed her eyes, debating what chant to use. There was one bit of Lightspinning she had yet to try. Should she risk a new piece of chanting, or try to make herself invisible while moving through a room? Invisibility in motion was nearly impossible; the choice practically made itself.

"*Loft not,*" Vi breathed, her own eyes feeling heavy and fluttering closed for a long moment. *Not* was a subset of *loft*—to sleep—and in the same family as *dorh*—to immobilize. The word was warm on her tongue and the glyph that haloed over the guard's head settled on his shoulders like sunset.

He let out a large snore and Vi crept though the room, still keeping the sounds of her footsteps silent. As soon as she was down the hall and out of earshot from the now slumbering guard, Vi let go of both glyphs and immediately whispered a few more words to step into the skin of one of the guards who had escorted her to the prison. With the man's face, she strolled easily through the halls and stairwells.

Vi ran her hand along the banisters as she ascended through the quiet passageways. The castle felt unnaturally empty. Servants weren't buzzing around and guards had seemingly limited patrols. It felt like a great beast, now slumbering, waiting until it would rise once more to be the bastion of the West.

Elecia had sent no shortage of maps of Norin and architects' drawings of the castle to Vi while she was in Soricium. She had deemed it "important for Vi to learn her heritage." Vi's chest tightened at the thought that she'd never have the opportunity to properly thank her cousin for how she'd prepared her.

Vi went up and up. She stepped through doorways and underneath carefully embellished archways. High above the royal family's quarters was the library. It was hexagonal in shape and extended five stories up with nothing but bookcases lining each wall. Had the original builders of the castle of Norin known of the Archives of Yargen? Were they aware of the distant influence that still held sway over their aesthetics?

Making her way up and around the library with a side stair, Vi paused at a doorway wedged between two bookcases. It was unassuming and unlocked.

The thick scent of roses assaulted her senses as Vi stepped out into the rooftop conservatory. Western breezes filtered through open windows in the high glass panels that capped the garden. The quiet sound of trickling water added a layer of serenity that had Vi's tense shoulders relaxing. She began to walk the gardens, looking at the various flora and fauna—mostly Western roses, Fiera's favorite.

"You're here."

Vi turned, meeting Fiera's gaze as the woman stood in the doorway. Fiera blinked with surprise, but it passed quickly and was replaced with a knowing smile.

"I am."

"I was wondering when you'd come."

"Forgive me for breaking free of your prison." Vi's attention shifted, turning to the sword still strapped to Fiera's hip. Her whole body ached at the sight of it and Vi barely held herself back from giving in to a moment of weakness and just ripping it from Fiera's body.

"Part of me suspects I should be pleased that you have."

"I mean you no harm."

"So you've told me, and so you've illustrated." Fiera took a step forward and lifted her hand. "Shall we stroll?"

For a quarter of one lap of the lush garden, they didn't say anything. Vi kept glancing at the woman at her side while Fiera kept her gaze forward and relaxed. Still, her hand remained on the sword hilt.

"I sense fate in you," Fiera said finally, "in a way I have never sensed in any other."

"I'm afraid I don't understand what you mean."

Fiera paused only long enough to glance at her from the corners of her eyes. "You're a poor liar."

"Don't mistake half-truths for a lie." Vi chuckled. "I don't understand what you mean when you say you 'sense fate.'"

"Yargen has chosen me to see along her lines," Fiera started, leaving Vi to wonder if her deflection had been so easily dispatched. "Sometimes, I feel compelled to look along those lines—more so than other times. Sometimes, I don't need to peer along the lines at all to know that someone or something has great importance in those designs."

"Or perhaps you are sensing places and moments where fate has been changed," Vi suggested, narrowly avoiding the term *Apex of Fate*.

"A good way to put it." Fiera gave a small nod. "You… you are the embodiment of that feeling. When I see you I feel I know you—like somehow I've always known you."

Fiera came to a stop and Vi with her. They faced each other, nearly identical in height and build. If anything, Fiera was slightly more curvaceous than Vi. But otherwise, they could be mistaken for identical twins at a glance.

"Perhaps it is because I look at you and see my face."

"An oddity, indeed." That was something she had no idea how she could explain away—not even with half-truths.

"Yet, this feeling runs much deeper," Fiera continued. "When I have tried to scry into the flames for you, I see nothing. The sight has been absent since we met, all other sensations dulled, save for you."

"But you told Richard Le'Dan you foresaw our meeting?"

Fiera laughed softly and shook her head at the mention of Richard. She wore a tender smile on her lips, one tinged with sadness.

"Richard wouldn't understand if I tried to explain it to him. He is not like you and me. He doesn't understand these feelings," Fiera said tenderly. "I told him that because I knew you would seek me out, as you sought me out the first time. My hope was that the more people I told of you, the greater the likelihood of you being led to me."

"How?"

"I had a feeling." Fiera shrugged and crossed to a bench. She patted it, inviting Vi to sit next to her. Vi obliged. "May I know your name now, traveler?"

"Yullia."

"Yullia, a beautiful and unique name." A knowing smile spread across her lips. "And tell me, Yullia, what is it you seek?"

The sword you carry. Vi knew it wouldn't be that easy. The crystal sword, known to the West as the Sword of Jadar, was a sacred relic. If she was going to steal it, she needed a bit more of a plan than grab and flee.

Move slowly, Vi reminded herself in Taavin's words. She had time, *decades* of time. She didn't have to take the sword in one night.

"I wish to be at your side—guiding and protecting as I am able," Vi said finally, after weighing her various options. "I can serve you in many ways, and perhaps we will find one that is the best for your needs. I am confident with a sword, and with magic. I am wise to the ways of the world. And I can see along the Mother's lines as well."

Fiera hummed softly. "I should tell you no. I wouldn't want to get a reputation for accepting people easily into my employ. Especially those who break our laws."

"Will you tell me no?" Vi asked, genuinely unsure of the answer.

"I will tell you that I am a woman of faith—and I believe in the Mother's will that guides us all. You feel of fate, and speak like one who has the sight." Fiera stood. "So kneel, traveler Yullia."

Vi pushed off the bench and did as she was instructed.

"Do you swear fealty and loyalty to me, and to the Solaris crown?"

She didn't even have to fake the broad grin at the question. "Yes."

"Then consider yourself a member of my guard, formerly the

Knights of Jadar…" A smirk pulled up the corners of Fiera's lips. It was somewhat coquettish and the first playful thing Vi had seen about the otherwise perfectly composed royal. "I'm still working on a new name."

"No names needed." Vi rose to her feet. "I am here for you, your highness. Not for a title."

"And I have been truly blessed in that." Fiera stood and began walking once more, but her shoulders had more sway to them, her steps far less rigid. Just like that, a barrier between them had been lowered, if not entirely removed. "You are not the first the Mother has sent to me in this way."

"Who was—" Before Vi could finish, three people appeared in the doorway.

"There she is." Tiberus let out a sigh of relief, crossing over to Fiera and scooping up her hands. He didn't even so much as glance Vi's way. Vi wouldn't be surprised if he didn't even realize there were other people around him. It was a far cry from the Emperor Vi saw in the great hall. "You worried me—all of us—wandering off without Zira at the very least. It's too dangerous still for you to do that. The association with me will have people out to harm you."

"No one in Mhashan would harm me. And I had to come and meet with my new guard." Fiera motioned to Vi and the Emperor slowly turned his head to look at her.

"You're the criminal."

"I'd prefer 'party crasher'." Vi shrugged.

The Emperor's expression grew more concerned at her nonchalance, but lightened instantly when Fiera let out a burst of laughter. He finally chuckled as well.

"You are an odd one, aren't you?" Tiberus shook his head with a slight smile, all the while his eyes still on Fiera. "I suppose if my beloved trusts you, so shall I."

Most of the stories Vi had heard of her grandfather were about him at the end of his decades of conquest. They were tales of an older man, hardened by war. The man before Vi now was barely in his thirties and he looked not a day past twenty-five.

"Yullia?" a familiar voice interrupted the conversation.

Vi grinned. "Hello, Zira."

"I thought it was you!" Zira hastily walked and clasped Vi's shoulder. "Forget how she made it out of the jail cell… how did you make it out of containment? You do have an interesting set of skills, don't you?"

"You could say that."

"A set of skills we will use for our Empire," Fiera insisted to Tiberus. "I have made her my guard and would seek not to have her punished for impersonating a noble tonight, or sneaking out of the soldiers' confinement. She was merely following the will of the Mother, and my will, to stand at my side."

"Then it shall be done." Tiberus gave a nod to Vi and, like that, she was absolved of all crimes.

"Thank you, my love," Fiera said lightly, almost sweetly. It was yet another stark contrast to the stiff, formal woman Vi had seen in the main hall.

"You are to be my Empress, the sword protecting my back, and will rule at my side. I wish for you to know always that your voice is heard." Tiberus cupped Fiera's cheek and Vi gave a glance to Zira, who was barely refraining from rolling her eyes.

"Zira, will you see that Yullia is settled in a room?" Fiera asked, turning away from Tiberus's affections. "There are more than enough open. You can place her wherever you think is appropriate."

"Yes, your highness."

"Zerian, please escort us back into the party. They'll wonder if we're gone for too long," Tiberus said.

"And leaving nobles to wonder only leads them to gossip." Fiera sighed. "You're right, we should be along." Tiberus offered Fiera his elbow and she took it, starting away. But not before Fiera paused once more to say, "I look forward to working with you, Yullia."

Vi stared at the familiar dark eyes. Fiera's spell-like quality of speech made Vi feel as if she were the only person in the world. Perhaps it was this quality that made others eager to bend over backward for the princess.

"And you as well, princess." Vi gave a small bow of her head. Zira and Zerian exchanged a nod and the man escorted the two royals back into the library. Vi glanced over at Zira, whose whole body now seemed racked with tension. "Is everything all right?"

"My eyes tell me I'm seeing the men who are responsible for King Rocham's death and the fall of Mhashan, while my mind reminds me they are no longer my enemies." Zira shrugged, shoved her hands in her pockets, and began strolling forward. "It takes some getting used to."

"I can imagine," Vi said thoughtfully and fell into step at Zira's side. "Does she love him?" As though Fiera's love would make the circumstances easier to bear for Zira.

"I can't tell," Zira answered candidly. Vi was grateful they'd already had the opportunity to build a rapport; talking came easily, and there was no need to dance around topics when they'd spent days imprisoned together. Then again, Zira didn't seem like the type to dance in any context that didn't involve holding a blade. "I know she loves her people. She loves this land. And if loving him saves those things, she will love him to the sun and back."

Her grandfather and grandmother's love had been the stuff of legend, and Vi had believed it. Though now, she wondered… A begrudging political arrangement wouldn't have done nearly as much to keep the West loyal and begin the slow process of endearing the South to their future Empress and Emperor. It made sense the story would be spun in brighter light. Vi's chest tightened and her breathing grew short, but not from the stairs she and Zira climbed.

Despite having been taught all her life that marriage was a political transaction for someone born to her status, Vi had looked to Fiera and Tiberus as a model for how a political union could straddle both love and politics. The thought suddenly seemed so naive now.

"Here, these quarters belonged to one of Fiera's other generals who's… Well, let's not linger on the details."

Vi walked into the room. It reminded her of a smaller version of the hotel in the Crossroads: a carefully carved sliding screen separated the bed from a sitting area, and two doors at her left likely led to a closet and bathing room.

The memory briefly misted her eyes. That hotel had been the last place she'd seen her brother. Those few weeks they'd spent together on the road were all she'd ever have now, and they weren't nearly enough.

"Make yourself as comfortable as possible," Zira continued, oblivious. "Do you have personal effects anywhere in the city I should collect?"

"No, I travel light."

"As a former mercenary of the Nameless Company, I respect that." Zira smiled. "I'm sure I can find more than enough spare clothes for you before morning. We'll need you dressed properly as one of her guards because tomorrow, you'll face something far scarier than an Imperial army."

"What?"

Zira turned from the doorway, a wry grin on her face. "The Royal Council."

Z IRA WAS GOOD TO her word and brought Vi two trunks of various clothing to choose from. As usual, the slim-cut styles of the West were nearly impossible to fit into if they weren't perfectly tailored to the wearer. But Vi found something that didn't look comically large or small.

She braided her hair in large parts, knotting the ropes together up and away from her face at the back of her head. There were already enough similarities between her and Fiera; Vi didn't want to encourage them further. Keeping her hair up rather than wearing it loose as Fiera did would be a good point of differentiation.

The council met just outside the royal quarters, which made it right down the hall and around the corner from Vi's room.

When she entered the chamber, she was greeted by only four familiar faces—Fiera, Zira, Ophain, and Zerian. Tiberus was surprisingly absent and everyone else was a wary stranger. Vi would tread lightly while she determined if she needed to earn their favor.

"We should discuss the matter of the soldiers first," Lord Twintle, councilor for maritime matters, pressed as soon as Fiera opened the meeting to concerns at large. "They are the men and women of the West, men and women who put their lives on the line for their kingdom."

"Their kingdom is no more," Zerian interjected. "In the eyes of the Empire they are war crimi—"

"They are equal citizens with a chance of serving the Empire," Fiera said, cutting him off quickly with a look before he could say something that would likely raise tempers. "Lord Twintle, I know your son is in one of the containment shelters."

"Containment shelter? You mean prison."

Fiera ignored the remark and continued, "We're doing all we can at the moment for our soldiers. But returning the city at large to a point of comfort and normalcy is our first priority. That way the soldiers see there is nothing more to defend and will integrate back with society more smoothly as citizens of Solaris."

"They will always want to stand for Mhashan," he mumbled. Fiera ignored him.

"Lord Twintle's eldest son is Luke," Zira whispered in Vi's ear. "He's been vying to get him out of the prison for weeks."

"Speaking of that normalcy, Lord Twintle, how is trade? And fishing?" Fiera asked.

"Fishing is better now that we aren't dodging Imperial vessels."

"And Oparium?"

"We're still talking with the dock master there regarding getting into port."

Vi stared at the notes, letters, ledgers, and maps spread on the table before her. She had heard of council meetings like this from her parents—even fantasized about one day being a part of them. Now that she was here, and with the knowledge she held, it was proving difficult to remain silent.

"Until trade improves," Vi began, and all eyes immediately swung to her. More than one councilmember looked surprised by her boldness. "Might I suggest we import additional rations from the East? I believe they are going to have a rather impressive year for grain; they might be able to spare more than they're letting on, in an effort to conserve in case of a poor harvest next year. But I'm confident the Mother will bless their fields again."

"And just who are you again?" Lord Twintle asked dully.

"My name is Yullia."

"I didn't ask for your name," he drawled. "Let me put it more simply for you: why should we care about your thoughts? Especially since they are the thoughts of a criminal."

Vi merely shrugged. "Care or don't. I merely offer my wisdom."

"And your wisdom is welcome," Fiera insisted with a glance to Twintle. "Yullia is gifted with the goddess's sight. Perhaps even more so than I." There were several skeptical glances at that statement. "I am certain when she gives us her thoughts, they are worth listening to. I'll speak with the Emperor regarding reaching out to the Lady of the East for additional supplies."

"Perhaps in that same missive he can introduce me to her," Ophain suggested from Fiera's right. "As I might need to deal with her directly in the coming years."

"I'll bring it up." Fiera nodded to her brother.

Vi studied Ophain as he leaned forward, making a few notes in his personal ledger. He seemed to be taking the situation with surprising grace. Then again, he was heir to the last king of the West and had somehow escaped being murdered following the end of the war. That would be enough to make anyone grateful.

"If we are thinking of asking the East for further assistance, we should check the current storerooms to ensure our counts are accurate," Denja, a councilor for commerce mused. She had a thick accent—one Vi couldn't quite place. It didn't sound entirely Western to her ears. "I have been sending messengers regularly, but I worry the Imperial soldiers have been dipping in without approval."

"Imperial soldiers would never," Zerian insisted.

"Then perhaps they haven't been taking careful notes." Denja smiled thinly.

"We shall go together," Fiera suggested.

"Do you think that's wise?" her brother asked.

"I've been shut up in this castle for too long." Fiera sighed and collected her papers. "The engagement has been announced and the people should know I'm not being held hostage until my wedding day. Besides, I'll have my knights with me."

Her gaze lifted to Zira and Vi. They both gave a nod to the princess.

"Knights," Twintle murmured. "But they're not anymore, are they?"

"I've yet to decide what the fate of the Knights of Jadar will be," Fiera said. She quickly returned the conversation to its previous topic, looking to Denja. "Do you have time now?"

"Of course, your highness." When the councilor bowed her head, the beads attached to the ornate headscarf she wore clanked softly.

"Excellent. I leave the other matters in Ophain's capable hands." Fiera started around the table. Denja, Vi, and Zira following behind.

"Where are you from, Yullia?" Denja asked as they walked. "You speak Southern Common and Mhashanese quite well."

"I've been gifted with languages," Vi said honestly. When Denja continued to stare expectantly at her, Vi knew she hadn't dodged the initial question. "I've traveled all over. I've never quite had a home and couldn't tell you where I was born or who my parents were." Vi kept Taavin's words in mind as she danced around the question; telling people who she was could have unintended consequences.

"How heartbreaking, an orphan alone in the world." Denja didn't sound for a moment like she was genuinely sympathetic. "And now you stand in direct service to one of the most powerful people on this continent. That's extraordinarily lucky."

This continent. The words stuck out to Vi like an absent compass rose on a map.

"And where are you from?" Vi asked, trying to keep her voice light. "You have the bright blue eyes of a Southerner." So blue they almost had hints of purple.

"I am from the south of Mhashan," she answered easily. "Right along the border. Some Southern blood made it into my family tree."

"I see." Vi didn't trust those unnaturally colored eyes, full of suspicious knowing. But for now, Vi put the sense behind her. She had other things to focus on—like getting a moment with Fiera to discuss the sword.

They stepped out into the royal stables and continued out toward the drawbridge that connected the castle to the city. However, before they could depart, an Imperial soldier blocked their way.

"Your highness, do you require a guard detail into the city today?"

"I already have my guards," Fiera motioned to Vi and Zira.

Even though Fiera's unspoken dismissal was clear, the soldier didn't move. "The Emperor has insisted that you are to be protected at all times."

"And I have told you that I will be. And I am quite able to protect myself, thank you." Fiera patted the steel sword on her hip and looked the man up and down. "I'd venture I was training long before you ever even saw a sword."

He pursed his lips together but managed to squeeze out, "This is an order from the Emperor."

"And I am the future Empress," Fiera retorted. "I wish to go out into my city without a pack of soldiers around me. The war is over, sir, and the people should know it."

"The city is unsafe."

"What do you know of the city?" Zira asked, a lazy grin on her face. "I think her highness and all her advisors have a clear sense of just how dangerous it is or isn't."

"Now, stand aside," Fiera ordered firmly. "If the Emperor has a problem, he'll take it up with me."

"Yes, your highness." The soldier finally relented and stepped aside. Vi could feel him and the others in his squadron watching as the four women passed.

"Do you think it's actually dangerous?" Denja asked.

"They're Southern. Judging by their sunburnt cheeks, they'll likely try and claim the sun itself is dangerous," Zira remarked dryly.

Fiera let out a low chuckle. "Perhaps, for soldiers, the city poses some threat. But I want the people to see me among them without Southerners surrounding me. To know that the Mhashan they once knew has not vanished, regardless of its name—and that I am still with them, regardless of mine."

After a beat of what felt like companionable silence, Vi cleared her throat. "Speaking of Mhashan," she began delicately. "The Knights of Jadar…"

"Don't start sounding like Twintle," Zira muttered with a roll of her eyes. "The man is relentless."

"Of course he is. He's one of the last living commanders of the Knights." Fiera sighed heavily. "It was an honor he doesn't want to see stripped."

Vi's stomach flipped on the thought and settled the wrong way. She couldn't recall Lord Twintle in any of her readings or discussions, but that didn't make him unimportant. From this point on, in Vi's world, the Knights had devolved into a shadowy, separatist organization that stood against her family.

"I don't wish to speak about the Knights a moment longer. That is my burden and decision. No need to cloud our otherwise good day with it." The note of finality in Fiera's voice brooked no protest. "Denja, can you please outline our goal for this excursion?"

"Certainly, your highness. There are new stores for grains and other supplies brought in by the Empire around where the old wall used to be…"

Vi tried to pay attention to the conversation with half an ear, but her eyes were on the houses around them. The dictates of martial law were being lifted bit by bit; citizens were getting a few more hours each day to be about. But this hour was not one of them, and the city felt like a ghost town.

She glanced over her shoulder, unable to shake the perpetual feeling of someone watching them. The silence in a city so large was eerie—an unwelcome fifth companion.

Slowing, Vi caught Zira's eye and the woman adjusted her pace until the two of them were side by side. Denja and Fiera took the lead, talking about current stocks and trade. Vi kept her voice hushed.

"Zira, do you feel like someone is watching us?"

"I feel like a thousand someones are watching us." Zira looked to the upper floors of the buildings around them. Vi saw a curtain abruptly close in one of the windows. "But that is the point of this, as our princess has decreed."

"Yes but…" Vi couldn't put her finger on the uneasy feeling that crackled up her spine like the phantom sensation of the red magic of an evil god. It was akin to the nervous energy she'd felt before sailing into Adela's stronghold. "I can't shake the feeling that *something* is about to happen."

"Should we head back to the castle?" The question was genuine, and Vi appreciated it down to her toes. Zira had no reason to give her so much faith, especially not when her worries were ambiguous.

"No, I don't want to turn us around for a mere feeling." Vi shook her head and tried to shake the sensations with it, but they clung to her like leeches. "I'm sure it's nothing."

The four made it without incident to the storehouses. Vi felt far better the moment she saw the Imperial guards standing out front of the large barn-shaped buildings. Vi and Zira walked a quick perimeter as Denja and Fiera consulted with the quartermaster. The whole affair took less than an hour and was blessedly over without incident. They were on their way back when bells tolled over the city, reigniting Vi's paranoia.

"The citizens are allowed out for an hour after the bells," Zira explained.

Sure enough, doors began to open and people wandered, blinking into the streets. They seemed dazed, their senses dulled by long hours cooped up inside. One by one, they turned their faces skyward; the sun was the first thing their eyes met, as if to burn away the haze in their eyes. As if to greet it like an old friend. For the first block, none of the people even noticed the princess in their midst.

"Y-Your highness." A woman was the first to turn their way. "You are free." She dropped to her knees.

"As I have always been. As are we all."

"The conqueror… what has he done to you, m'lady?" another young woman dared to ask.

"Only steal my heart." Fiera gave a smile so tender and warm it could melt ice.

One look, and Vi nearly forgot all her prior questions about the genuineness of Fiera's love for Tiberus—only to have them rushing back even stronger. Did she have a genuine smile? Or was it the look of someone desperate to save their home—someone who knew the safety of her people depended on them believing a beautiful lie?

It wasn't her business, Vi tried to remember. She was here for the crystal weapons. She had enough on her plate when it came to love.

"He has stolen your heart, and your fire." A male voice cut through Vi's thoughts. The little crowd collecting around Fiera suddenly seemed far larger as Vi searched for the speaker. "The Fiera who led the Knights of Jadar, who was truly blessed by the Mother above, would've never given into the false sun."

Vi's eyes settled on the man, who had short black hair and a closely trimmed mustache. Zira took a step closer to Fiera, situating herself between the princess and her detractor.

"You might not be able to understand," Fiera said, keeping her composure rock-solid and voice as soft as feathers, "but I truly do love him. He brightens my fire. And I will ensure he protect us all."

Motion from Vi's left caught her eye.

Like a bull rushing forward, a cloaked man pushed through the crowd. Vi's eyes barely had time to land on a flash of silver. Zira wasn't moving and wouldn't notice in time, Denja had yet to react, Fiera was looking the other way—

"*Mysst soto larrk,*" Vi hissed under her breath, moving as she spoke. She drew her hand across her chest, moving as though she was drawing the blade from a hidden sheathe in her sleeve. Vi hoped it was enough to hide the flash of the glyph that created the weapon she now held.

Steel met steel as Vi pushed Fiera aside, stopping the assassin's blade. But the hooded man paid her no heed. Instead, his dark gaze swung to Fiera.

"You should've died with your father," he uttered darkly. "Traitor."

9

T HE WORDS WERE THE man's last.

The hand-guard of Vi's dagger was flush to his blade. She slid it upward, the short pommel of hers butting against his. Vi used the force to beat the blade away; she had momentum, and the man was caught off-guard by the sudden assault.

Twisting, Vi threw her body into a lunge and sank her blade into his ear. As Vi withdrew, he crumpled.

She spun in place. Zira had already engaged the man who had first drawn their attention and had him on the ground in an instant. People were screaming, fleeing; chaos radiated around them, but Vi's eyes scanned the windows and rooftops. The memory of the Knight's attempt on her mother's life at the Crossroads was suddenly fresh and—

Motion caught her eye.

Vi lifted a hand and sent a tendril of flame in a burst toward a rooftop. She used the motion to release her dagger back into her sleeve, the flash of fire and fabric hiding the unraveling remnants of light. Whoever had been on the roof darted away and didn't return to the building's edge. Vi linked arms with Fiera, briefly startled by how warm the woman was to her touch.

"Your highness, we must move you—"

"I will not be moved." Fiera pulled her arm back, an offended expression at being manhandled briefly taking over her features. She spun in place, looking to the man Zira held at sword-point on the ground. The princess crossed over like a beast stalking prey. "Who sent you?"

"No one sent us." The man narrowed his eyes at Fiera. "We didn't need to be sent by anyone, because we no longer need a leader. We shall lead ourselves as we stand by our mission—to defend Mhashan from Southern invaders."

"The war is over."

"The war is only beginning." A smile spread across his mouth. "Kill me, like you did the other Knights of Jadar. Those who made the mistake of being loyal to you until the end."

"You are not my knight," Fiera whispered.

Vi continued to scan the buildings. Denja, for her part, remained incredibly calm—far calmer than Vi would have expected from a commerce minister. Vi's attention landed on her and they locked eyes for a long moment.

Denja had been the one to suggest going to the storerooms, hadn't she? It wouldn't have been hard to find dissenters and organize an attack with a few hours' notice.

"No, I am not *your* knight. I am Mhashan's Knight, one of the true Knights of Jadar," the man insisted. "We have broken free of you. We do not need your orders."

"You speak treason like it delights you."

"Truth is what delights me."

"I will not give you another chance to—"

"No, you won't," the man interrupted. "Just like you did not give your once-loyal Knights another chance on the docks that night."

Vi frowned. Of course word would spread of what had happened at the docks. Most likely, Luke or Kahrin had started the rumors—Zira wouldn't. Luke was Twintle's son and Twintle could connect back to Denja. Lines of betrayal unfolded like a deadly map before her, one where a single misstep would lead one to death.

"What will it be, princess?" the man continued. The commoners watched from a wide distance. "Will you—"

Fiera clamped her hand over the man's mouth. Fire poured from between her fingers and down his throat. Vi did not grimace or turn away; this was how Jax had described her father's method for killing people.

Vi wondered if Aldrik was even aware of the similarity with his late mother. That the action was a dark, unlikely, perhaps even unintentional connection between them.

The man collapsed to the ground, his skin red and bubbling as Fiera straightened away. She smoothed out her clothes and tossed her hair over her shoulder, starting for the castle without a backward glance.

"No one touch them," Fiera declared as they passed the ring of wide-eyed onlookers. "Do not burn them this evening for a Rite of Sunset. I want them to be strung up and branded as traitors. Let there be no doubt that my Empire has no room for those who stand against me. The only true knights are those at my side."

Every man and woman seemed to hold their breath while Fiera's eyes were on them. They were utterly captive to their fear. And while Vi could see a certain amount of shock in their stares, she was keenly aware that none of them seemed surprised.

Fiera was a double-edged sword. One side of her could slice through a man's most iron-clad defenses with startling sweetness. The other side of her could cut a man down beginning with his ankles and working up from there.

The most fearsome thing was that Fiera clearly knew what she was, and had learned to wield her skills with deadly precision.

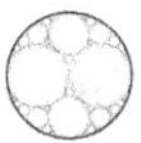

"Knights of Jadar," Fiera muttered, pacing her personal quarters and worrying the heavy silver ring on her finger. Immediately after returning to the castle, Fiera had made her will known regarding the bodies of the traitors, sent Denja away, and summoned Vi and Zira to her rooms. "They called themselves 'true Knights of Jadar.'"

"They wouldn't be able to pass even the initial tests to become a Knight," Zira muttered. She lounged in a large wingback chair by one of the windows of Fiera's room, one leg draped lazily over the armrest. "They are cutthroats turned opportunists."

"They make a mockery of my family." Fiera clenched her hands into fists so tightly they trembled. Tiny tendrils of flame snaked through the air around them. "Being a Knight of Jadar was the greatest honor in all the West."

Vi watched Fiera's rage from where she leaned against the wall by the doorway, arms folded and holding her elbows. She tried to keep herself detached from the princess's plight by reminding herself that this Fiera was not her family. Vi was merely here as a traveler, doing what she needed to do before leaving without a trace.

Yet the raw hurt that swirled almost visibly in the air around Fiera brought up emotions from the void that was always threatening to swallow Vi whole. Fiera's eyes were glassy, as though she was nearly at the point of frustrated tears. Still the fire within them burned.

"What do you think?" Fiera asked Vi.

"Pardon?"

"I asked your thoughts, Yullia." Fiera motioned toward her with an open hand, flames still writhing around her fingers. "Do you agree with Zira that these are opportunists and I do myself more of a disservice by giving them a platform with my anger?"

Vi only had to make a show of thinking about the answer. "I don't think this was an isolated attack, unfortunately."

"You don't." Fiera's hand dropped to her side.

"I think there are those who cling to old Mhashan like a security blanket. Those who would've rather fought with every last breath for every last brick, regardless of the cost."

"Those like my father." Fiera pinched the bridge of her nose with a sigh and shook her head, walking over to one of the three large windows that dominated one wall of her sitting room. They towered over her, making even Fiera seem small. "He wanted to defend Norin until it was ashes. He would've seen every last man and woman of the kingdom die if that's what it took to prevent Mhashan bending to Solaris."

"Foolish men and their foolish honor." Zira tipped her head against the side of the wingback, looking to Fiera. The princess was still avoiding eye contact with both of them.

"Foolish people who cannot see the world changing around them," Fiera said thoughtfully. "We are a people surrounded by desert. Yet somehow, there are those who cannot see how power shifts like sand in the wind. It blows one way, then another. You can never expect it to be in the same place for long.

"Mhashan was not made strong because of our cities of immovable stone. The Ci'Dan family did not rise to prominence because we were rigid. It was because we could adapt."

Vi continued to stare at the princess's back. Fiera would give up everything to save what she loved. Not to preserve the world as she knew it, and had always known it—but to see it thrive, to continue on even if that meant letting it change.

A thought settled at the forefront of Vi's mind: when she had gone to Meru to be the Goddess's Champion, what had she been fighting for? Had she wanted to see her family thrive in whatever form that took? Or had she only wanted to see her family as she had envisioned them?

"The fact remains that not all possess your wisdom," Vi said, silently including herself in the sentiment. "And those men and women will band together."

"He said the war was only just beginning." Fiera turned away from the window at last. "You said you believe the attacks will continue. How do you think they'll strike next?"

"All wars need a general. In the case of the Knights of Jadar, that general is designated by a singular object—"

"A sword," Fiera finished for her. "They will never lay their hands on my grandfather's sword."

"It sees the light of day rarely enough," Zira murmured.

"They will go after it though, regardless of where it is. If they even sense the edge of its power, these false Knights will hunt it." Vi braced herself for what she needed to ask next. "If I'm to be effective as your guard, I need to know where it is."

For the first time, Fiera didn't immediately acquiesce. Vi supposed she should be grateful; Fiera's caution surrounding the sword was their first line of defense.

"It took me three years to lay eyes on it." Zira stood. "Why do you think she should show you? You've only just entered her service."

"Because my only goal is to protect it," Vi said as earnestly as possible. She pushed away from the wall and allowed her arms to fall to her sides, abandoning her previously defensive position. "Because I have a sense about it, just as I had a sense earlier this day about the attack."

"What sense?" Fiera looked between her and Zira.

"She did tell me as we were walking to the storehouse that she felt uneasy. But then again, we all did."

Fiera debated this a moment before slowly approaching Vi. She searched Vi's face and narrowed her eyes slightly, as if she could extract any falsehoods from Vi's eyes alone. Vi worked to make sure she didn't hesitate, which seemed nearly impossible under the woman's relentless inspections.

"I need more from you," she said finally. "Your words, the feeling of fate steeped in the air around you... it has gotten you this far. But I need more from you if I am to bestow this most prized secret on you."

It was fair, more than fair. Vi had earned Fiera's trust thanks to the woman's senses. But she'd found the extent of that good will and now the real work would have to begin. Taavin had cautioned her as much.

"I see more than the future," Vi confessed softly, her voice nearly quivering. She was walking a very fine, very dangerous line. "I was chosen by the Mother herself to defend this world and the sword will play a role in that. Keeping it from falling into the wrong hands is all I desire."

"Chosen by the Mother?" Zira repeated, though Vi couldn't tell if her tone was one of belief or incredulity.

"It's true," Vi continued, speaking directly to Fiera. "And if you take me to the sword, I can give you proof of my claim that will satisfy you." Fiera was immobile as a statue, listening, waiting. It was that expectant tension that had Vi adding, "Should it not, then kill me there and I will take the secret of the sword's location to my grave."

The princess took a step backward, then nodded. She glanced to Zira and said, "I'm going to accept Yullia's offer. Keep your blade ready."

Zira gripped the pommel of her sword and Vi's heart began to race.

Fiera was ever the double-edged sword and Vi walked the ridge down the middle. Would she end on the side that would protect her? Or was the sharper edge about to be turned against her?

Her future with Fiera balanced on what happened next and, unfortunately for Vi, she had no idea what she was about to do to earn the trust she needed.

10

L UCKILY, VI HAD A bit of a walk to think about her plans. Even better, the walk was done entirely in silence. Fiera led them down through the castle with Vi in the middle and Zira behind her.

As Vi walked, she scribbled down a mental list of things she could do to prove to Fiera she was meant to have the sword. She could try to look into the future and if that didn't work, perhaps summon a glyph? That would seem mysterious enough.

They entered through empty passages clearly meant for soldiers—those men and women still locked away at the order of the Emperor. Fiera led them past a desk that must once have belonged to the quartermaster, and through one of three doors that led to a mostly empty armory. Every part of Norin had been impacted by the ten-year siege. The city was like a carcass that the Empire was slowly, bite by bite, licking clean.

Fiera went to a door in the back, lifted a key with a chain around her neck and, with one more glance back at Vi, opened the door.

Beyond the threshold, a narrow hallway glowed orange thanks to a curtain of swirling flame burning at its end. The fire was nearly white-hot and would no doubt be difficult for even the most powerful of Firebearers to pass through.

Fiera waved dismissively and the flames vanished. Vi was left blinking into the sudden darkness in the moments before the princess summoned a mote of flame for them to see by.

"How difficult is it to maintain that flame all the time?" Vi asked.

"I've grown accustomed to it," Fiera answered. "At first, it seemed like a great deal of power constantly draining from me, making me weak. But our magic is like our muscles—the more we stretch and flex our powers, the stronger they become. I hardly notice it now."

Vi believed her. Fiera's powers were as breathtaking as all the stories she'd been told growing up made them seem.

They continued forward, past the stones that still glowed faintly from the residual heat of the flames and into a tiny room. It was unadorned, save for the sword hung on the wall before Vi, and a narrow table beneath it. Fiera reached for the blade without hesitation, unsheathing it.

"The Sword of Jadar," she said with quiet reverence. "Bestowed by King Jadar onto his youngest son—the one who did not inherit his flames—so he could use its powers to defend Mhashan and the throne." She held out the blade, pointing it directly at Vi. "You have seen it. And now I will have the proof you promised."

She should feel threatened. But Vi's heart raced purely because of how close the crystal was. She could feel the waves of power rippling from it. Every swirl of the magic within it delighted her, enthralled her.

Vi's plan to prove her good intentions had been formed out of a series of guesses. But in that moment, she no longer needed a clear way forward. She didn't need to overthink.

She acted on instinct.

Lifting her hands, Vi's fingertips lightly landed on the edges of the blade on either side. It was sharp enough that it could bite into her flesh but it didn't. It wouldn't. This was the will of the goddess; Vi and the sword were of the same make, now, and it would not harm her.

Power lifted off the blade. The faint glow that perpetually surrounded the sword curled like tendrils of smoke, reaching for Vi with a nearly sentient quality. Like the scythe, the power crashed on her, and the sensation of being two places at once overtook her.

They stood in the center of the Dark Isle.

Two women and two men were semi-circled around one older man who had the same pointed ears as Taavin. He still appeared youthful, yet his eyes were ancient and ringed with dark circles. Clutched in his left hand was a tall staff of glittering crystal as bright blue as a clear morning sky.

Vi knew the man was the former Champion. Looking at him was like looking in a mirror that twisted her outside reflection while exposing what was within. He spoke to what she assumed were his children, but his eyes remained on her—as if he could see the one who would come after him, even then. As if somehow, across all time and space, he was aware of the future Champion in his midst.

Lifting the staff, magic burst from his hands, merging with the glow of the crystal as he broke off the first quarter of the staff.

The fragment glowed so brightly that Vi was left blinking, struggling to make out what was happening; the four kneeling before the Champion covered their eyes. But the light and magic faded, revealing a scythe he bestowed on his youngest daughter.

The Champion repeated the process, giving an axe to the next daughter, and a sword to his youngest son. On his eldest's brow, the Champion settled a crown of crystal.

As soon as the man's hands left the crown, his body aged. Vi watched as the magic left him like fireflies returning to the sun high above. He swayed from side to side as muscles vanished and his clothes became limp sacks. His skin and hair grayed and his lips curled in.

But his eyes—those eyes that had witnessed the passage of time from beyond its reach, thanks to the hand of Yargen—stayed the same. They were not surprised. They were not in pain.

Vi only saw acceptance and relief in the man's final moments.

All at once, her awareness returned to her physical body.

As it had with the scythe in the Twilight Kingdom, a soft glow coated her skin, extending from the sword. The magic disappeared like smoke as the vision left her. Fiera and Zira looked at her with startled and slightly worried expressions.

Vi lowered her hands from the blade, taking a step away. She moved slowly so they wouldn't spook and attack her, and because her head was still spinning, settling back into this time and place.

That vision had been far more vivid than the last. With the scythe, she'd experienced shifting images, feelings, sensations that connected into a story Vi could piece together. This had been a complete scene from start to finish.

"They glow blue, not red…" Zira whispered. "Like the sword."

Vi lifted her hand to her temple and wished there was a mirror in the room so she could confirm Zira's murmurings were about her eyes.

"What are you?" Fiera asked as she lowered the sword.

"I am chosen by the Mother to defend this world," Vi repeated softly, hoping this act of exposing a part of her true nature didn't adversely affect the future she was working toward. For reasons she couldn't quite explain, Vi trusted Fiera and Zira more deeply than she likely should. "You will not understand who—what—I am. But you must keep what you have seen a secret. The fate of your world depends on it."

Zira took another step back. But Fiera was less shaken. She delicately rested the tip of the sword on the stone floor and sank to one knee. She bowed her head.

"Chosen of the Mother, you have my allegiance."

"Fiera—"

"*Zira*," Fiera interrupted sharply. "You saw her. You witnessed her magic. Her blue eyes. Her communing with the sword itself. You must have felt it too—the sensation of fate."

Zira looked between Fiera and Vi. She swayed slightly, but dropped to her knee after only a moment's hesitation. "My fate is linked with yours, Fiera. It was declared by the Mother. If you are loyal to her, so am I."

Vi took a slow breath. Yargen's power still surged through her. The blade beckoned her with whispering invitations only her ears could hear.

"I require the blade."

"Require it?" Fiera lifted her head first, then the rest of her. Zira followed the princess back to her feet as well. "This blade has been in my family for—"

"Hundreds of years," Vi finished. "Yet you do not know where it came from… not really. Nor what it can be used for." She motioned to the sword. "In that blade is a great and terrible power. The longer you wield it, the more you risk it twisting your body and mind, as well as the bodies and minds of those around you. It calls out to the false Knights of Jadar who rely on lore they don't understand in an attempt to return themselves to prominence."

"I cannot give it to you."

"You must," Vi insisted.

"The princess said she cannot, so she cannot." Zira stood, her hand back on the sword at her hip.

"The sword will be used in my wedding to the Emperor as a ceremonial piece," Fiera began. For the first time, Vi saw doubt on the ever-self-assured woman's face. "But… after… I had intended to seal it away. Even had you not said so, Yullia, I'm aware that this weapon holds a great power that mortal men aren't meant to hold. Perhaps, I might entrust it to you at that time." The princess shook her head, as though she was dismissing the notion as soon as it came to her. "No… I must think on it."

Vi wanted to insist on Fiera's compliance, but she'd already made progress. The longer the princess simmered on what had transpired here, the closer she'd be to realizing the truth of Vi's words.

For now, an openness to giving up the sword would have to

be good enough for Vi. Pressing the matter, looking desperate, wouldn't suit her.

Fiera returned the sword to its scabbard, the scabbard to the wall. No sooner was it back on its pegs than footsteps sounded in the hall. All three women turned, startled.

Two figures approached from the darkness of the hall: Tiberus and Denja.

"There you are, my bride." Tiberus, once more, went immediately for Fiera. For him, nothing else seemed to exist in a room when she was there. "I have been worried to the sun and back for you."

"I'm fine." Fiera squeezed his forearms lightly and took a step away. Even though she wore a smile on her lips, Vi could see the discomfort behind her eyes. She didn't appreciate the suddenly crowded room any more than Vi did.

"Denja told me what happened on the streets, and that you refused your guard detail."

"I had a guard detail." Fiera motioned to Vi and Zira. "Why don't we all head to a sitting room to discuss these matters? It'll be far more comfortable."

"What is this place anyway? You've not taken me here before…" The statement trailed off as the Emperor looked around. His attention was quickly consumed by the sword. "This was what you held that night… This must be the Sword of Jadar."

These weapons attract power-hungry men. Vi keenly heard the words of her father once more. If Tiberus's expression was any indication, the Knights of Jadar were no longer the only ones who were out for the sword.

"Yes," Fiera said begrudgingly as she stepped in front of her betrothed. She rested her hands lightly on his upper arms in an attempt to guide him away. "We shall use it at our wedding to bless our union and then it will be sealed away forever."

"Here? Will it be here?" Tiberus asked, a little too eagerly.

"No, I will find a new spot for it." Fiera swept her gaze across the room, landing on Denja. Vi didn't miss the subtle confusion that furrowed Fiera's brow. "Too many people appear to know of this location." Then, like magic, her whole expression softened. Fiera gave Tiberus the sweetest, most endearing smile one could imagine. "Now, my love, come with me to procure some refreshments? I'm both parched and starved from all the excitement this morning."

"Yes, the excitement…" Tiberus looked back to Fiera and his focus returned. "You must tell me what happened."

"Of course." Fiera linked their arms, leading Tiberus out of the room. Denja fell into step behind, Vi and Zira pulling up the rear. Fiera locked the door and Vi could feel the *pop* of magic as she lifted the curtain of flame in the hallway once more.

"Zira," Vi said lightly, loud enough for Denja to hear but not so loud that it distracted Fiera and Tiberus. "Do you have time now to show me that sword technique you were telling me about earlier?"

"Yes, I think now would be a wonderful time," Zira said easily, without even missing a beat.

"Excellent."

They paused at a landing, Zira taking the lead. "If you three will excuse Yullia and me, there's something I promised to show her in the training ring."

"Good of you to do so." Fiera picked up on the ruse. "I appreciate you taking such an active interest in Yullia's training."

"I have other matters to attend to as well," Denja said stiffly, adjusting the scarf around her head. "If you'll all excuse me."

"Thank you again for informing me of the incident today," Tiberus said to the blue-eyed woman. "I appreciate that someone made it a point to notify me of actions taken against my betrothed."

"Certainly, your grace." Denja bowed. "I am here to serve." After taking two steps backward, Denja turned, disappearing down the hall.

Vi bowed as well, Zira mirroring the motion before leading them in the opposite direction as Denja. They rounded down two staircases, to a storeroom attached to an empty training pit. Zira closed the door behind her and settled on one of the room's many unmarked crates before asking, "You wanted me alone and now you have me. What is it?"

"Denja. How did she know of that room?"

"I don't know, but I don't think Fiera told her."

"I don't think so either." Vi paced, running her hands along the dusty boxes of training equipment. "Which means she figured it out, interrogated someone else who knows, or followed us."

"Before today, only Fiera and I knew of it."

"Not even her siblings? Ophain?"

"If they know, I'm unaware. But I doubt they would've spilled the secret just because some random councilor asked."

Vi stopped pacing. With stilled feet, her mind felt like it could move faster. "How long has Denja been in the employ of the royal family?"

"Right around the time the war began, I believe. I've only served our princess for three years, so I can't say for certain." Zira pushed herself off the crate. "Long enough that if there was something to worry about when it comes to Denja, they would've already found out."

"Not always," Vi said softly. "Some betrayals take decades to mature." *Like Jayme.* "In the coming months, we must protect the sword at all costs."

"So you've said. What happens if it falls into the wrong hands, as you say?"

"Would you believe me if I said the end of the world?" Vi gave a bitter grin. Zira let out a laugh that told Vi just how seriously she took the warning.

"You really are an odd one." Shaking her head as the laughter faded, Zira started for the door. But her hand stalled on the handle. She looked back to Vi and—for one brief second—Vi could see the woman taking the words seriously. "We'll keep it safe."

"I hope so."

Zira gave her a nod and left. Vi crossed over to the window that overlooked the empty training field. They would keep it safe this time. She wouldn't allow the world to repeat itself once more. There wouldn't be another Vi pulled from her home to be Yargen's Champion. There wouldn't be another Taavin to suffer at the hands of fate.

The cycle *would* end. Now that the sword was within her grasp, the real work could begin.

IN THE DEAD OF night, the halls were empty, and the castle was quiet.

Vi made her way with ease, glyphs wrapped around her wrists. One masked her sounds. But should someone see her, the other gave her the face of a random Imperial guard.

Once in the armory, Vi closed the door behind her, grabbed one of the swords off the racks, and propped it lightly against the handle. There would be no surprise guests this time. She wanted to know the moment someone came in.

Though, hopefully, her paranoia would prove unfounded.

The lock on the door to the sword's chamber was easy to melt away with her magic. She repeated the same process she had in the Archives to get to Taavin after Ulvarth had locked his door. Vi melted and bent and separated the ring holding the lock in place, rather than destroying the lock itself, and set it aside. That way, she could return it to its previous position.

As a Firebearer, Fiera no doubt knew of this flaw in the

protection of the blade. That was why she kept the curtain of flame burning at all times within the hall. But the princess had also said she barely noticed the magic leeching away from her anymore. Vi surmised that if Fiera were asleep, she wouldn't notice any slight fluctuations in that magic at all.

Lifting her hand, Vi moved forward deliberately. Her fingertips dipped into the flames first. It was warm—Fiera's power undeniable. But it didn't burn her.

She didn't want to assume full control of the flames, merely adjust them. Pushing her magic out from her extended hand, a hole barely larger than her wrist appeared in the wall of fire. She extended her magic further, stretching the opening little by little until it was wide enough for her to step through, flames raging right at the edge of her power.

On the other side of the fire, Vi released her hold, allowing the flames to ease back into place.

"*Narro hath hoolo,*" Vi uttered, her eyes locked with the sword on the wall. She didn't so much as look at Taavin when he appeared.

"This is record time for you getting here." He took a step forward, looking up at the sword. "What did you do?"

"What you told me to: I befriended Fiera and found the sword. Then I came to it." Vi crossed in front of him, lifting the weapon off its pegs.

"You need to be more specific. It's my duty to record all you do, and because I keep that memory, you do better every time… until, eventually, we succeed."

"We'll succeed this time," Vi insisted, focusing on the scabbard.

"While I admire your confidence, we won't know for sure until your sight shows us a future where Raspian is safely sealed away."

"Have a bit of faith." She finally allowed her attention to stray to him. His eyes were twice as brilliant and three times as hard as an emerald. "Believe in me."

"I do."

"You don't." Vi set down the blade on the table, taking a step away from it. Every time she was near the weapon it consumed her attention—but she wanted to give Taavin her undivided focus. "You don't think we'll succeed this time, otherwise you wouldn't be so cautious."

"I'm cautious because the world needs me to be."

"Because you think I'll fail."

"It's not what I think that matters. It's what's happened ninety-two times…" he murmured, glancing askance. Vi refused to allow it, stepping into his field of vision.

"When you look at me, you see me combined with ninety-two other versions of myself. You see actions I have not taken, but still could. Moments when I succeeded and, more often than not, failed. You see me in a way that I can't even imagine myself." She looked at him from head to toe. "But when I look at you… I only see one Taavin. The Taavin who taught me my magic and guided me across Meru, who betrayed me and my father. The Taavin I still loved even when I thought one more betrayal would break my heart. The Taavin I watched burn—" Her voice broke and she allowed herself to fall silent.

She didn't want him to sweep her into his arms and kiss her fiercely with lips that weren't really there. She wanted to feel like he understood—like he heard her. When he remained silent, she continued.

"All I have is you, Taavin," she whispered. "But you're stuck with those other ninety-two versions of me, and part of you is already expecting to meet the ninety-fourth. You'll never be with just me again."

"You're wrong," he said hastily. Emotions broke through all at once. His eyebrows pinched, his lower lip quivered slightly as he spoke. His hands trembled, as if wanting to reach for her, but they remained in place. She wondered if he, too, was held by the same invisible tethers that kept her rooted to the floor. "You are the only one I am with… the only one I have ever been with.

"You consume every thought I have. There's not a corner of my mind you don't fill. Or—" He was before her now, toes nearly touching. So close she could feel the phantom warmth that radiated off him like magic and sunlight. Vi raised a trembling hand, resting it on his chest, feeling the simple fabrics where there had once been intricate embroidery.

"Or?" she repeated, looking up at him through her eyelashes.

"Or my heart," he said finally. "You vex me. I have hurt you and you've hurt me in ways I cannot describe. And even now, I love you. I love you in a way I don't know if I deserve."

"You do," she whispered. She needed him here, now. She needed this love as much as she wanted it.

"I'm not sure." Taavin chuckled softly. The tip of his middle finger brushed against her temple. Soon his fingertips were in her hair, smoothing it away from her face, knotting in the strands at the nape of her neck.

"It's not your decision to make." Her head tilted upward, obliging his unspoken guidance. Her eyes dipped closed. "You'll be hurt again," she breathed across his lips.

"So will you."

It wasn't quite a kiss, but a trembling of lips brushed together. Vi pressed forward eagerly, and Taavin obliged. His arms tightened and she was swept against him.

Vi pressed her eyelids tighter together. This kiss… *it wasn't the same*. She willed her mind to ignore the slight shimmer of magic, the heat of the glyph at the watch that brought him into her world, the thin barrier that couldn't be lifted between them. She wanted to scream, and the only way she could keep the feeling contained was to smother it with his mouth.

When they pulled apart, his cheeks were lightly flushed. His fingers caressed her face.

"What should we do now that I have the sword?" Vi pulled away, flashing him a smile when she saw the confusion in his eyes at the swift change in topic.

"You still need to tell me how you got to it so swiftly." Taavin rested his palm on the small of her back.

"Right… Well, I went to the ball just as we had discussed…"

Vi recounted the events of the morning, the attack on Fiera, and her efforts to convince Fiera to take her to the sword.

"What did you say to her, specifically?" Taavin didn't miss when she'd glossed over that part. "Usually Fiera is far more cautious with the sword."

"I told her I was chosen by the Mother herself to defend this world and that I need to prevent the sword from falling into the wrong hands."

"Vi, you can't let them know who you are and why you're here. If the Dark Isle gains knowledge of the Champion, it could change the course of events."

"Just how easy is it to change the course of events?" Vi asked. "If I've failed ninety-two times, it must not be that easy."

He crossed his arms, a sour expression dousing his features. "You're right. It's not entirely easy." Taavin sighed, bringing his hand to his forehead. "Think of time as a river, flowing along. There are three types of things you will find in that river.

"The first are leaves floating along—these are people, pulled along by the course of fate, thrown this way and that by the flow of the world around them.

"The second are stones—things that are immovable. They will happen regardless of what you do. The river runs around them, its current and pace distorted by these events." He held up two fingers.

"So… some things can't be changed?" Vi said quietly. Taavin nodded. "What if Raspian being set free is one of those things?"

"It's not," he said quickly. "Raspian being set free is a result of other actions, not an action itself."

Vi thought about that a moment and finally hummed in agreement. Raspian was set free because of the crystal weapons being destroyed. Prevent those actions, and he wouldn't be freed.

"And the third thing in the river?" she asked.

"You—the dams and floodgates you create to guide the currents. The few locations where the river is quiet enough, or shallow enough, or narrow enough, to change how it flows."

Vi leaned against the table, Taavin at her side, the sword behind her. She hung her head, eyes on the floor, staring at nothing. She had to function like a surgeon of fate—cutting and stitching carefully, or the whole world would bleed out and die.

"The Apexes of Fate," she said slowly. "I can *make* them?"

"Yes. You, the previous Champion, and the crystal weapons."

"That's why there were so many in the North," Vi realized. "Because the axe was there for a long time and helped shape the North itself?"

"Exactly."

"So here in Norin, there must be many, too?"

"Indeed. And now that you have access to the sword, we will seek them out in time. At the Apexes, you will peer into the future, and there we'll learn if your actions have led to a change in fate overall."

"So where is the first one?"

"Don't be so eager. You've done enough for now. Lie low for a bit, build trust."

"There isn't time," Vi said hastily. "Fiera will be wedded soon, and then Aldrik will be born. That's when the Knights take the sword, and my father told me that Fiera dies trying to protect it. We have months, Taavin, to prevent that from happening."

"Remember what I said about stones in the river," he said cautiously. Vi didn't miss the ominous undercurrent to his words.

"Are you saying Fiera is—" Vi didn't have a chance to finish.

The flames at their right brightened as a woman pushed her way through. The fire licked around her skin but didn't touch it, thanks to a protective barrier. When she was through, that barrier shattered with a snap of light.

"*Mysst soto sut,*" Denja said instantly. Light spilled from her palms, weaving and solidifying into the shape of a war axe she hoisted with ease. Her muscles bulged against the thin fabric covering her arms. Her bright blue eyes leveled with Vi, Taavin having vanished. "We should talk, you and I."

M AGIC COLLECTED UNDER HER palm, ready to be unleashed. Vi bet they were about to do a lot more than talk.

"We clearly have a lot to discuss." Vi's eyes darted to the weapon. Denja was a Lightspinner. No wonder Vi didn't hear the crash of the sword she'd propped against the door. Denja had likely used *durroe sallvas tempre* to hide her movements. "Why don't you release that, and we can do so calmly?"

"Why don't you summon one of your own like you did in the streets?"

Damn. She'd seen. Vi pressed her mouth into a thin smile. "I really don't want to hurt you."

"I've yet to decide what I want to do with you," Denja said casually. "I know you're not one of the queen's women. And I'll assume you know that travel to the Dark Isle isn't permitted, so I'll give you one chance: why are you here?"

What Vi wouldn't give to have a simple answer to that question. Instead, she said, "How do you know I'm not one of the queen's agents?"

"If you have to ask, you're not." Denja had some kind of communication with Meru, Vi would bet. "You're wasting a lot of what could be your last breaths not answering my question."

Vi locked eyes with the woman, swiftly debating her options. She could fight her way out—kill Denja. It wouldn't be hard to get in a *juth calt*. Even Taavin had been surprised when she'd used the words in that way. Then again, there was always *juth mariy*—destroy magic; Denja would use that on her the moment she started chanting.

Firebearing, then?

No, killing one of the Queen Lumeria's agents would create more problems than it would solve.

"Really? Nothing to say for yourself?" Denja narrowed her eyes, blue and almost purple-ringed. She slid her feet forward and sank into her stance. "Then—"

"Your name isn't Denja," Vi whispered. Her whole body relaxed, overcome with a sense of knowing. But this wasn't magic. What she felt was the overwhelming relief of recognition. How had she not noticed sooner?

"What?" She seemed genuinely startled, her grip relaxing slightly. Perhaps, Denja recognized her too, with some phantom echo of past lives they'd shared.

"Deneya?" Vi asked softly, trying to superimpose the face of the slightly older knight who had taken her to see Queen Lumeria over top of the woman before her. "It's Deneya, isn't it?"

"So you know my name. That's possible for any good spy to find out." Deneya tightened her grip again. "Especially one who could be working with the elfin'ra."

Vi balked. "The elfin'ra are still sealed away on their island, aren't they?" They should be, if Vi's memories and understanding served her. The elfin'ra were sealed away along with Raspian, a barrier on their island tied to the Crystal Caverns.

"They're constantly looking for ways to escape. Or finding agents to serve them who are not limited to the island." This woman was vastly different than the level-headed, quiet knight Vi had met briefly. Yet her eyes were the same as the woman who had found Vi in the Archives.

"Deneya, a world away, you promised me that I would have your sword if I sought you out… Well, here I am, seeking you out."

"What're you talking about?" Deneya chuckled. "You're not going to distract me, agent of evil."

Vi sighed heavily. There was no way Deneya was going to believe her, not without doing something drastic. Vi would just have to hope Taavin forgave her.

"I'm going to use *narro* now, to summon someone who can help explain things. Will you allow me this?"

Deneya seemed to weigh her options. She lifted her axe, resting it over Vi's left shoulder. The blade was a hair's width away from the flesh of her neck.

"If I hear even the start of a chant that begins with anything other than *narro*, your head comes clear off."

"Fine," Vi agreed easily. "*Narro hath hoolo.*"

Taavin appeared off to the side as he usually did—rebuilt from glyphs of light until he looked nearly solid. Only the faint outline of magic around his form betrayed that he wasn't actually there. He looked from Vi to Deneya, then back to Vi.

"Well, this is early," he murmured. Then, with his attention squarely on Vi, "Did you miss where I told you to keep yourself a secret and act cautiously?"

"Believe it or not, I'm actually trying to keep myself alive right now." Vi ground out the words. Couldn't he see she had a war axe at her throat?

"What sorcery is this?" Deneya whispered, staring at Taavin.

"Can you tell her who I am? You know her from before, right?"

"Yes, I do." Taavin turned to face Deneya. "Deneya Tallois, daughter of Arullia and Rox. Currently the first knight in Lumeria's Order of Shadows. She who has been on the Dark Isle defending the Caverns for the past hundred years… It is a pleasure to meet you, again."

"H-how?" Deneya stuttered. The axe at Vi's neck quivered and nearly bit into her flesh. Deneya was too startled to notice. "Begone elfin'ra specter!" She swung the weapon toward Taavin. It cut straight through him as though he was made of nothing but mist. It didn't seem to harm him, but the sight was a phantom blow to Vi's gut.

"I am not wicked. I am the eternal Voice of Yargen," Taavin continued calmly. "I have served her for hundreds of years. In my last lifetimes, in this, and in the next."

"You are not the Voice of Yargen. She is—"

"Fathima, and she has been the voice for the past two hundred years," Taavin finished. "And she will perish in the next twenty to thirty years… depending on certain factors, which will give room for Ulvarth to make his power play against Lumeria."

Deneya frowned, lowering her weapon—though she still held it so tightly, her hand trembled. Vi took it as a good sign that she had yet to brandish it against them again.

"Earlier, you said *hoolo*." Deneya looked to Vi. "One of Raspian's words? Is this man his work?"

"No," Vi said quickly. "You would feel it if it was." She remembered the sensation of the elfin'ra using the word on Adela's Isle of Frost. It was unmistakable.

"And the dark god is sealed away, unable to give new words," Taavin continued for Vi.

"Then… what are you?"

Vi took a deep breath and Taavin remained silent, yielding her the floor. Deneya finally relaxed, releasing the axe. It unraveled into strands of light and disappeared.

"I realize that what I am about to say is hard to believe," Vi began, working up her courage. "I am the Champion of Yargen, and I have been placed here by the goddess herself to defend this world from Raspian's return." Vi worked on bite-sized pieces of information.

"The Voice would've sent word if Yargen was giving us a Champion once more," Deneya said cautiously.

"As far as this world is concerned, we don't exist." Taavin smiled bitterly.

"Think of us more as travelers, passing through," Vi added.

"If you're truly the Champion, prove it to me. Tell or show me something that only the Champion can do."

"Have you ever met a Champion before?" Vi asked.

"Well, no…"

"Then how will you know it's something only the Champion can do?" she challenged.

"I…" Deneya let out a low chuckle. "You're almost drawing me in to this insanity, both of you."

"Deneya," Taavin said firmly, silencing the woman. "With the help of the proctor, you cheated your way through the written portion of your examinations to enter into Lumeria's Order. You did so not because you couldn't remember the information—but because the words dance on the page before your eyes, and you knew you wouldn't be able to finish in the allotted time."

"How do you—" Deneya took a step back, horror overtaking her features.

"Your tutor, the proctor, died in a skirmish in the south of Meru, leaving you alone with the truth of what you both did. Despite his assurances, you have always worried that you are not good enough for your post."

"I…" Deneya looked between the two of them. Vi could see the hasty rise and fall of her chest as her breathing quickened, panic settling in. "I never told anyone that," she whispered.

"You told her." Taavin gave a nod at Vi. "In a past life. You trusted her because she is the Champion and because she is a woman worth trusting."

Vi felt a frisson of heat rising to her cheeks at his praise.

Deneya took a step backward, her back meeting the wall. Slowly, she began to laugh, shaking her head. "This is madness. This is impossible."

"But here we stand," Vi said.

"Glad one of us knows where we stand because I'm not sure which way is up anymore." She cast a wary eye over Vi and Taavin. "I need time to deal with all this."

"Fine." Mother above, even Vi was still processing what was happening to her. And she had the benefit—if one could call it that—of living through the goddess rebuilding her body to send her back in time.

"But while you do so, swear you will not act against the Champion. And swear you will not report back to Lumeria or anyone else on Meru of her presence here, or of my existence," Taavin cautioned.

"Why?"

"I'm walking the razor's edge of fate and the only way we're all getting out of this alive is if I have as much control as possible," Vi said confidently, perhaps more confidently than she felt. "I don't need more variables I can't control complicating an already-complicated situation. You're the only one in this world who knows who I am. I don't want to regret that trust."

"Not even Fiera?" Deneya had a look of genuine surprise.

"No." Though Vi suspected Fiera had some inkling of what Vi was, even if she didn't have the words to describe it. "Do I have your word?"

"On one condition."

"I don't remember this turning into a negotiation." Vi folded her arms over her chest.

"It's not every day I get to negotiate with the agent of a goddess." Deneya smirked and swung her eyes to Taavin. "You seem to know so much. Perhaps you know what I'm about to barter for?"

"It varies." Taavin's answer only seemed to unnerve Deneya more. She stared at him for another long second, but abandoned whatever thought she had as she looked back to Vi.

"You give me no reason to suspect you're up to anything. No funny business. Be on your best behavior." Deneya's attention turned to the sword. "And that… I don't know what it is you intend to do with it. But if you're seeking it out, you must have some plan for it. Whatever that is, you don't get to act until you tell me. I'm on this Yargen-forsaken rock to watch over those weapons and the tomb. So if you do something with the sword—or any other weapon—you're right in the line of my duty."

Vi looked back to the sword, then Taavin. He had told her they needed to act slowly and be cautious. Making this promise to Deneya seemed in line with that objective. Vi also couldn't make her play on the sword until after Fiera's wedding.

"Fine, I accept your deal," Vi said casually, trying not to convey any hesitation or doubt. The Champion wouldn't waver. She had to be steadfast in her decisions.

"Good, because I'm tired and desperately want to go to bed and find out this was all a bad dream." Deneya yawned for emphasis. "When I see you tomorrow, it should go without saying, none of this happened." Vi locked eyes with the woman and gave a small nod. Deneya returned it, stepped backward, and uttered, "*Wein.*"

A glyph shot out from her midsection. Splitting into two, one rose vertically to the crown of her head and the other dropped to her feet. The two circles of light faded as they swirled around Deneya, as though they were wrapping her up in a magic casement. Power glittered across her skin as she stepped back through Fiera's flames unharmed.

"*Wein,*" Vi repeated thoughtfully. Just like Taavin's word, *uncose*, it did nothing for her.

"She received that word from Yargen before she came to the Dark Isle. It acts like a personal shield from attack. It's most like what you know as Groundbreakers' stone skin," Taavin said factually, as though it were obvious.

"If you know so much, why didn't you warn me she was coming?" Vi rounded on him.

"I didn't think it'd happen so soon." He lifted up his hands defensively. "Perhaps it's your recklessness that's speeding things up. Recklessness… like summoning me to appear before her."

Vi cursed under her breath, working to calm the spark crackling up her spine. "I didn't know what else to do. And when I figured out she was from Meru, I just thought…" Vi shook her head, feeling the spark abate. "I don't know what I thought."

"I'm sorry for snapping, too." Taavin heard the apology in her tone. His hands clasped over her shoulders. "This is exactly what I'm trying to protect you from—what I was telling you earlier. There is *variance*. Very few things are perfectly identical in any of these recreated worlds. Even though there are stones in the river, the little leaves bob and sway along the water's currents—each acting according to its own will."

"Even so, you could've told me it was going to happen eventually. You could've prepared me so I wasn't caught off-guard."

"Foremost, I didn't think it'd happen for weeks yet. And truly, I didn't see how it would have helped you any. I couldn't give you specifics even if I wanted to. Maybe you would've had this confrontation in a council room after everyone had dispersed. Or on a training field. Or in a hall one night on your way here." He spoke with such certainty that Vi had no doubt all of those things had, at some point, happened. "All I would've accomplished by telling you would have been putting you on edge nearly all the time."

"I want to know," Vi insisted. "You want to know what I do in this timeline? I need to know what I've *done*."

"I don't want you to act rashly." He smiled tenderly. But Vi only felt more frustrated. "Take things slowly. We'll figure out the best way to take the sword when the time is right."

When would the time be right: before or after Fiera's death?

Vi kept the question to herself. She didn't want to worry him more. And there was only so much she could accomplish in one night. It had been a long few days, and she was very tired.

"Very well," Vi agreed finally. "I trust you."

"And I trust you." He leaned forward, placing a gentle kiss on her forehead. It was little more than the ghost of warmth. "Now, go rest. I can feel your exhaustion."

Vi nodded and released the glyphs.

"Do you trust me?" she whispered to the empty air. If he trusted her, he would arm her with information. But all Vi was getting were crumbs and a heavy dose of skepticism from him; should he give her anything more, she'd take it and run head-first into the end of the world.

13

"YOU MUST SET them free." Fiera slammed an open palm against the council table. "It has been long enough."

"*Weeks*, it has been weeks," Tiberus growled. His patience was visibly running thin, the man's hair a mess from constantly raking his fingers through it. "It's not nearly enough time to let loose those who called not only for my death, but the death of my men—and perhaps now the death of you, since you are to be my wife."

"They are my soldiers and would never harm me," Fiera insisted.

"Like those men on the streets would never harm you?" He arched his eyebrows.

"Those were riff-raff, not my men." Fiera leaned forward. "All you are doing, Tiberus, is risking gratitude turning into resentment."

Vi volleyed her attention between the two most powerful people on the continent. Technically, Tiberus's say was the only one that mattered. But he deferred to Fiera in a far greater way than an Emperor should. She still didn't know what Fiera felt for the man.

But Tiberus's feelings were clear enough in his actions.

Zira leaned over, whispering, "Do you think they'd notice if we just walked out?"

"Be my guest and risk it if you'd like," Vi mumbled.

The whole council had been confined for at least a half hour as the debate raged on. Everyone looked uncomfortable.

Vi caught Deneya's eyes across the table, but the woman glanced at her for only a second. The fact that it had been a week and she had yet to say anything to Vi, or act out of the ordinary, was a testament to her training from Queen Lumeria.

"You're being utterly unreasonable." Fiera threw up her hands. "You were the one who set out to conquer. You can't expect the rest of the continent to roll over like Cyven."

"I do not expect the West to handle their change in rulership with the same grace as the East." It was a low jab from Tiberus, one that made Lord Twintle's head turn and eyes narrow.

Vi closed her eyes and took in a slow breath. She had to work to prevent it from coming out as a heavy sigh. Fiera was all fire and passion, no doubt playing up those traits because of how easily they got under Tiberus's skin. Usually, this enabled her to push him in the direction she wanted him to go.

"May I propose a compromise?" Vi asked, allowing the remnants of her years as a royal to seep back into her tone. She couldn't tolerate this a moment longer.

The Emperor appeared startled she'd spoken up, but Fiera gave her a trusting smile and said, "I'd love to hear it."

"Thank you." Vi stood. "Your graces, I think I—we all—understand your respective wishes. My proposal is this: release the confined soldiers in several rounds in the coming weeks. The first round would be soldiers willing to put their skills to use and serve in their new Empire's army. Also in that round would be the sons and daughters of any nobility."

She gave a look to Twintle, remembering Luke, who was still trapped in the encampment.

"The next round would be those who do not wish to fight, but have a valuable trade skill. Put them to work and keep their hands and minds busy with rebuilding their city, so they do not think to turn against you.

"The final round would be those remaining." Vi thought a moment, running the suggestion over a final time in her head. "If any have nefarious intentions, they will likely show their colors as they lose patience."

Vi finished and glanced between Fiera and the Emperor. The former had gone stony faced and Vi couldn't discern if the suggestion was pleasing or upsetting. The Emperor on the other hand was far more transparent with his emotions, giving Vi hope when he finally said, "Your new knight speaks wisely."

"Thank you, your grace." Vi bowed her head and sat.

"What do you say, my love?"

"It's a fair suggestion," Fiera finally relented. "A week between each round?"

"A month," Tiberus fired back.

"Two weeks." Fiera's mouth quirked into a tiny grin. Fondness alighted in her eyes, brought out by the banter.

"Very well." Tiberus chuckled. "Two weeks, and let none claim that Tiberus Solaris does not bend before his bride." He stepped away from the table and everyone stood on cue. "Now, may I steal that bride for a drink before dinner?"

The royals departed, and everyone in the room seemed to immediately sit straighter, a weight lifted.

"About time." Twintle gathered his papers, shoving them unceremoniously into his folio. "Our loyal Westerners have rotted in their prisons long enough."

"They have been kept comfortable," Zira said firmly.

Vi remembered her time in the "containment shelter" and how quickly the once-glorious manor house devolved into squalor when crammed with soldiers who didn't have proper access to something as simple as a bath. She wasn't sure if *comfortable* was the right word.

"Comfortable? You think confinement is comfortable?" Twintle grumbled. "I cannot wait to hear just how comfortable my son has been these past weeks when he is back in his home where he belongs."

"Luke comes from good stock. He'll be—"

"Good day to you all," Twintle cut Zira off curtly, striding out of the room without a backward glance.

The other councilors gathered their things quietly, the tension in the air slowing their movements to a glacial pace.

"What a mess," Zira mumbled.

"Empire building is rarely tidy." Vi stood. "At least we found an acceptable solution."

"One can only hope they both think it's acceptable come morning."

"What about Kahrin? Will she be out with Luke?"

"No, she'll likely get out with the tradesmen. She's the daughter of a miner to the north of Norin and became a Knight seeking glory. I think she's had enough of fighting for one lifetime." Vi could only hope that was true. The fewer angry Knights of Jadar she had to contend with, the better. Zira sighed. "I really do hope this is the last of it. Fiera needs to focus on planning her wedding… it's coming up soon."

"Yullia," Deneya interrupted them. "May I borrow you for a word in my office?"

"Certainly."

"This way." Deneya started out the room. Vi shrugged at Zira as if she had no idea what this could be about, then followed the minister down the hall and into a closet-like office. She closed the door behind them, locked it, grabbed Vi's hand, and uttered, *"Durroe sallvas tempre."*

A glyph formed between their locked palms.

"You certainly have my attention." Vi looked between their hands and Deneya's face.

"I didn't want to risk anyone else overhearing." Deneya's grip was firm and unflinching. "I've been thinking about what you said and I must ask, what is your goal here?"

"I already told you, I—"

"Yes, agent of Yargen or some such." Deneya shook her head. "What are your goals as that agent—Champion, rather—acting on behalf of Yargen? What are you hoping to achieve?"

"To protect—"

Deneya pressed her free palm to her forehead and sighed. When she spoke again, it was with the same tone Vi would use to explain a difficult concept to a child. "I understand all that. You're here on behalf of Yargen, protecting the sword. Our goals really aren't that different."

"I doubt they would be," Vi said cautiously.

"If you're truly are here on behalf of the Goddess, it's my duty to assist you. Tell me how I can do that."

"Information," Vi said after a moment. "You've been ingrained in this world longer than I have. I need information on people, specifically the Knights of Jadar and those associated with them before the fall of Mhashan. They've already begun moving against the sword."

Deneya thought about this, humming softly. Then, as if her mental tally came up with the same answer Vi already knew, she gave a nod. "They haven't been too pleased with Fiera's engagement."

"If their attack on the street is any indication."

"That's only the start of the whispers I've heard."

"Oh?"

"Information gathering is part of my duty to the queen. I go out at night and sit in taverns. Most don't recognize me, so I hear murmurs of the citizenry. Some seem content—they're happy the war is over. But others are more in line with the thinking of the old king. They'd rather burn than bend the knee. They see Fiera doing so as the ultimate betrayal."

"Foolish…" Vi mumbled. They couldn't see, or were willfully ignoring, that Fiera's engagement was likely what saved them all. And was possibly the ultimate sacrifice on her part—to be married to a man who had conquered her land for the sake of her people.

"I'm sure the rumors will get worse when the soldiers are set free. A lot of the Knights are still in there. I'll work on procuring the full roster of names for you."

"Thank you," Vi managed, somewhat surprised by the sudden kindness. "Let me know when you have it." Vi moved to leave, but Deneya held her hand firmly, almost yanking her back.

"Be careful," Deneya said solemnly. "Getting close to the royal family without having eyes on me took me years. You've ascended swiftly and publicly… They're already whispering about you."

"I'm not worried," Vi lied. In fact, she was suddenly very worried. This whole time her eyes had been on Fiera, at the expense of noticing who had their eyes on her. "I have this under control."

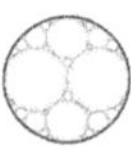

Vi hefted the Sword of Jadar overhead and brought it down in a vertical slice. She slid her feet to the side, dancing around an unseen opponent, drawing the blade in a side slash. She stepped back, shifted her grip, and thrust forward into a lunge. Her movements were slow and deliberate, more meditation than combat.

Soon enough, Deneya would arrive to go over the list of Knights she'd procured. And before then, Vi needed to speak with Taavin.

She went to put the blade on the table, pausing. The vision of the Champion splitting the staff remained ever-present in her mind. *How had he known how to do that?* Vi tried to push the question from her mind, uttering, "*Narro hath hoolo.*"

"You're back here again." Taavin looked around.

"Yes. I've been doing just as you asked for the past two months and laying low." She stared at the sheathed weapon on the wall. Despite herself, the memories of the last Champion still lingered. "Taavin… do you think there's a way to manipulate the crystal?"

"Why do you ask?"

"My last vision… the last Champion split the staff. Do you

think I could split the sword?"

"We're trying to preserve Yargen's power, not split it," he needlessly reminded.

"What if—"

They were interrupted by Deneya emerging through the flames at the entrance to the small room. The woman's bright blue and purple-rimmed eyes darted between them.

"Sorry to keep you waiting."

"It's all right. Tell me what you've found?"

"You're not going to like it." Deneya frowned. "The Knights of Jadar are picking right back up where they left off. Nearly all of them."

"How so?"

"They've been gathering at Twintle's house at odd hours."

"When?"

"In secret, at night... I've reason to believe they're meeting right now."

"Then what are we waiting for?" Vi started for the flames. "We should go and see what they're—"

Taavin stopped her by grabbing her hand with his ghostly grip. Vi swung around to face him. Her heart began to beat faster, already knowing what he was about to say.

"No."

"But—"

"*No*," Taavin said more firmly. "Our goal is not the Knights of Jadar."

"The Knights of Jadar are trying to take the sword. They're likely plotting it right now. Knowing what they're scheming will only help us."

"She has a point," Deneya muttered, and Vi liked her that much more for it.

"You know why you can't." Taavin leveled her a look that told Vi everything.

She couldn't, because her rebirth wasn't yet assured. She hadn't given the watch to Vhalla Yarl yet. So there was no guarantee of a new Vi Solaris, a new Champion, if she failed.

If she failed.

"What if this is what I need to do for us to succeed, and I'm not, because we're being so cautious?" Her words were softer than she expected, nearly pleading.

"What we need to do to succeed is keep the sword safe."

"And if we know what the Knights are doing, then—"

"I don't want to see you risking your life. I can't live with that knowledge," he added, softer. Vi hated his tenderness and how it quelled her frustrated anger.

"Hello." Deneya waved, drawing both of their attention. "Yes, hi, I'm still here." She smiled broadly. "How about this? If you can't go for… whatever reasons the Voice has, I'll go in your stead? I'll just keep watching them as I have."

"A fine suggestion," Taavin said. He had yet to release Vi's hand.

Both eyes were on her. Vi bit the insides of her cheeks, but finally said, "Fine, go now… and let me know what happens."

"They'll be none the wiser, I promise! *Wein*!" Deneya dashed through the flames, gone as quickly as she'd come.

Vi stared at the fire, her hand still in Taavin's. When he finally released it, it fell limply at her side.

"What is my purpose here?" she whispered.

"To protect the Crystal Caverns."

"Is it?" Vi spun, rounding on him. Fire was alive in her, burning down her arms, cracking into life around her knuckles. "Or am I just a vessel shepherding us into another repeat of the world's end?"

"Of course not."

"Then you must let me act. The Knights of Jadar are gaining strength while I help Fiera pick out flowers for the Cathedral of the Sun and minstrels for the reception. They are going to act against my family for generations. They will *kill her* if I don't stop them."

"Your only focus should be the sword," Taavin reminded her

gravely. "What happens to everyone else—Fiera, Zira, Tiberus—is not your concern."

"They are my family!"

"Your family is gone and will never come back!"

The words echoed through her ears; Vi staggered back. She swayed, but righted herself. A buzzing sound vibrated her brain and the world blurred for a moment, tilting in a sickening way. He'd only spoken the truth, a truth she'd known. Why did it hurt so much?

"Vi, I'm sorry," Taavin said hastily.

"No," Vi whispered. "You're right." She forced a smile, but felt her cheeks curve into what was certainly more of a snarl. "My family is gone, and I'm clearly a fool for caring about these people."

"That's not—"

"Leave me." Vi waved her hand and released the glyph. Blissful silence filled the air as Vi was left alone with the sword. She stared at it, wondering how a single object could cause so much pain.

Vi approached the weapon slowly. Her eyes were on the sword, but her mind was on the Knights of Jadar. While she was here, waiting, they were plotting. Everyone else was acting as Vi drifted along.

This feeling was worse than being in bed for a month with autumn fever. Worse than waiting her whole life for her family to retrieve her.

"Nothing good comes of a Solaris with a crystal weapon," Vi murmured, putting her hand on the scabbard. "You were right, Father."

She hung her head and felt her eyes burn. Vi took a shaky breath, and then another. She remained like that until her muscles were stiff and her feet ached. She stayed in that tucked-away armory room for so long, the sun was streaming through the windows as she made her way back to her quarters.

There she remained until she was certain she wouldn't betray Taavin's trust and run off after Deneya.

14

VI STARED OUT THE window at Norin. For months, it had been slowly blossoming before her eyes like a bloom that had been trapped in the permafrost of war now poking through the snow. People were beginning to take to the streets again; the Western militia in its entirety had finally been freed of their confinement.

She was used to looking down at cities. She'd spent the vast majority of her life doing just that as she was kept in the fortress of Soricium. Now, it was Taavin's caution keeping her here. She was relegated to council meetings, training grounds, and working with the crystal sword in secret, trying to figure out the depths of its power… As Deneya did the real work of keeping track of the Knights of Jadar and their ever-growing strength.

"… ask her again. I don't think she's listening," Zira said from where she and Fiera stood.

"Yullia?" Fiera repeated herself.

Vi jerked. "Yes? Sorry."

"Don't apologize, all this bores me to tears, too." Zira collapsed into a chair, her long legs kicking out and falling limply over the armrest.

"It's not that bad," Fiera mumbled. "Yullia, I was wondering what you thought of the dress color. Of course, silver or red would be traditional Western colors, but white or gold would be more fitting from an Imperial standpoint."

Vi walked over to the table, looking at the swatches of fabrics the royal tailors had sent for Fiera to review. The whole, cluttered mess represented what Vi had always expected of a royal wedding—a political headache where one misstep could be the difference between a smooth ascension and a long-term nightmare.

"If I'm honest, I think the white and gold is stunning." Fiera lifted a scrap of fabric covered in layers of golden petals. In the light, it sparked almost like flames. She layered it atop pure white silk, humming. "Yet I worry it will ruffle a few feathers in the Western Court if I don't show anything of home."

"The Western Court is a relic now and they need to get over themselves," Zira muttered, tipping her head back. If Vi had to bet, she would guess the woman found the toils of war easier to bear than wedding preparations.

"Even if Tiberus has formally disbanded the Crimson Court, they are still influential families in this land. And he also invited most of the members to be a part of the Southern Court whenever they choose to attend."

"And how often do you think they'll head south?" Zira asked dryly.

"That's not up to me." Fiera's usually composed tone slipped to the edge of annoyance, prompting Zira to stare out the window as Vi had been. "Anyway, Yullia, what do you think?"

Vi took the fabrics from Fiera's hands, feeling the sumptuous textiles between the pads of her fingers. Her clothes had once solely been made from cloth like this. Now, Vi felt as though she shouldn't be touching them. She returned them to the table after only a few seconds.

"I'm inclined to agree with you—all white and gold could spell disaster. The nobility of the West finally seem to be settling with this idea, and you've ensured Mhashan you will still rule as their princess while being a Solaris."

"She should wear what she wants," Zira insisted. "It's her wedding."

"It's not though," Vi said before Fiera could get a word in. "She is a symbol first and everything here—" Vi swept her arm over the table "—conveys a message about what that symbol stands for."

Zira blinked blankly at Vi. Her mouth opened, closed, and she looked away again. Vi turned back to Fiera only to be met with a strange expression.

"I hope I didn't overstep." Vi bowed her head.

"No, you stole the words from my mouth," Fiera said brightly, patting her shoulder. "You really are a natural at the ways of diplomacy." Vi snorted at that. "Now, my astute friend, tell me what color my dress will be."

"How about a compromise? Wear gold on white for your dress. But then your jewelry could be silver and red."

"Yes, a silver crown inlaid with Western rubies." Fiera's expression lit up at the idea.

A silver crown. The thought drifted through Vi's mind on a memory. Her mother had held her once as she'd fallen asleep, indulging all of Vi's then girlish curiosities on the details of her wedding to her father. She had worn a silver crown…

"I think a silver crown would be beautiful," Vi said in a tone softened with nostalgia.

"It's settled, then!" Fiera clapped her hands together. "I love it."

"Excellent." Zira pushed herself away from her chair. "Is that all we had for today?"

"For now." Fiera placed a hand on her stomach. "I'm starving."

"After all the breakfast you ate?" Zira gave her a startled look. "I wouldn't eat for a month if I cleaned my plate like that."

"Planning takes a lot of energy!" Fiera gave a laugh and started for the door alongside Zira.

Or she was already eating for two. Fiera had given birth to Aldrik in all-too-short a time after the wedding in Vi's history. Just long enough that no one questioned her father's legitimacy, especially since the Emperor had always acknowledged him as his son.

If she was pregnant, that meant they were headed along the same path as Vi's world. Not that she could've expected it to have changed; she hadn't done much to shift any fated events.

"Yullia, are you coming?" Fiera asked, pausing to glance over her shoulder.

"Yes, of course," she said. What she really wanted to do was stay in that spot and beg Fiera to listen to her as Vi warned her against all that was to come. For it wouldn't matter what dress she wore, or who she upset, if she was just going to end up dead before the year was up.

"Zira, while I'm at lunch, will you do me a favor and fetch the sword? Tiberus and I will be rehearsing the ceremony with the Crones this afternoon."

"Why not just use a regular sword instead?" Vi asked. She didn't like taking the sword out of its hiding place.

"I suggested as much," Fiera sighed. "But Tiberus was insistent… He's not been quiet about finally seeing the legendary Sword of Jadar. I hope if I indulge him some, it'll lose its wonder."

It never would, but Vi didn't have the heart to tell Fiera that. "Are you rehearsing at the Cathedral of the Sun?"

"No, we'll do it here."

"At least it's not leaving the castle, then."

"My thoughts exactly." Fiera gave them both a smile and passed the key to the armory over to Zira. "Now, if you'll excuse me, I don't want to keep Tiberus waiting." Fiera turned, starting up the hall.

"Princess—" Zira began, quickly stopping herself.

"Yes?" Fiera looked startled at the outburst.

"It's nothing." Zira put her hands in her pockets and smiled. "Have a good lunch."

Vi followed Zira down toward the armory. If the sword was being taken out of its hiding place, then she was going to stay glued to its side. But her thoughts wandered from the sword.

"What was that?" Vi finally asked, when it was clear Zira wasn't about to say anything.

"What was what?"

"The thing you were going to ask Fiera."

"It's nothing."

They arrived at the armory and Vi held her breath as Zira undid the lock, waiting to see if she noticed anything amiss. But if there was a sign of Vi's nighttime experimentations and practice with the sword, Zira overlooked it. In fact, even as she took the sword off the wall, her gaze was a thousand miles away.

"Zira—"

"My family is here," Zira finally let out with a heavy sigh. "My mother and daughter."

"Raylynn?"

Zira froze for a full half-minute before turning slowly. "I don't recall ever telling you my daughter's name."

"Perhaps you… forgot?"

"I think I'd remember."

"Perhaps the Mother gave me a vision of the girl."

"Did she…" Zira murmured, looking at Vi as if seeing her for the first time. "Perhaps you can help me."

"With what?"

"Come, and let me tell you on the way."

They strolled through the castle, winding down the now-familiar pathways. She ran her fingertips along the walls, feeling the grooves of the stone underneath her nails. There had been another Vi before her who had walked these halls. Had she made the same motions? Were her fingerprints running along the tracks of the fingerprints of ninety-two other Vis throughout time?

"A few years ago, Fiera told me that when she met Raylynn she would look into the girl's future," Zira started.

"Like a curiosity shop?"

"Yes, exactly. I made the mistake of telling Raylynn and now she won't stop asking about it. I think that's part of how she convinced my mother to drag her here." Zira looked to Vi with pleading eyes. "I know I shouldn't ask this. But I don't want to trouble Fiera, not now, not with all that's going on. And I know that five is a little young to scry into a child's future, but—"

"I'll do it," Vi interrupted, touching the woman's elbow. "I'll pretend to be Fiera and try to peer into the future."

"Are you sure?"

"It's the least I can do after all you've done to help me." She smiled, hoping the expression hid her uncertainty. Unlike the future-seers at curiosity shops, Vi had much less control over what she did and did not see. But she also had Lightspinning at her disposal, and could make a convincing show of it.

"Thank you." Zira squeezed her hand once as she led them through two side rooms and into a mirrored reception area with a few low chairs.

There, an older woman sat on her feet and held up her palms, as a young child punched and kicked them.

"Faster, Raylynn," the elderly woman demanded sternly. "You're spending too much time on both feet. Bounce!"

The girl tried to do as her grandmother bid, focus knotting her brow. Her golden hair, a striking contrast against the deep tan of her Western skin, swished as she moved.

"I don't think she's meant to be a brawler. I think she'll hear the song of the sword like her mother," Zira said.

"Mommy!" the girl squealed, sprinting over to Zira. Zira crouched down, taking her daughter into her arms. "Can I come live with you in the castle now? I want to defend the princess, too."

"You will defend whatever and whoever you wish." Zira tapped Raylynn's nose. "When you are old enough to hear the calling."

"But I can fight." Raylynn wriggled from her mother's grasp, bouncing from foot to foot. She threw jabs into the air identical to the ones she'd been practicing with her grandmother.

"You can fight better than half the men I train, my little dagger." Zira laughed, ruffling her hair. The woman's tone was entirely different around her daughter. She still had the sharp edge about her that Vi would always associate with Zira, but it was tempered with a tenderness unique to a mother's love.

"Thank you for gracing us this day, your highness." Zira's mother dipped into a low bow, her forehead touching the floor. "You honor us."

"Princess, I will be your new guard!" Raylynn proclaimed, thrusting a hand into the air. "I am here to report."

Vi let out a laugh and crouched down as well. "You will be a mighty guard indeed, someday. Though you should listen to your mother and give yourself time to see what cause calls you."

Raylynn lowered her arm, thinking about this. "If you say so, your highness."

"Now you've met my daughter, Raylynn." Zira scooped up the girl, pulling her into her lap. "And this is my mother, Sophie."

"It's an honor to meet you both." Vi gracefully eased herself onto one of the legless and armless chairs across from the family. Raylynn's golden hair was a stark contrast to the rest of them. Her father's identity was a mystery Vi would not be asking about, given that the girl was conceived after the South invaded. "Zira has told me so much about you."

"She told me you would look into my future!"

"Raylynn, please," Sophie half scolded, half sighed.

"Yes, I will. Would you like me to do that now?" Vi glanced over at Zira. The woman bobbed her head yes.

"Yes please." Raylynn bounced from her mother's lap. "Gran and I brought things to burn. She said this wouldn't be like a normal curiosity shop, so we'd better be prepared."

"Your grandmother is very wise. Be sure you continue to listen to her."

"You hear that? Even the princess says you should listen to

Grandma Sophie," Zira said.

"Yeah, yeah." Raylynn rolled her eyes at her mother. "I know that." She hastily returned to Vi with a collection of items retrieved from the satchel at the older woman's side. "Here, I brought these."

Vi scanned what a five-year-old girl had determined was precious enough to burn for a sacred purpose. She held a clump of cotton, two dried leaves, and a bottle containing a shot of amber colored liquid.

"Are they good enough?"

"They're wonderful," Vi assured. "I'm going to hold out my hands and make a fire; you drop them in one by one, all right?" Raylynn nodded, an adorable intensity overtaking her. "Here we go."

Vi rested her elbows on her knees, sitting cross legged. She leaned forward, made a bowl out of her hands, and allowed her spark to fill the empty space. Fire ignited, eagerly filling her cupped palms. It burned brightly, shining off Raylynn's delighted expression.

One by one, the girl dropped each item into the flames, almost reverently. After uncorking the bottle and pouring the liquid over the fire, her hands clutched the dagger that was attached to the small belt on her hips. Three items to burn, one to hold. Vi took a breath, readying an illusion with *narro*, but as her eyes caught the flame, the genuine sensation of future sight overtook her.

The world blotted out, blurring into white, and Vi found herself standing a mere stone's throw from the castle her body was in.

Fiera and Tiberus stood together at the center of a crowd, hands joined with a red ribbon wrapped loosely around them. Zira stepped toward them, drawing the crystal weapon she wore on her hip. A Crone of the sun spoke, though Vi couldn't hear the words. Even if she could, her focus remained on the glimmering Sword of Jadar.

Zira lowered the sword with purpose, resting the flat of the blade over top their joined hands. Flames sparked, harmlessly singeing the ribbon to ash. Tiberus beamed and Fiera returned the smile. Zira lifted the sword once more and as she held it aloft—

A blade gouged through the soft flesh of her neck. Blood ran down the ceremonial armor Zira wore in a river that raced to pool at her feet. The phantom sounds of gurgling, of Zira's knees hitting the ground hard as the blade was withdrawn, filled Vi's deaf ears.

She watched with disturbing detachment as a man she didn't recognize grabbed for the weapon. Chaos collapsed in on the couple. The last thing Vi saw was Tiberus pulling Fiera close to him, panic in his eyes.

Vi blinked, suddenly seeing the flame in her open palms again. Straightening, she let go of the spark and looked out the windows along one wall to avert the worry in her eyes.

"What did you see?" Raylynn asked eagerly.

"Give the princess a moment, her eyes haven't even stopped glowing." Zira hushed her daughter sternly.

"I saw…" Vi started softly, but lost all train of thought. That certainly hadn't been how Vi expected this to go. Her future sight wasn't a trained skill like it was for the purveyors of curiosities. Her future sight only happened at places where fate changed. Would the Cathedral of the Sun become an Apex at Fiera's wedding?

Her eyes drifted from Zira to Raylynn.

She'd heard stories of Raylynn Westwind, the only female member of Prince Baldair's illustrious Golden Guard. She'd joined shortly before the young prince's untimely death. The stories Vi had heard were striking—the sort that stuck with a girl first learning to hold a sword.

"Your life, Raylynn," Vi finally began with confidence, "will follow your mother's in service. But where your mother follows a crown of silver, the one you serve will be a crown of gold, like the hair of your head."

And the hair of Prince Baldair's head. Perhaps Raylynn could prevent Baldair from meeting his young death if she felt she were destined to be his guard. If she grew up to become even half the swordswoman her mother was, it could be enough to change his fate. Memories of her father talking with such longing about his brother, a broken relationship he could never repair, flooded and propelled her.

"You will live by the sword, and through it you will fulfill many duties. These duties will be heavy, but you will carry yourself gracefully till your final hours. And through it all, you will find your home." Finishing with something ambiguous seemed far wiser than getting too specific. As much as Vi wanted to meddle with the outcomes of history to spare her family, Taavin's cautions stuck.

"You honor us with your sight of the Mother's plans." Sophie dipped once more into a low bow. Zira stared in slack-jawed awe.

"Do you hear that, mommy?" Raylynn stole her mother's attention. "I will carry a heavy sword, just like you!"

"That you will, my little dagger. But the sword I'm carrying today isn't heavy. In fact, it's very special. I only have it now for the princess's wedding. Would you like to see it?" Raylynn nodded and Vi was forced to watch as the crystal sword was unsheathed once more, casually exposed to even more eyes. "This sword is—"

"The Sword of Jadar," Sophie gasped.

"Is it so special?" Raylynn asked, running her little fingers along the flat of the blade. The girl was calm and at ease, even in the presence of a legendary weapon.

"Very special. Can't you hear its song?" Zira tilted her head. "Remember, we must—"

"Listen to the blades, and dance and sing with them." Raylynn finished. She tore her eyes away from the sword. "Did you give my mother this sword?"

"It belongs to my family," Vi answered doggedly.

"Can you give me a sword when I am in service to the golden crown?"

"Perhaps."

"I want a sword like mama's."

"A sword like this cannot be made. It came from the Mother herself, very long ago." Zira sheathed the weapon.

"But her visions come from the Mother, and she's so powerful!" Raylynn looked between them all, as if one of them could explain why this fact wasn't obvious. "If you can't make another sword, can you give my dagger power just like it?"

"Stop bothering the princess and mind your manners, Ray," Sophie said sternly, cutting off the conversation. She stopped the girl from unsheathing the dagger.

"Now, the princess and I have to go get ready for her wedding. It'll be very soon." Zira gave Raylynn one final squeeze and stood. "I'll meet you both tonight for dinner. Thank you again," Zira murmured as her mother and daughter exited. "Do you think I'm a bad mother for this deceit?"

"No." It was Vi's turn to give Zira's hand a squeeze. "I think you just did a very, very good thing."

If Vi's suspicions were right, she had just witnessed her first real opportunity to change fate.

15

V I GAZED UP AT the domed ceiling. A statue of the Mother held out a giant basin of fire that lit the entire cathedral—the second-most impressive structure in all of Norin. It was yet another piece of architecture that reminded her of the Archives in Risen.

Beneath the great statue were smaller ones of the Mother in various poses and expressions. Those statues melted into the relief sculptures of the Father that rounded the room. He looked up at the visages of the Mother above in yearning.

Vi inspected the tender face of the deity who would be Raspian. The sculptor knew nothing of the god's actual likeness, just like the Dark Isle knew nothing of his real relationship with the Mother. All Vi saw in his longing eyes was a drive to once more subdue the goddess that ruled above him.

"So much history they don't even know they're a part of." A familiar voice startled Vi from her thoughts. Deneya had seemingly materialized at her side. "Every time I come here it reminds me of home—in a strange, not-quite-right sort of way."

"It's a bit like a distorted mirror, isn't it?" Vi murmured.

"That's one way to put it." Deneya glanced at her from the corners of her eyes. "Now, why did you summon me?"

"I need your help today."

"Oh?"

Some Crones emerged from a nearby door, beginning to light sconces throughout the room. Vi walked in the opposite direction, keeping her voice so low it was barely audible over the echo of their footsteps in the cavernous space. "I need you to protect Zira."

"Zira has always struck me as a woman capable of protecting herself."

"The Knights are going to make a play for the sword. I had a vision."

Deneya stopped walking. "When?"

"About two weeks ago."

"You didn't think to mention this when we spoke with Taavin last?" Deneya arched her eyebrows. The three of them had been meeting weekly.

"Slipped my mind."

Deneya rolled her eyes. "Whatever you have to tell yourself. That's between you and him."

"Exactly," Vi said firmly. Her stomach was still in knots because she had yet to tell Taavin of her vision, her slight maneuvering—*encouragement*—of Raylynn, or her bold plan. But this was her moment to spare Zira from an untimely death *and* prevent the sword from falling into the hands of the Knights of Jadar. Asking for forgiveness would be easy when she succeeded. She hoped. "At the point in the ceremony when Zira lifts the sword overhead, she'll be struck from behind. I need you to move through the crowd and counter the attack."

"So just focus on Zira. Not Fiera or the sword?"

"I'll worry about the sword and Fiera. Just save Zira."

"Simple enough." A smirk curled Deneya's lips. "I always wanted to run circles around the Dark Isle dwellers with Lightspinning. But it's against my code while I'm here."

"But you'll help me do this?"

"Of course. You're the Champion—exceptions can be made for you." And Deneya looked all too eager to make those exceptions. "Things were boring before you came."

"Hopefully, if I do my job right… they'll be boring again." Vi's attention was drawn to the main doors of the cathedral—the only entrance and exit onto the streets. As if sensing their discussion, Zira appeared. "Now, if you'll excuse me."

Deneya fell into step, whispering hastily, "I have something else I need to tell you, when it's all over."

"What?"

"No time now." She lifted her eyes, looking to Zira. "Good day, captain."

"Good day, councilor. Is everything all right?"

"Yes." Deneya smiled. "Just checking in with Yullia here about the final count of the guards so I can ensure they are paid correctly. Now, if you'll excuse me, I need to change before the ceremony." Deneya bowed and departed.

"Are you ready for today?" Zira asked.

"I think so. You?"

"No," Zira answered bluntly. "I've fought countless men in dozens of battles. But this has my hands trembling."

"You'll be fine." Vi patted the woman on her shoulder.

"Do you mind if I go over the ceremony once more with you? I don't want to forget." A nervous Zira was more endearing than Vi could've imagined.

"Not at all."

"Thank you." Zira promptly turned to a back door.

Vi's eyes were drawn to the sword on her hip as Zira moved. Vi's head bobbed along as Zira went through the ceremony a final time. But her attention was on the sword.

She would protect it, and the woman, at all costs.

She wouldn't accept any other fate.

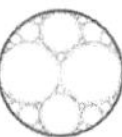

Two hours later, Fiera arrived by covered carriage. Soldiers stretched sheer panels between poles that obscured her as she entered the cathedral. The gathered crowds cheered and threw flowers, praising their soon-to-be Empress, as if their happiness for the union had been there all along.

Vi watched from an upper floor, scanning the guards that lined Fiera's walk. How many of them were Knights of Jadar loyalists? How many were ready to stab the woman in the back if the opportunity presented itself?

When Fiera entered the cathedral, Vi spiraled down the narrow iron staircase that took her from the top of the spire she'd perched in down into a side wing, and out into the cathedral proper. The main chamber was beginning to fill with nobles and dignitaries and Vi stepped lightly, unnoticed by most.

She scanned the crowd carefully, trying to discern who might be surreptitiously positioning themselves, waiting for the time to strike. Vi made a note of every man and woman who chose to stand behind where Zira would be in less than an hour. By the time she waded through the sea of people, Vi had committed their faces to memory.

Vi slipped into a back hall that connected to a waiting room where Fiera sat in a chair by the window—looking far more composed than Vi had expected.

"Are there a lot of people yet?" Fiera asked, perking up when Vi entered.

"It's filling quickly." Zira was nowhere to be seen. Having the sword out of sight put Vi on edge. She glanced at the two handmaids who hovered in the corner of the room. "Out with you both."

They glanced at each other, but left when Fiera commanded a gentle, "Please excuse us a moment." The princess turned back to Vi, dark eyebrows arched in question.

Vi stared down at the woman, wondering countless things at once. Was the cut of her dress—tight below the bust, but flowing loose around her abdomen—happenstance, or an intentional concealment? Had she looked into the future at all during these past weeks? Did she have any sense of what was about to transpire?

Not knowing the answers to those and several hundred other questions, Vi slowly drew her sword. Acting on instinct, she rested the point of the weapon in a crack of the floor and knelt before Fiera.

"Princess, soon to be Empress…" Vi looked up over top of her white-knuckled hands. "I shall not abandon my post before your throne, on this day or any to come. I am loyal to you, and any actions I take are an extension of that loyalty."

"What have you seen?" Fiera asked. "Tell me. I am burdened by the sight as well, and accustomed to living with its revelations. You do not need to shoulder this truth alone."

"There will be an attack during your ceremony."

"Who else have you told?"

"No one," Vi lied easily, and Fiera believed it without question.

"Not even Zira?"

"I need her to act without knowing."

"I see." Vi actually believed she did. "What do you need from me, then?"

"Faith. Trust."

"You have had those from the first moment I laid eyes on you," Fiera said softly. It was a gift Vi still didn't feel she'd earned, but was grateful to have.

"When the moment comes, trust me to protect you."

Fiera nodded just as their conversation was interrupted by the door opening. Lord Ophain stood in its frame. He was dressed in deep crimson finery from head to toe, a heavy silver pendant around his neck that Vi recognized as the mark of the Lord of the West.

"Dear sister, it's time," he said gently, walking over. Vi stood and stepped out of the man's way, allowing him to take both of

Fiera's hands. Ophain was accustomed to servants and guards in his presence; he didn't so much as look at her twice. "Are you ready to do this?"

"I am," Fiera said with a small smile. "There is only happiness and love ahead. The war is done, and this shall put it to rest."

The fight for Fiera's life was only just beginning. But Vi said nothing as they left, arm in arm. She slipped out through the side door and joined the masses gathered to watch the first Empress Solaris be crowned.

It had become difficult to walk in the great room of the cathedral. People had filled it to the point of pressing against the guards on the outer ring. Vi looked for the faces of the men and women she'd seen earlier. She sought out people she might know. Some she was certain she recognized, others she was certain she didn't. But her recognition or lack thereof was not a reliable measure for traitors. Vi could thank Jayme for that lesson.

Soft gasps and murmurs distracted her when she was halfway through her first sweep. Vi jerked her head upward, toward what was stealing everyone's attention. Fiera had entered and, at the same time, the Emperor made his grand entrance from the upper doorway in the dome. As Fiera walked, her gold-trimmed train stretched behind her in equal measure as the Emperor's golden cape.

They made their way to each other in the center of the room. There, in an outer circle, was a row of soldiers. After that, a row of Crones, Fiera's sisters, and Zira.

"My lords and ladies of the West, our esteemed guests from the South and East, I welcome you all to this most joyous occasion," Ophain's voice boomed as they reached the middle of the chamber. "It is my honor as Lord of the West to present my sister to our Emperor so they might be joined in marriage." Ophain presented the hand of his sister to Tiberus.

"Eons ago," the head Crone began to speak, wasting no time. "The Father lived in a land of eternal night. It was in that darkness that he met the Mother. She was a brilliant star..."

Vi tuned out the ceremonial storytelling. Her eyes continued to scan the crowd, even more attentive as she positioned herself directly behind Fiera. Deneya would defend Zira, and from this vantage Vi would get a look at the attacker if she was lucky. But her vision hadn't shown her the aftermath of the attack, and Vi would be ready for whatever came.

"The Mother watches over us, bringing life and joy. The Father watches over our timelessness, seeing us safely into the lands beyond." The head Crone produced a long red ribbon from inside her robes. It was the same one Vi had run back to the castle for earlier. She pushed forward into the crowd, ignoring the glares and rude gestures of those around her. "From our births to our deaths, we are bound to the plans they have laid. We walk the red lines they have given us."

Not if I have something to say about it, Vi silently added. She was the one who could change those red lines—if she was bold and brave enough.

"By this, it is not for us to question those who are called to each other, just as it is no more our place to question those called to greatness. To do so would be an affront to the divine."

Vi heard the scoff of a man to her left. She looked in his direction. He murmured something to another gentleman beside him. Vi stepped through the crowd, squeezing through an opening to get closer to the man. The ripple effect of shifting people caught his attention.

Their eyes met and he gave her a thin smile before looking forward again. The other man he'd been whispering to shuffled through the standing masses. Vi caught only a glimpse of the back of his head. *Luke?*

"Princess Fiera Ci'Dan, daughter of the last King of Mhashan, may the Mother bless you with the greatness of her warmth." The Crone carefully laid the ribbon, looping it over the couple's joined hands. Vi looked between them and the man who had vanished into the crowd. She couldn't go chasing after him. She had to stay close to Fiera; the time was near. "Emperor Tiberus Solaris, first

Emperor of this great land, chosen by the sun, may the Father bless you with his resolution."

The Crone carried on with her blessings, wrapping their hands with each one. At the same time, Vi worked her way through the mass of people, pushing bodies aside when they refused to move. She was right behind Fiera as she and Tiberus recited their vows to each other.

For a brief moment, the world was calm. Happy, even. Fiera smiled brightly as she promised to be the Emperor's, to honor him, to serve him, to hold him to a standard befitting an Emperor of all, for all. The Emperor nearly teared up as he promised the same—that he was hers, that he would love and cherish her, that she would forever be the brightest ray of the Solaris sun.

The future was hopeful in that breathtaking minute. And Vi witnessed the first glimpse that told her, beyond all doubt, this unlikely couple had come together to be greater than the sum of their parts.

Then the Crone spoke again: "The Mother bestowed on Mhashan a weapon to guard us all." Zira unsheathed the sword. "May your love be as strong as this blade, as unyielding as its edge. And, should she above bless this union, may her fire touch the fate that binds you both."

The Crone stepped back as Zira raised the sword above her head. Movement caught Vi's eye. Zira dramatically lowered the weapon over top their joined hands. Vi sank into her legs, ready to spring. Women around her wept tears at the ceremony's beauty. Vi readied herself to kill.

Fire ignited between the ribbon and the blade, burning it away as ash. Vi held her breath as Zira lifted the sword. *This was it*. This was the moment she died.

Instead, like the fire that burned in the sculpted brazier above the center of the room—flames erupted at Fiera's back, igniting chaos in the crowd.

16

ZIRA SCREAMED, STUMBLING FORWARD.

Vi launched herself forward as well, pushing a Crone and Princess Tina out of the way to barge into the inner circle of the wedding ceremony. Zira's back was singed, her clothes hanging by threads. But for the time being, she was very much alive.

People began to move, the crowd rumbling as if the earth itself trembled beneath them.

"Everyone stay back!" Vi shouted at the top of her lungs. She reached for the head Crone, pushing the elderly woman away. Vi spun, grabbing Zira and pulling her toward her, Fiera, and Tiberus in the same moment.

"How dare—" the Emperor grumbled. Before he could finish, Vi conjured a thin wall of flame with a thought. It burned white-hot and towered above them, nearly touching the bottom of the stone basin the statue was holding aloft in the dome above.

"It's an assassination attempt." Vi glared at Tiberus. "Keep your wife safe and don't move."

Sweat dotted his brow, but the Emperor kept silent, the reality of the situation sinking in. He clutched Fiera to him, so tightly that Vi couldn't make eye contact.

"Zira, stay here and protect the sword."

"I can fight," the woman insisted, pain turning her voice into a snarl.

"You're hurt and—"

"Mother above I will turn this sword on you if you don't let me at the bastard who did this!"

"Fine." Vi was grinning like a fool. As if this was something she wanted. Something she enjoyed. "Fiera, you guard the sword."

"It has always been my duty." Fiera pushed the Emperor away enough to take the sword from Zira's hands. She looked the least frightened of them all. The only thing that filled her dark eyes was the light of Vi's flames, and absolute trust that Vi had only ever seen one other time—in the eyes of the men and women who had followed Fiera into battle that night.

"Ready?" Zira asked over the crackle of flames.

"Take this." Vi quickly drew her sword, handing it to the woman.

"What about you?"

"I'll find—"

A sword sliced through the wall of fire, nicking the Emperor's side. He yowled in pain and turned with a growl. Blood stained his hip red, but it wasn't a fatal wound.

"We've wasted enough time." Vi grabbed Zira's hand and pushed an opening into the fire, just wide enough for them to slip through, before closing it once more. They ran head-first into a man on the way out.

Head over heels, the three of them tumbled. Vi rolled, stomping feet around her crushing her back and ribs as the panicked masses fled. Grunting, she pushed herself off the floor, flames following her every movement, sending those who would run into her away in burning pain.

"*Mysst soto larrk.*" A sword appeared in Vi's palm, her flames masking the strands of light and glyphs that condensed into the weapon. In the back of her mind she continued to focus on the wall of fire protecting Fiera and the Emperor; at all costs, she'd maintain it.

That brought her attention back to the barrier. Three men were slashing at it blindly, getting as close to the flames as they dared. They must think the wall of fire was Fiera's and that the princess was the one to kill to see it undone.

A dark delight filled her at the notion. This was becoming too easy.

More fire erupted at her side, identical to the flames at Zira's back and stealing her attention. Zira pushed the charred man off of her, scrambling to her feet.

"Thank you, a second time."

She'd thought Vi was behind the fire. "You're welcome," Vi said as she rapidly scanned the shifting crowd for where Deneya was firing off *juth starys*. But the woman had hidden herself well, and Vi brought her attention back to the men slashing for the Emperor and Fiera. "Let's take care of them."

"My pleasure."

They moved in tandem. Vi had been running drills with Zira long enough that she was familiar with how the woman moved. But moreover, she was confident with a sword now. Killing came easily. Vi sliced the first man down without a thought before moving onto the second.

Zira parried another. They fought off the immediate threat with backs to each other in an odd dance of death.

Vi bared her teeth, panting and snarling as she looked across the blood-smeared floor of the cathedral for more threats. Most people were out now, the other conspirators included. They must've turned tail when they realized their plan wouldn't bear fruit.

"We need to follow them!"

"No." Vi stopped Zira with a straight arm. "You get the Empress and Emperor to safety. Bar up the room she was in earlier. Let no one in but me. I'll go after them."

"Yull—"

"This is an order!"

Zira blinked, startled at Vi's audacity. Vi kept her brow furrowed, lips pursed, and the tension in her muscles the same as when she had been in battle. Zira's mouth fell open, shock softening her jaw. She closed it with a nod.

Vi released her control of the flames. "Go!"

The Emperor and Empress looked around, dazed. Tiberus blinked several times, no doubt seeing blue from the fire. Fiera was faster to recover, swinging her gaze from Vi to Zira.

"This way." Zira stepped forward.

If Vi left now, she might have a chance to follow any remaining attackers. It'd be the best opportunity to weed out those who were actively hunting the sword. Vi looked over to the group of royals, nearly at the door.

She wouldn't leave until they were safely away. Vi tightened her grip around her sword. Zira was still alive. She wasn't about to see her killed now.

As soon as the door to Fiera's preparation room closed behind them, however, Vi was off. She raced behind the last of the guests flooding out onto the streets.

"*Durroe watt radia,*" Vi whispered as she crossed the threshold of the cathedral. When she emerged, it was in a new skin.

Vi swung her head left and right. She decided on the direction where the majority had gone. Moving quickly to catch up with those still fleeing, she listened carefully.

"The new Empress is dead."

"She's not dead!"

"They really did it."

"The Knights actually did it. He pulled it off."

"He didn't pull off anything. That was an utter failure."

Vi spun in place, trying to locate the speakers. She slowed her pace to a walk.

"What do you think they'll do next?"

"They can't accomplish anything without the sword."

Two men were walking into a bar not far from her. Vi stepped lightly behind them, trusting her Lightspinning to prevent them from identifying her.

"I think I know a way they could get it."

"*Shh*, you idiot, not on the streets." The taller of the two men glanced over his shoulder, but his eyes swept over Vi as they hastily entered the bar.

She was quick behind them.

"... him at the warehouse. I think the next meeting is—" Vi caught the last of what the tall man was saying as she entered.

"Excuse me, miss, we're closed for the day," the barkeep interrupted abruptly. The two men startled and looked directly at Vi—but what they saw was the face of a random woman who attended the wedding. A woman who, blessedly, neither of them recognized.

"I'm sorry." Vi put on a thick Western accent. "I got separated from my companions, I didn't know if they'd come in here."

"They're certainly not in here. Closed to mourn the tragedy at our princess's wedding. Out with you," the barkeep barked.

Mourn? Or conduct private business? Vi looked between the groups of men, but merely gave a sweet, innocuous smile. "I'm sorry for interrupting."

With that, Vi left.

The streets were mostly empty as she trudged back to the cathedral. When she ascended the stairs once more, it was as a woman the world knew only as Yullia.

"Using your spinning to conceal yourself like that is clever." Deneya leaned on a column by the doors, arms folded. "You have other tricks for the words?"

"Maybe. And maybe I'll show you if you continue to be useful to me." Vi couldn't tell if the curve of her mouth was a roguish smile or a more threatening display of teeth. She was in a deadly mood.

"I'm useful enough to keep Zira alive like you asked." Pushing off the column, Deneya walked over to her. "I also saw who delivered the first blow," she said in a hushed tone, looking out over the city while Vi stared absently into the cathedral.

"Meet me later in the usual place, then."

"Usual place?" Deneya groaned. "It's dark and dull and hard to get to. Let's go out tonight."

"It's secluded and no one will overhear us." Vi shot her a glare. Deneya just grinned as though her goal all along had been to rile Vi up.

"My office instead? I have their fire whiskey, good stuff—"

"Fine." Vi was beyond arguing. She still had work to do. What they were doing could be a game to Deneya, a fun opportunity to meddle with the affairs of the Dark Isle. But every action had the highest stakes for Vi. "I don't know when I'll be there, so you'd better wait."

"All the more reason to meet in my office." Deneya strolled down the steps. "I'll have my books and bottle to keep me company while I wait."

"Keep your head about you," Vi called down.

"Won't be a problem." She raised a hand, touching the scarf on the side of her head, just where the tops of her ears would be. *Elfin.* The woman was elfin, Vi realized. That was why she was never without a scarf.

Vi shook her head and went inside, heading right for Fiera's door. She knocked softly.

"It's me." She heard the locks disengage and the door cracked open, Zira brandishing the sword. She relaxed the moment her eyes met Vi's and opened wide the door.

"You find the bastards?"

"Unfortunately not. They blended into the crowd." Vi stepped inside, still locking the door behind her. "Is everyone all right?"

"Tiberus is—"

"It is just a nick, do not fret," he interrupted Fiera. "I've had worse out in battle. You, however, will need to see a cleric."

"You worry for nothing," Fiera mumbled, glancing askance.

"We'll arrange for a guarded carriage to take you both back to the castle. There, you can both be looked at by clerics," Vi said. "And following, we'll need to discuss protection of the sword going forward."

"I have every intention of sealing it away." Fiera shifted in her seat.

"Sealing it away?" Tiberus muttered. "Why seal away a weapon like that, when you could turn it against your enemies?"

That was the last thing Vi wanted. She stepped forward, kneeling before the Emperor and Empress. For a brief second, her breath caught in her throat at the sight of them—a regal couple, young and strong. She was witnessing a moment that even the most skilled painters never could have captured. A moment she should never have witnessed.

"My Emperor and Empress," Vi started reverently. "I am your loyal subject. I defer to you in all things. But if you will, I implore you to accept council from this lowly one." She was laying on the decorum thick, but Vi knew enough about Tiberus now to know he was one to appreciate it. "The Knights of Jadar will grow in strength with or without the sword in their possession. They see it as their right."

"Which it certainly is not," the Emperor snapped. "Treasonous scum."

"It is not," Vi agreed. "But reality and the perceptions of men rarely overlap."

"What would you have us do?" Fiera asked.

"Hide it as you intended," Vi said delicately. "But it needs to be a place no one will know—a place they cannot even hunt you to find."

"How do you suggest I do that?"

"Give it to me," Vi said boldly, her gaze unwavering. If she didn't exude confidence, how could she ever expect them to invest it in her? "Give me the sword, and then not even you will know of its location. You cannot be captured or killed to find it."

"You think we should trust *you* with the sword? You overstep much for a guard," Tiberus said down his nose at her.

"She knows her place and acts within it." Fiera reached out to touch her husband's hand lightly. "It is something I have considered before. Furthermore, she's right... this is not something either of us should do. We do not live for ourselves any longer. We live for our Empire—and for our unborn son."

Fiera rested her hand on her stomach. Vi had never been so fixated on something that couldn't be seen. One motion could say so much, but Vi didn't know what language the message was in. Did this mean she was pregnant now? Or was Fiera merely referencing the prophecy Vi had given her months before? She narrowly resisted asking outright.

"You..." The Emperor seemed torn. Torn between his growing family and the peace a contented royal family would foster, and his thirst for conquest. His gaze volleyed among the sword, Vi, and Fiera. But ultimately his wife and unborn child won out. "You are right."

"Then I will entrust the sword to you, Yullia." Fiera's mouth turned upward into an easy smile. She almost looked relieved. "Tell no one what you do with it."

"I will take its secrets with me to my grave."

SHE HAD THE SWORD.

Vi had to replay the day's events in her mind as she stared at the faintly glowing weapon in her bedroom that night to make sure she wasn't dreaming. There had been the preparations, the wedding, the attack. She had summoned a carriage to take Zira and the royals back to the castle before slipping out a back door herself, the sword wrapped tightly so that not even a glimmer of its divine blue light could be seen. Her shoulders had been tense as she wove through the city, the grin she wore so wide that it hurt.

Her heart was still racing as she summoned Taavin.

The man looked from Vi to the sword on her bed. Like a moth to a flame, he slowly crossed to it, entranced. Taavin ran his fingertips along the blade. Yargen's magic sought him out as it did Vi. It seemed to seep into him and, for a brief, breathtaking second, the thin lines of magic that hummed around the edges of him faded.

He was there, in the flesh. She crossed over to him and rested a hand on his shoulder. He turned, startled. His eyes widened. He must have felt it too.

"Taavin, you're…" He was solid underneath her fingertips. Vi snaked her arms around his waist, acting on instinct and awe. She could feel his heartbeat racing. Or perhaps the frantic beating was actually her own.

"Vi—" Taavin moved to embrace her and lifted his hand from the weapon. The shimmering magic returned to his form. The warmth and smell of him vanished.

"The sword," she whispered. "It makes you… real." If she could string it around his neck, she would.

"Yargen's magic is a power unlike any other. It's the embodiment of life itself," he said thoughtfully, more to the sword than her. But Taavin brought his gaze back to Vi, his thumb caressing her cheek. "But I am always real, for you."

Vi put on the bravest smile she could, unable and not trusting herself to say anything else.

"Now, tell me, how did you manage to procure it so quickly?"

Her arms tightened around him. "Don't be cross with me," Vi started, already searching his eyes for the edges of anger.

"*How* did you procure it?"

"I had a vision," Vi began hesitantly.

"When?"

"About two weeks ago."

Taavin released her and took a step back. "Two weeks, and you didn't tell me? Where did you have it? What was your vision of?"

Vi finally told him of Zira's request, looking into Raylynn's future, and what it had ultimately led her to. She watched his expression darken more with every word. Her heart was now racing for an entirely different reason—the adrenaline of warring emotions.

When she finished, Taavin turned, putting his back to her.

"Taavin, I was only doing what I thought was best. What I thought would lead this world—"

"No, you were doing what *you* wanted to do," he interrupted harshly. "You weren't acting on behalf of this world. You put yourself in danger to strike against the Knights of Jadar. You didn't even consult me."

"You would've told me not to do it."

"Of course I would've!" He spun, looking at her with rage-filled eyes. "You're not thinking this through."

"I am," Vi insisted. "I played it safe. I did what you asked. And all it led to was the Knights of Jadar gaining enough time to strengthen and organize an attack. If I had been acting offensively sooner, then maybe I could've prevented the attack on the wedding from ever happening." He was silent, glowering at her. "If I hadn't acted, Zira would be *dead*."

"That's it, isn't it?" Taavin whispered.

"What?" Vi was taken aback by his sudden quiet.

"This wasn't about the sword, or the world. It wasn't about dealing a blow to an organization that threatens your family. This was about her."

"It was about the sword," Vi insisted.

"No, you wanted to save Zira." He took a step forward, raising a finger and pointing at her. "You wanted to save her, because you *always* want to save her."

"And is that so terrible?" Vi met him step for step. "What's so awful about not wanting to see a little girl grow up without her mother?"

"Because you can't save Zira." Taavin shook his head sadly. "And you can't save Fiera, either."

It was an arrow that fired straight and true, landing right through her heart. Vi staggered back. She grabbed her chest, clawing at the physical ache there.

"You don't know that," she whispered.

"Their deaths are stones in the river."

Vi shook her head, as though she could shake off his words. She couldn't—they'd burned her. His words singed her chest, making her feel hot all over, like her bones had become cinder. "No," she said softly.

"Vi, listen to—"

"You listen." She brought her eyes back to him. "I saved my father when the world presumed him dead. I saved him from Adela. I had a vision of Zira dying today, and she yet lives. I am the one who is to change fate and save this whole, damned world. Do not tell me I can't save two women."

"It doesn't work that way." The pity in his eyes was the worst part.

"Have I ever saved her before?" Vi volleyed back to him. He narrowed his eyes. "Has Zira ever survived the wedding before?"

"No," Taavin reluctantly admitted.

"Then you don't know." Hope was a wave crashing down on her, extinguishing the blaze that had nearly consumed her. "You don't know, because this is new."

"I have ninety-two other histories that guide my wisdom."

"But you don't *know*."

"I know there are some things that, no matter how hard you try, don't change."

"Then I will try harder," Vi insisted.

"I grant you that you've kept Zira alive longer than ever before. But Yargen will come for her life, as she will Fiera's. Perhaps the assassin that came in the night ten attempts ago will return once more, looking for the sword—"

"Then I will have guards posted at her door."

"Two attempts ago she was involved in a skirmish with the Knights while patrolling the city and was cut down."

"Then I will do the patrols," Vi continued to counter. "Rather than tell me what I can't do, help me accomplish what I can. Help me find all these avenues to spare her by telling me how she's died before."

"Or she dies at the hands of a thief who gets the jump on her while she's sleeping along the road during one of her trips, long after you've left her side." Vi narrowed her eyes slightly and balled her hands into fists. Before she could say anything again, Taavin continued. "And if you save Fiera from one death, she's murdered in equally horrible ways. Or falls victim to an accident no one could prevent."

She stared up at him, searching for a lie in his words. But Taavin's eyes were stony clones of their usual warm selves, cold and unfeeling. The backs of her eyes prickled, though Vi couldn't quite explain why. She hadn't felt like crying in months. Why now?

It wasn't that she knew Fiera *that* well. Certainly, she'd come to love the Empress in an unexpected but not entirely surprising way. And the woman did have her undeniable aura that made people willing to follow her to the ends of the earth.

But this feeling was more than that.

This was her stomach flipping upside down until her throat knotted. It was her eyes burning and her breaths becoming shallow. This feeling was worse than staring down Adela, or Ulvarth… perhaps even worse than burning Taavin alive.

"Why?" Vi whispered. "Why would Yargen do this?"

"There is the greater cycle of fate, the one we are trapped within and trying to free ourselves from. But there are also smaller turns, turns within families. Cruel fathers who raise cruel men who become cruel fathers themselves. There are some things we cannot escape."

"No." She shook her head. "I am here to change it—to break those cycles. And I refuse to believe that a goddess who supposedly wishes to look after all her people would trap them in destructive cycles they can't free themselves from. If anything, that is the work of Raspian, and I will give it no credence."

"I know your pain," Taavin said firmly and with a slightly pleading edge. "I understand your hurt. Watching the ones you care for suffer, over and over again. Being helpless to stop or change it, no matter how hard you try. Seeing someone you love more than anyone or anything else in this accursed world trapped in a loop for nearly a thousand years.

"Feeling every blow, pain, and betrayal as though it's your own.

Each one worse than the last. Yearning not to feel… but you—I can't avoid feeling, because the moment I lay eyes on you, I feel everything."

His hands were on her face. Vi blinked up at him, startled. She hardly remembered him crossing to her. His words were more entrancing than any of Yargen's. The way he said them was like a prayer, or a Lightspinner's chant.

Taavin's thumbs smoothed over the curve of her cheeks and he held her there. In his eyes she saw all the wonder and pain the universe had ever held. It was enough to make her knees weak and heart ache.

"If you know this pain… then help me end it," Vi whispered. "Help me break not just one cycle, but all of them. Then we'll all be free."

He smiled sadly and his eyes drifted from her lips to her forehead, where he placed a tender kiss. Vi pressed her eyes closed, a deep ache reverberating through her. She needed him. Her hands grabbed the back of his arms above his elbows.

"I'm trying to help you," he murmured. "But you have to let me. You have to listen, and be careful. The best chance we have to end this is caution. But if we don't end it, we have to see you reborn. Be careful until then."

Taavin pulled away and when Vi opened her eyes again, he was gone. She spent a moment focusing on every long breath of air, but each one felt thinner than the last. When he left, he took all the oxygen with him.

Vi grabbed the sword as though she could somehow strike down the barriers that stood in their way. But all she did was sheathe and hide it. The currents of emotion she was wading through were her own. There was still work to be done—work that wouldn't end just because she wanted and needed more time to sort through her own experiences.

The castle was alive now, even at night. Servants tended to duties they didn't have a chance to get to during the day. Vi donned the skin of one random helper she'd seen most afternoons in Fiera's chambers as she made her way to Deneya's office.

Two raps on the door and it opened promptly. Deneya looked her up and down.

"I heard you needed help sorting your bookcases," Vi said, keeping the masquerade even though no one was around.

"My bookcases are fine. Though I wouldn't mind help with laundry. Folding is a pain." Deneya gave a smirk, one Vi returned. "Come on in." Vi entered and released her illusion. "It's just *durroe*, right?"

"Yes, though it helps if you pick a real person. It's harder to fabricate someone who doesn't exist with enough detail to keep the illusion stable."

"You speak from experience?" Deneya walked over to her desk, where there were two glasses set out alongside a half-empty decanter. Deneya had started without her.

"I do." Vi adjusted the sword at her belt to sit in one of the chairs facing Deneya's desk. "Though, I admit, it's been a while since I first began using *durroe* this way. Maybe I would have more luck with a fabricated person now."

"It seems to be working well, no point in pushing to change it." Deneya glugged a heavy pour from the decanter into each glass.

"That's precisely the reason to change it." Vi wore a grin as she accepted her glass. "Given the reactions I've received from the people of Meru, it's been far too long since someone re-imagined how the goddess's words can be used."

"Some would say re-imagining the words of the goddess is blasphemy."

"Beware of the ones who do—they're the real enemies of Meru. And, as the Champion of Yargen, I say it's fine."

Deneya chuckled and held out her glass. "I like you, Yullia. Cheers to saving a royal family today."

"Cheers." Vi tipped the edge of her glass against Deneya's and took a long sip of the dark amber liquid in her glass. It tasted of spiced caramel, surprisingly sweet. "And it's Vi. My name is Vi."

"Vi," Deneya repeated thoughtfully. "Why Yullia, then?"

"It didn't feel right to use my name when I came here, for a whole host of reasons." She watched the liquid swirl in the glass as she slowly rotated it.

"Then thank you for telling me."

"I know your true name. It's only fair," Vi answered offhandedly. As though she hadn't just allowed Deneya past a barrier.

Deneya took another sip of her drink and Vi did the same. She vaguely remembered the drink Erion Le'Dan had given her all those months ago. Was this the same? Or different? Better or worse?

She fought to dredge up the memories—the only proof that that time had existed at all. Vi set her glass down on the armrest of the chair.

"You said you saw who was the first to attack?"

"Yes."

"What did he look like?"

"Western, tall, bushy mustache… you couldn't see it in what he was wearing, but he has a scar on his forearm, too."

"You know him then?" Vi asked hopefully.

"*Know* is a strong word. I've seen him before." Deneya set her glass down and crossed her arms.

"Where?" Vi settled back into her chair, quickly adding, "No, let me guess. Heading in and out of Twintle's estate?"

"Half right. One of Twintle's warehouses down at the docks."

"Idiots," Vi half sighed, half mumbled. "They're no longer meeting at the estate?"

"I'm not certain. They've become much better at hiding their tracks," Deneya said with a note of frustration.

"Either way, Twintle is their ringleader."

"It seems so, and that brings me to the other thing I had to tell you." Deneya's eyes sparked with knowing. "Twintle contacted Zira, offering to resume some of his old Knightly duties and assist overseeing security at the last minute. Said it would be his honor."

Vi was sure she hadn't heard of it because Twintle no doubt hated her after she suggested the soldiers be released in stages, resulting in them being imprisoned longer. He would've done everything possible to keep her out of the decision-making process. "Slimy snake," she mumbled.

"He's definitely the one leading. He has the means and the coin," Deneya said with a note of agreement. "But I think Luke is helping organize. He's a convenient mobilizer so Twintle can continue to fulfill his duties and keep suspicion off his family."

"I see." Vi swirled the drink in her glass, thinking back to her conversation with Taavin.

"So, who do we go after? Luke, Twintle, or neither? I doubt Taavin would approve," Deneya said, not knowing how spot-on she was.

"No, he wouldn't." She took a long sip of her drink, savoring the burn while she thought about what Taavin had said. He'd claimed that, regardless of what she did, there were people she couldn't save. But that wasn't about to stop her from trying. She was in uncharted territory now, after all. At the very least, she'd make the lives of those who would harm the family of a future-Vi as miserable as possible. "We're not going to go after Twintle or Luke."

"Who, then?"

"All of them. Every Knight that would ever swing a sword against Zira or Fiera." She had saved Zira once. Now, Vi had to keep her alive, and prove to Taavin that boldness was the key to ending this vicious cycle once and for all.

"Where has Twintle gone, exactly?" Vi asked as she and Deneya walked through the midday streets of Norin toward the port.

"He has a manor between here and the Crossroads, not too far from the latter. Last I heard he was taking a short leave of absence to return home and spend some time with family before summer is up."

Houses in the city, houses in the Waste. The old noble families of Mhashan had more homes than Vi currently had pairs of trousers and seemed to change them with equal frequency.

"Family, or networking with the old lords and ladies who still harbor ill will toward the new Empress along the way."

"My money would be on that."

"Mine as well." Though Vi also entertained the idea of him turning tail, embarrassed by his failure at Fiera's wedding.

"Then this is a boring gamble." Deneya chuckled lightly. Sometimes, like now, Vi deeply appreciated her casual disregard for the weight of the situation surrounding her. Perhaps it was because Deneya didn't see herself as a part of the Dark Isle, and its trials were mere amusements to her. Or perhaps she'd genuinely been so bored for so long here that even the slightest activity was a genuine delight.

Either way, it forced Vi to relax some. Her demeanor had Vi working to remove herself in a similar way—look at all that was happening from the outside. It didn't directly affect or relate to her, not really. She only had one goal and that was to do whatever it took to prevent the Crystal Caverns and weapons from being destroyed while saving as many people as she could in the process.

Of course, this distance was fabricated and skin deep. At her core, Vi couldn't deny the simmering hatred she felt for the Knights of Jadar for what they had done and would do to her family—a hatred that only grew by the day.

"Either way, he won't be here to deny the search, and no one else in his employ should be able to refuse me."

"You're confident in that?" Vi asked, glancing over at Deneya. The world blurred at the edges of her vision with bright shifting light. She was using *durroe* for an illusion once more. This time Vi had experimented with basing the masquerade off the face of a real person and the body and clothes of a different real person—a hybrid of real to make something fake. According to Deneya, her work was as flawless as it was the first two times she'd seen it.

"Look at me. Do I look like a woman who has ever not been confident in her life?"

"No." Vi refrained from bringing up Taavin's mention of her cheating on an exam during their first interaction. She'd looked very uncertain then.

"Good. You play your part, I'll play mine. We start with the two warehouses on the left side and work our way to Twintle's."

Vi didn't quite like the plan. The idea that they would go to other warehouses under the guise of a surprise inspection before arriving at Twintle's—theoretically giving Twintle's men time to learn they were coming and hide any evidence of the Knights—still rankled her. But Deneya was confident in the best approach and Vi would give the woman the benefit of the doubt. She'd yet to disappoint her.

The first warehouse was on the far end of the docks; Vi could smell it long before they arrived. It belonged to a prominent fish trader and Vi resisted the urge to cover her nose as she perused the rows of fish nearly the size of her, laid out for bidding. She was more than ready to depart when Deneya issued them the all-clear.

The next warehouse belonged to a logger, barging lumber from the North. Vi stared up at the massive chunks of wood, knowing they were mere fractions of the sentries she'd grown up in. She wondered how long until this man's business was shut down due to the Emperor's encroachment on Shaldan.

Finally, after spending the better part of the morning in the first two warehouses, they were on to Twintle's. His was around the middle of the bustling docks, toward the richer side of town. Vi paused, staring out at the ships. Her eyes swung to the far corner, the oldest stretch.

On all of her maps, those docks had always been there. They were the humble start of the greatest port on the Dark Isle. They had been there... when the scythe left.

The vision Vi had on Meru was in the forefront of her mind: an Eastern man with hazel eyes, standing at those docks, bestowing a scythe-shaped velvet-wrapped parcel on a ship captain. That was the spot where the scythe had left this land and—

"Are you all right?" Deneya startled her from her thoughts.

"Wh—oh, yes." Vi glanced back to the far end of the port.

"What is it?"

"Nothing, it's nothing." She shook her head. "Just remembering something. Let's carry on."

There were two men posted as guards on either side of the narrow entrance to Twintle's warehouse.

"Good afternoon gentlemen," Deneya said lightly. The two men gave gruff nods, regarding them warily. Deneya leaned over, glancing at the ledger Vi held open. "I see this is... oh right, Lord

Twintle's storehouse. Of course."

"What business would you have here, ma'am?" the shorter of the two men asked.

"You might not know me, but I am Denja, the councilor for commerce." Deneya held out a hand and Vi slipped a piece of paper into it, just as they had for the first two warehouses. On it was Fiera's handwriting and both the royal seal of Mhashan, and a much more recent Imperial seal. "Everything should be in order verifying my credentials."

"Yes, councilor, how may we assist you?"

"I am performing inspections on warehouses today at the docks. Standard procedure to make sure all goods have been properly accounted for and the recent Imperial taxes levied against them."

The two guards shared a glance. Vi couldn't tell if they were genuinely surprised or not to see them and it made her shift her weight uncomfortably from foot to foot.

"We're afraid the Lord isn't present at the moment."

"Oh, that's right." Deneya brought her index finger to her jawline. Feigning ignorance was not the woman's strong suit. "He is traveling right now, isn't he? But here or not, this is something none of the traders are exempt from. If you could just allow us inside, my assistant will catalog goods and I'll cross-reference that against taxes paid yesterday."

"Lord Twintle explicitly instructed that we were to allow no one in until his return," one of the guards said hesitantly.

"As I said, no one is exempt." Deneya put her hands on her hips. "Please don't make me hike all the way back to the castle to get the Imperial guards and do this by force—none of us wants that."

The guards had a quick mental conversation that ultimately ended in a shrug from the taller man and an indifferent expression from the shorter.

"All right," he said. "But be quick about it. And we'll need to escort you the whole time."

"Very well."

With that, they were inside.

The warehouse was a simple build—little more than a brick box. Windows lined the upper portion of the walls just under the roof, no doubt to let out the rising heat from the Western sun. But they were currently shuttered, which meant the building felt like an oven.

It was surprisingly empty. Larger crates lined the walls along the outside. Rows of smaller ones that came up to Vi's waist stretched away from the door for about half of the space. In the other half, they were stacked in mountains. The logic of the two sorting methods was lost on her.

"While my assistant verifies the goods, could you please show me the most recent ledgers?"

"Of course." The shorter man went off to a far corner with Deneya, rummaging through a chest. That left the taller man with Vi.

She walked down the first row of crates, straining to open a heavy lid. Inside the box, settled on a nest of wood shavings, were some of the largest sapphires Vi had ever seen. Most were rough-cut, but they would still produce several stones of enviable quality in the hands of a skilled jeweler.

"Jewels," she murmured. "I thought Twintle was keeping fish and food?"

"That was only for the siege. His fleet was the smallest and fastest—they could slip past any Imperial vessels. Now he's sold off most of those wares." The man paused, narrowing his eyes at her. "I would think you would know that as the assistant to the councilor."

Vi laughed brightly and moved onto the next crate. "I'm sure you know how it is… they never tell the help *anything*. Just expect us to read their minds."

"Isn't that the truth." He shook his head sadly.

"So he deals in gems now." Crate after crate was filled with sparkling items that would fetch incredible prices. Where did Twintle get the money to invest in such a pricey business? And just how much was here?

"Rumor on the docks is the Le'Dans are quite sour because of it."

"Oh?" Vi paused, sliding up to the man. She made it a point to glance over at Deneya and the other guard. "Say, what's your name?"

"Adeem."

"Adeem," Vi repeated. "I do love good gossip, especially when it involves nobles."

"Who doesn't?" He chuckled. "All I know is that Richard Le'Dan has come by twice and both times were… quite contentious."

"I see."

"Twintle said that's part of why he's hired us to guard the place. He's worried the Le'Dans will come during one of his secret meetings."

"Secret meetings?" Vi could feel the muscles around her ears tense, as though they were trying to widen themselves so she could better hear what he would say next. This was what she had come here for.

"They happen at night. I think it's Twintle's suppliers and movers. Men and women—mostly men, though—come carrying crates in and out."

"What do they look like?" Vi asked, trying not to sound too eager.

"Twintle is very secretive about his trading practices… They all wear red hoods, like a Crone."

Vi laughed. "How odd," she said lightly, though inside she was barely bottling her excitement. Twintle had moved the meetings of the Knights of Jadar from his home to his warehouse and he was amassing wealth for the Knights there. He was likely distributing it as well. Everything lined up with the bits of information Deneya had collected. "Do you know when the next meeting is?"

"I imagine when the Lord is back. He usually holds them once per week, right at the end." The guard shrugged. "Though, again, it's not as if they tell me anything."

"Right…" Vi's eyes landed on a stretch of chests locked with heavy padlocks. She began rummaging through her bag. "Adeem, can you be a dear and please go fetch me a quill? I seem to have misplaced mine."

"Of course." He eagerly scampered off.

Vi leaned over, crouching behind one of the chests to hide her motions. "*Juth calt.*"

The lock was off and Vi set it aside. She opened the chest hastily, not even wasting time with a glance in Adeem's direction. Rubies winked up at her in the low light of the warehouse's flame bulbs.

Rubies… Vi closed the chest, straightening away and looking at all the other identically locked chests. Chests of Western rubies.

"Here you go." Adeem had returned, and he wasn't alone.

"Everything checks out on my end," Deneya said in a tone that implied she wouldn't be able to stall for much longer. Which was fine—Vi already had the information she needed.

"Mine as well. Thank you both for your flexibility in this." Vi made some marks in a ledger and smiled brightly at both the guards, imagining her illusioned cheeks dimpling.

"Yes, thank you." Deneya started for the door. "I'll be sure to let Twintle know that he has cleared inspection and remains in good standing with the crown." They emerged back into the sunlight. "You two have a lovely day."

Vi gave a wave, hastening beside Deneya before there were any further exchanges.

"Find anything?" Deneya asked when they were out of earshot and halfway to the next warehouse. They had three to go to ensure the surprise inspections couldn't be questioned.

"Two things, actually."

"Oh? Do tell," she asked eagerly.

"The first is that he has chests of Western rubies."

"How many?"

"I counted at least eight."

Deneya hummed. "That should be past the legal limit. King Rocham imposed mining sanctions on the stones about two decades ago. Though, knowing Twintle, he'd argue that it was a law made by an old king and is currently unclear under Imperial law."

"So not illegal, and not inherently nefarious?"

"Not nefarious, though suspicious… Good Western rubies fetch prices that can make your head spin. The reason Rocham banned them was because of an attack by Adela on a mine not far from the coast at the southern border. Combined with the difficulties surrounding their mining."

"I see," Vi murmured, eager to change the topic off Adela as quickly as possible. "The guard—Adeem—also told me that Twintle has been hosting gatherings of his 'suppliers.'"

"Now that sounds interesting." Deneya stopped walking to give Vi her full attention.

"It was. Men and women apparently coming and going in red hoods. Hiding their faces. Keeping others out at all costs." Vi glanced back at the warehouse. "I think we might have discovered the Knights of Jadar's new meeting spot and, even better, I think I know when the next meeting is."

And that meant the next time all the Knights were gathered, she would be ready to strike.

19

TWINTLE WAS GONE FOR about two months. His absence forced Vi to be patient, and to sit with her decision to take an active position against the Knights. The time also gave her ample evenings to continue working with the Sword of Jadar.

After Raylynn questioned if Vi could make the girl her own crystal weapon, Vi was no longer practicing with it as she would any other sword. Now, she focused on the magic, imagining it brightening and changing underneath her fingertips as it had with the ancient Champion.

The sword was suspended between Vi's knees as she slowly pushed and pulled at the magic that surrounded it. The magic was becoming a tangible thing, like a taffy that oozed between her fingers if she tried to hold onto it for too long, but solid enough for her to get good draws against it. She could sit for hours, moving it between her hands. Each time she turned it over she felt something new and different, as if a distant corner of her soul was ignited by it.

"As fascinating as it is to watch," Taavin said from where

he sat across from her, "I'm still not sure what you're trying to accomplish."

"That makes two of us," Vi murmured, holding her focus. She'd made a cage of her fingers, the air within shimmering. "But you said I've not tried to manipulate Yargen's magic or the crystals the ninety-two other times. So why—" Vi glanced at him and her concentration was broken. The magic snapped back into the sword with a palpable *crack*. Vi sighed. "Why not be rebels and explore this as a possible tool to help us end this cycle?"

"The way we end this cycle is by making sure nothing happens to that sword and, sooner over later, getting it as far as possible from this city." He stared at her for a long minute, shook his head, and proceeded to become fascinated with a corner of the room. Vi hated how even when she was frustrated with him, the angular lines of his heartbreakingly beautiful profile softened her. She returned her attention to the weapon.

"I think I can do it, because I think I've made crystals before," Vi confessed.

"*What?*"

"It was when we were on Meru. When I crossed the shift to enter the Twilight Kingdom."

"You told me nothing of crystals then."

"I had a lot on my mind." Twist, pull, hold. Vi wrangled the magic like her memories. "I was more focused on keeping you alive and saving my father than anything else. There were those tears in the shift, formed by the red lightning. When I passed through on my own for the first time, the magic in the watch protected me."

"You mentioned that. How do crystals come into play?"

"Well, when the magic emerged from the watch, there was shimmering blue. It condensed and hardened around my feet. It protected me. When I made it through to the Twilight Kingdom, tiny shards of obsidian surrounded me. The shards looked identical to dormant crystal."

"I see…"

"It makes sense, don't you think? The crystals were formed

from Yargen's power. They contain her power. It's as if the magic condensed…" Vi put pressure on the ball of magic she held in her hands. "… enough that…" Sparks flew between her fingers, increasing in brightness and density. "… it was given physical—" All at once the magic broke free and snapped back into place "—form," Vi finished and finally turned her eyes to him.

Taavin gazed at her with a peculiar intensity she hadn't seen from him yet. Only he could make her feel on edge and completely relaxed at the same time. "Perhaps you're right."

"Mother above, did it hurt to admit that?" Vi tilted her head back and let out a burst of laughter. Lifting the sword off her lap, she set it to the side and gave Taavin her full focus.

He ignored the remark. "Perhaps that's the variable I haven't been considering."

"The incident in the Twilight Forest?"

"Yes. All this time I focused on what you did and what happened to you when you were sent back. I never stopped to consider how the events that happened *before* you fully assumed your mantle as Champion shaped and formed what came after."

It seemed rather obvious to her, but Vi resisted saying so. She'd already made one playful jab and they were having what seemed like productive discourse.

"I think there was a unique sequence of events at play," he continued. "Lightning strikes, you getting to the Twilight Kingdom, noticing the obsidian, and piecing together how those shards relate to the watch's magic… all random variances between worlds."

Taavin stood with purpose. Holding out his hands, his lips began to move quickly. It never took him too long to draw on the wisdom of his past selves. When he finished, his attention was on her.

"Well?"

"I already knew there was no record of your obsession with manipulating crystal, but that confirms it."

"Does this mean we can say with certainty we're on a new timeline?" Vi jumped up from her chair. "Zira is alive, nothing has befallen her—"

"And some events will still transpire regardless," he said firmly.

"Maybe not, you don't know."

"I—"

"You don't *know*," she emphasized, then waited for his challenge. It never came. "We could be on a new timeline. Possibly a successful one. There's only one way to find out."

"You want to go to an Apex of Fate."

"Yes, and I think I know where one is." She'd been waiting for a convenient opening to convince him this was the right course. Tonight was that night.

"Where?"

"The port… where the Eastern descendant of the Champion gave up the scythe to send it to Meru." His frown told her she was right in assuming it was an Apex. "The port is safe. I can conceal myself. It's low risk." Taavin ran a hand through his hair. He clearly didn't want to agree with her. Vi persisted in the wake of his silence. "The wedding might have changed everything, and we don't know."

"You're right. You need to look into the future. And I know I must let you do this. Yet…" Taavin crossed over to her, scooping up her hands in his. His thumbs ran against her knuckles.

"Are you really the same person who had me sailing to Meru?" Vi said softly. "You fret over me leaving the castle now."

"I'm not the same person." He gazed at her through his lashes. "That man didn't understand the cost of losing you—not for the world, and not for him."

"But I am the same woman who made that journey," she said tenderly, tightening her fingers around his. "I am the same woman who boarded a vessel and left her home behind, who fought pirates and *won*, who accidentally made crystals. I might look like those ninety-two other women, but I'm not. I'm me, Taavin. Regardless of who I look or sound like, I am unique. This chance, this very moment, is ours alone. Don't condemn me for others' failures."

He nodded. "I know." She wasn't sure she could believe him. "Which is why I'll merely ask you to be safe on this excursion."

"I will." His warming up to her boldness only made her feel all the guiltier for keeping her other actions regarding the Knights from him. But hopefully, by the time he learned of them, she would be telling him their future was secure.

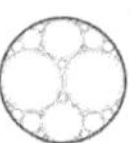

The port of Norin was bustling at all hours of the day. A vessel was always coming in or leaving. Fish needed to be hauled for the morning's market. Sailors looked to blow off steam before they returned to the sea.

Yet there was a unique quiet to the port at night. People went about their business with the hushed tones darkness brought. Most saw by the lights of lanterns at pubs, the glow of their pipes, or stars in the sky.

Vi was reminded of a different time she'd journeyed to the port of Norin in darkness. Jayme had been with her then. Those days had been her final moments on the Dark Isle of her world.

She paused, sweeping her eyes across the port, remaining alert, before tucking her head back down and starting off toward the oldest section of the docks. The salt covered stones beneath her feet had seen more history than libraries. And, if she was lucky, they would show her history yet to be made.

At the far end was the old dock, rotted and sagging. A mix of nostalgia and respect still kept its pylons in use, but only dinghies were tied up here now.

Vi stared out at the sea, envisioning what the scythe had shown her. She saw the slow curve of the land to her left, the cliff rising up to support the rich section of Norin.

"It was here," Vi affirmed to herself. She glanced around. A man slumbered against a doorstep. The houses were dark. No eyes seemed to be on her. Still, her heart raced.

She crossed over to the sea wall and sat on its edge, her feet dangling just above the dark water. With one last glance around, Vi cupped her palms in her lap and summoned a mote of flame.

It didn't take long before the world was overcome with white.

Color came into focus first. Then, blobs formed hazy shapes that quickly gained clarity and form. A mass of people moved together. They swayed and swirled in time to music Vi couldn't hear.

Their faces were painted with expressions of joy. Hands clapped soundlessly. Golden strips of paper rained from the sky. Vi held out her hand, trying to catch a piece of confetti. But it fluttered straight through her.

Pennons bearing the seal of Solaris reached out for the breeze, their golden stitching picking up the sunlight. It was a celebration unlike any Vi had ever seen, in a place she had only ever imagined.

Surrounding her was a semi-circle of triangular bleachers that rose up like points on a sun. Men and women were packed within them, drinking, talking, cheering. She didn't need to hear their joy; she could feel it. It was a palpable, pulsating thing.

The song stopped, and with it the dancing. The crowd turned their focus to the high stage lined by wide columns. This was the Sun Stage. She recognized it from the drawings Romulin had sent her.

Then, as if by thought, he appeared.

Every emotion welled in her all at once at the sight of her family. Her father led, mother at his right hand. His hair was salted as she remembered it. Her mother's was perfectly coiffed. It was a trick of the mind, but Vi could almost smell the faint scent of eucalyptus that was always in their perfumes. Romulin was at their side, just as she remembered him.

Which meant…

Vi searched for her future self.

She wasn't there.

Her heart started to race. When was this? What was this celebration for? Was she in the North *or*… Had she changed the future so dramatically that Vi Solaris was no longer a part of it?

Vi's thoughts came to a screeching halt as Romulin collapsed.

The young man seized on the ground. Vi tried to take a step forward, but she was rooted to the spot. People were running around her, guards were being called. Her mother held her brother, hoisting him upward. Her father barked orders. Romulin's head rolled back, his mouth hanging open like the gaping mouth of Raspian himself.

Red lines ran down his cheeks—tracks of bloody tears. They had the same glow as the red lightning cracking through the sky. Romulin's sky blue eyes had gone milky, and a pale white foam oozed from his mouth.

Vi screamed. She screamed and screamed but no sound came. She flung every curse she knew at the world, at the heavens, at the injustice of it all. She screamed until there was nothing left to say, and the vision came collapsing back in on her.

She panted, back on the sea wall, her fire extinguished, her body doubled over on itself. Her throat was raw, so raw she could vividly imagine Raspian ripping into it. She slowly raised her head, staring out across the sea.

If the White Death still came for this land, she had changed nothing.

"No," Vi rasped, forcing her spine to find strength enough to straighten. If her brother was the one who was diseased—not her mother—*something* had changed.

Vi pushed herself away from the wall, pulled her hood tight and started off, her bones shaking with every step.

She had begun to shift fate. But she hadn't altered it enough. Saving Zira, working to thwart the Knights' attention at the wedding, and getting the Sword of Jadar sooner than she ever had before... none of it was enough to stop Raspian from being set free.

Clenching her jaw, Vi glared at Twintle's warehouse as she passed. Changing fate would take something bolder, and more daring, than anything she'd tried until now.

20

"YOU AREN'T EXPERIMENTING as much with the sword lately," Taavin observed.

"I know." Vi yawned so wide her jaw popped. "I'm too tired these days." Vi was nearly going cross-eyed from exhaustion.

"What has you burning the candle at both ends?" he asked thoughtfully.

"By day I fulfill my duties to the crown, enough to keep a low-profile here… I train with Zira, lunch with Fiera… and most evenings I have nightcaps with Deneya." That wasn't all she'd been doing at night.

"You don't have to do this, you know." Vi knew what he was about to say before he said it. It was a discussion that was creeping up more by the day. "You have the sword, Fiera has trusted you to hide it—you can leave."

"If I leave too quickly, people will notice and might suspect I have the sword."

"It's been months since the wedding."

"And all it takes is one suspicious act." Vi gave him a tired smile. "Weren't you the one telling me to be cautious?" She stepped behind a folding screen set before her closet, changing into a nightgown as she spoke.

Taavin averted his eyes. "I am, but at a certain point, inaction is just as risky."

"Make up your mind." Vi emerged from behind the screen with another yawn.

"At some point, you'll have to take the sword and go."

"I know. But I'll do it when the time is right. And that time isn't tonight."

"Yes, I'll let you sleep." Taavin walked over, cupping her cheek thoughtfully. His eyes scanned her face. "Do try to get some rest tonight. You look exhausted."

"I will." The lie cut her gums on the way out. The smile that followed it hurt more.

"Sleep well." Taavin leaned forward and planted a gentle kiss on her forehead, vanishing before he could lean away.

Vi stared at where he'd just been, steeping in the guilt. It wasn't the right time to take the sword away. And it wasn't the right time to get some sleep.

She went back behind the screen, changing into dark clothes and grabbing a blood red hood that matched Adeem's description of the robes worn by the men and women who attended Twintle's meetings. This way, she could blend in without need of an illusion. Vi wanted both hands free in case she needed to use her Lightspinning when she entered into the lion's den.

Twintle had returned from his travels a week ago and Vi had been perching herself on a rooftop several down from his warehouse each night since. She suspected he'd call a meeting sooner rather than later and she wanted to be ready the second he did.

Her feet knew the way to the docks by heart. She'd practiced the route to and from the warehouse each night. She knew that when the time came, she would want to be able to run through the back alleys and keep off the main roads without second-guessing herself.

Tonight, she sank into the shadows of an alleyway as two men caught her eye—Twintle and Luke. They spoke to each other in hushed and hurried tones on their way to the dock, though Vi couldn't make out any individual words. Vi waited until they were down the road before hurrying through a back alley to lean against the corner of a building to watch them proceed. The men were none the wiser to the woman following in their wake.

She took the back way around Twintle's warehouse. There was only one entrance and exit, so Vi waited, crouched low, listening to the murmuring voices within and the footsteps approaching without.

Every man and woman uttered a soft phrase, "Rulliad," before being permitted entry.

Rulliad meant loyalty in the language of old Mhashan. Really… one would think they would be more creative than that when it came to their passwords. Still, it made things easy.

Vi yanked the hood she'd fashioned over her head.

With nothing to protect her but confidence and trust in her magical skills, Vi strode to the entrance. Neither of the guards were the ones Vi met when she had come with Deneya, which made her wonder how often Twintle's paranoia had him changing his hired swords. She hoped she and Deneya's inspection hadn't cost the others their jobs… but didn't linger on the thought.

She had more important concerns.

"Good evening," one of the guards said in Southern Common.

"Rulliad," Vi replied without preamble. He gave a nod and she walked in.

Everyone gathered around the mostly open area with the stacks of crates. There wasn't much mingling and most people kept to themselves. Not one person had lowered their hood, which made it easy for Vi to remain hidden.

"We'll begin in another two minutes—we're waiting on just one more," Twintle said, stepping forward. He and Luke were the only two people who had lowered their hoods. Likely because everyone knew exactly who was behind the organization of this meeting. But there was safety in anonymity among the rest of the members—they couldn't out each other if captured.

As soon as one more man entered, Twintle began as promised.

"I know it has been some time since we all last met. But today I come to you with exciting tidings." Twintle turned to address the crowd in full. "I left our beloved city of Norin and returned to the Waste. There, I communed with the people we fight for. Those who still stand with the Mhashan we have always known.

"Here in this city, they call us extremists. Those beyond these walls see that if we are extreme, we are only extreme in our love for this land. Those beyond these walls stand by us, cheer us on, to stand by our rich heritage. Those beyond call us heroes."

"Don't be taken in by Solaris!" a man from across the room called out.

"Yes, yes my brothers and sisters, we are the ones impervious to the allure of Solaris lies. Solaris claims they stand for the West, but they are making the West poor with their demands of tithing to pay for the remnants of their war. They are the ones making the West weak by sending our girls and boys south to fight for their cities of stone and ice."

"We shall stand against them!" another called.

The whole room was being worked into a frenzy by Twintle's words. People shifted in place. Murmurs of support grew to outright cheers.

"We shall be the ones to stand against Solaris tyranny!" Luke stepped forward. "We shall be the ones who honor our oath to defend the poor. To upkeep tradition. And to honor the sacrifices of all those who came before us."

"But we cannot do this with our glorious fervor alone." Twintle's voice dropped to a hush and everyone hung on his next words. Vi had never seen an orator quite like him. It was more than the skill of a virtuoso musician. Every man and woman Twintle had gathered was their own instrument, and he could play the orchestra. "To restore Mhashan to its former glory, we need a power that affirms our divine right."

More whispers, all resounding to an eerily soft chant, as if everyone gathered was under some kind of spell. A single word passed from person to person in hushed tones: *sword.*

"Yes, we need the Sword of Jadar. The sword once bestowed by King Jadar on his magickless son. The sword that was destined to defend Mhashan. We are its rightful owners now that the blood-traitor princess has turned her back on our ways. And with the sword's power, we can restore the throne to someone befitting of its honor. We will not be like the coward whore to the sun. We will unlock the power it was made to unleash on this world and with that power we will liberate ourselves from the tyranny of Solaris."

Applause, cheers. Vi watched as some men got so overwhelmed with excitement they nearly threw off their hoods. It was a type of spell that had just as much power as Yargen's words. Though Vi found herself immune. She watched it all unfold, trying to detach herself from the situation.

Yet in the back of her mind… a bonfire of rage burned for all the hatred and hurt these words would sow.

"You've made progress on the sword, then?" a man asked, more skeptical than Vi expected.

"I have," Twintle said proudly. "With this last trip to our brothers and sisters in the Waste, we have established a network that stretches far beyond this city. We have amassed wealth. And, in this, I have procured access to the one person who can steal from Solaris—the one person who has evaded Tiberus ever since she cut down his father and stole his family's treasure."

"You're mad," a man near Vi murmured. No one but her seemed to hear.

Twintle was mad. Because if he was talking about the one person Vi was thinking of, it would mean he had made a deal with—

"Adela," Twintle finished her thought. The fires that had been burning in the back of her mind crackled against her clenched and shaking fists.

"The bane of the seas?"

"The pirate queen?" another gasped.

"Yes, the *pirate queen*," Twintle proclaimed, glaring around the room as if challenging anyone to move or speak against him. No one did. "Sometimes, the enemy of our enemy is our friend. Adela will gladly help us strike against Solaris. She has even reduced her rate for the delight of this job."

"You would trust the sword to a pirate?"

"She'll just take it," Vi mumbled. Luckily no one heard. None of them had ever dealt with a force like Adela Lagmir before and it showed. Adela would gladly take the job, pocket every Western ruby she was likely demanding of them, and take the crystal sword for herself if she even had an inkling of the power it held. The mental image of the Knights scrambling to get it back—of them being betrayed like her family had been—delighted her like a black flame, dark and burning.

"She will lend us the help of her crew. Through them, she will provide knowledge and manpower with the wild magicks of the Crescent Continent. We shall steal the sword back when it is being transported to the South with the Imperial party. From there, it is not far to the Crystal Caverns." Twintle held up a worn journal. Vi squinted but she couldn't make out the writing. "I have procured the writings on Jadar's search for Windwalkers, about his belief that the sword could unlock enough power to see Mhashan rule for millennia to come. This is only a fraction of what was collected from the Burning Times, but it will be enough that we can access the true fount of power in the depths of the Crystal—"

Twintle paused, lowering his hand slowly. All eyes were dragged to the doorway where Twintle was now focused. There a man stood, leaning against a crate, panting heavily.

"Forgive me, brothers and sisters, for my delay," he huffed. "I was—"

Twintle held up a hand, stopping him. His eyes swung across the room, lips moving in a silent count.

"Bar the doors," Twintle commanded, deathly quiet. "There is a stranger hiding among us."

Everyone looked around and Vi did the same, not wanting to be easily identifiable as the odd one out. She could use *durroe* to hide herself. No, they'd already accounted for her. They'd launch a search if the count was off now. But they wouldn't find her if her illusion was solid enough.

"We are the sword—" Twintle started loudly.

"That stands against the darkness!" Everyone answered boldly, proudly, and in unison.

"Her," a man next to Vi shouted, approaching. "She didn't say anything."

"You there, lower your hood," Twintle demanded.

"Tell us your name," the man asked.

"My name?" Vi said softly, looking up at him through her eyelashes and past the edge of her hood. She should run. She *should* get out of there as quickly as possible—Vi had her information on what the Knights' next move was and they still didn't know who she was. This could still be salvaged without taking too many actions that risked fate.

But something rooted her to the spot. The spark that had been crackling within her was ready to ignite into flames. And as she gazed up into the eyes of this spiteful man—a man who would kill everyone she'd ever loved if given the chance—something within her snapped with an audible crack.

"Your name." The man reached for her hood, catching hair with fabric. But she didn't cry out in pain. She didn't even give any indication he was hurting her. She calmly met the eyes of the Knight she was about to kill.

"My name is *juth calt*," Vi whispered darkly.

He shuddered, stumbled, and fell back—dead before he hit the floor. Several other Knights jumped away and drew their swords. These were men trained in war. They weren't about to be swayed so easily.

The first lunged for her and she just stared at him, smiling.

"*Mysst xieh,*" Vi hissed. The words blurred together, but a shield of brilliant light sparked in the air before his blade could hit her. Vi ignited flames around the shield with a thought. He stumbled backward.

"What sorcery is this?" The man looked at his sword as though it had betrayed him and blinked at where the fire had been.

"The sorcery of the Mother." Vi waved a hand and cast an arc of fire around her. It burned white hot—hotter than it had burned for Taavin. Men and women bounced backward, throwing hoods from their heads, exposing faces of pure ugliness beneath.

The fire caught, leaping from crate to crate. Soon, the warehouse would be up in flames. Its contents wouldn't burn—the jewels would survive. The masonry of the building would endure. But she wanted to see them scatter like rats.

She wanted to see them burn until they were husks. She didn't care about fate or crystals. She wanted vengeance.

She wanted—

"Firebearers, get those flames under control and get her!" Twintle's voice cut through her thoughts.

Vi blinked and it was like coming out of a trance. Bloodlust had made her foolish. "*Durroe watt radia.*" Vi did what she should've done the whole time and made herself invisible.

The Firebearers among those gathered finally got control of the flames, but not until after they had consumed a fair bit. Others had already run out of the warehouse.

"Where is she?" Twintle demanded. Nothing more than a small spark illuminated the area. "Where did she go?"

"Father, there was an arc of flame all around." Luke moved the dark soot with his boot that formed a crescent shape around Vi. "We would've seen her—"

"She said she was the Mother," someone else whispered.

"Impossible." Twintle approached, blessedly stopping at the line she'd created in the stone floor. "The Mother does not have mortal flesh, and if she did… she would stand beside our noble cause."

None of the other men and women questioned his claim, though

Luke seemed skeptical.

"A Waterrunner must have helped her escape. Search the area," Twintle commanded, then looked back in her direction, ignorant that their eyes were locked. "Turn over the whole docks. I don't want anyone to rest until the strange sorcerer and her accomplice are brought to me."

21

IT WASN'T UNTIL AFTER they left that Vi's heart decided to knock against her ribs. Nausea rose up and she brought her free hand to her mouth, holding in quivering breaths.

She would've killed them all and delighted in it, even if that meant this world ultimately failed. Some part of her, a part she desperately wanted to ignore, knew that if she indulged in these urges there was no recourse. The worst that happened was the world ended, again. It'd be the ninety-third time. How bad could it really be?

Vi shook her head and closed her eyes, urging the thoughts away.

Yet they lingered.

They clung to her like Raspian's magic, the tiny sparks of red lightning that had danced underneath her skin after she'd used the tear his magic had made in the world to get to the Twilight Kingdom—after she used his words. But she had also witnessed Yargen purge those tendrils of his magic from her when she was being remade.

These urges were her own. She couldn't blame a dark god or desperation born of a dying world. Controlling herself and staying the course was on her own shoulders.

Taking a deep breath, Vi forced herself to calm and began moving. She relaxed her spell and pulled up her hood once more. She could hear people moving outside, low voices drifting in through the doorway. Vi crept forward, scanning the docks; most of the Knights had fanned outward and were now far away.

When she slipped out, the nearest Knight had his back to her, and Vi disappeared into the side alleyway.

She ripped the hood from her head, throwing it on the ground and running from it as though it was about to give chase. As though that was the source of the darkness she'd felt. She weaved through the city, eventually sprinting onto the main road. The castle grew in her field of vision and Vi didn't even bother slowing her pace as she dashed by the guards stationed at the end of the drawbridge.

"You there—"

"It's Yullia." Vi spun, bouncing from foot to foot, stalling long enough for them to see her face before turning and resuming her run. They didn't give chase.

Her side burned as she took the castle stairs two at a time—up the main staircase, then through a door into a narrow spiral stair. She bounded down a hall, not far from where the council chambers were. Vi didn't even bother stalling to check if Deneya was there. Instead, she went right for her room.

The door snapped against the wall, reverberating with a low thud as she threw it open. Vi had to resist the urge to slam it in her haste. Instead, she slowly closed it, locking it behind her.

She raced to her bedside and hoisted the heavy down mattress, flopping it over onto itself. Underneath the mattress were woven grass panels, supported on slats of wood. Vi dug her nails into a panel, prying it upward. She set it aside and then carefully removed one of the wood slats.

With trembling hands, Vi retrieved the Sword of Jadar from its hiding place.

She clutched it to herself, shaking, holding onto it like a child she thought she'd lost. As though the Knights had found it while she was gone. As though she was the one being played the entire time.

Vi cursed under her breath and ran a hand through her hair, trying to get a hold of herself. She had killed before, she'd kill again. Yet something still rattled her about the feeling of how… *easy* it could be. She loathed the delight she could find in it, the feeling that there would be little repercussion.

Risking the end of the world should be repercussion enough. She'd sworn to end this and wouldn't let her emotions get in the way.

Staring at her hiding place and reflecting more calmly on the events of the night, Vi knew it was time to act. Taavin had been right—she had to get the sword away from Norin, especially with Adela closing in. A plan formed in her head and Vi stood, starting for the door once more.

Down the hall and to the left was another room, nearly identical to hers. Vi gave a few soft knocks. Zira was a light sleeper. Anyone who made a living fighting for their life and others had to be.

"Yu—" Zira's eyes dropped to the sword the moment she opened the door. A frown crossed her mouth briefly before it formed into a hard line. "What is it?"

"I have a task for you," Vi whispered softly. "But it won't be an easy one."

"What is it?"

"I need you to die."

"Excuse me?" Zira narrowed her eyes slightly. Vi had the distinct feeling that if she hadn't built up such a solid rapport with the woman, she would already be cut down.

"Not literally. May I come in and explain?"

"You'd better." Zira stepped to the side and Vi entered. Her fingers had gone numb from how tightly she was clutching the weapon.

"The sword needs to be hidden—above all else."

"I don't disagree."

"I want you to take the Sword of Jadar, tonight, and flee the city." Vi leveled her eyes with Zira's, knowing full well what she was about to ask. "I need you to take it, and I need you to die in the eyes of the people."

"So no one comes after me?" Zira reasoned.

"Exactly. We will say you were doing rounds and were cut down by a man in the alleyways." The alleged attacker would, of course, be revealed as a Knight of Jadar. "I will procure a body and there will be a Rite of Sunset held for you tomorrow afternoon."

"Fiera will know then."

Vi had been debating this ever since the plan began to solidify in her mind. "Yes. We can trust her with the knowledge that you are alive. But she won't know you have the sword. She can't know."

"What will she think then?"

"I will tell her we devised a plan to counter the Knights, and they needed to suspect your death. Which isn't untrue." Vi wiggled her fingers on the blade and tried to relax the bowstring-tight tension in her shoulders. It did little good.

"And what will I actually be doing while I'm 'dead'?" Zira asked.

"Take the sword and go to the Nameless Company, visit your daughter, and stay hidden for a time. Let no one there know you have it."

"But they can know I'm alive?" Zira arched her eyebrows.

"Am I wrong to say I trust the Nameless Company to keep the secret?"

"Not in the slightest." She grinned with pride. "The Nameless Company would all die fighting before they gave up my secrets… and we don't discuss the business matters of others."

"Go and hide there." Vi took a deep breath. "After a month… maybe two—enough time that things have calmed here—begin to head East with the sword." The crystal weapon needed to get as far out of reach as possible from the Knights of Jadar. And the East had managed to keep a crystal weapon safe before. She hoped they could do it again. "I'll meet you in Cyven. Linger near the old senate hall there."

Zira looked away and Vi could almost see the wheels turning in her mind as she ran over everything once more.

"If I leave now, wait two months, and then head East, there is a chance I won't make it back for the birth of Fiera's child."

"I know." Fiera was already well into her second term. The primary cleric overseeing her care was fairly tight-lipped about exactly when she suspected the baby had been conceived, which meant Vi's suspicions about her pregnancy during the wedding were likely well founded.

Aldrik's legitimacy was shaping up to be a thinly veiled lie. He had surely been conceived out of wedlock. But the Emperor was adamant that nothing untoward had happened before their wedding night. And if the Emperor declared his wife could have a child in less than the normal term, such would be the official truth as far as the rest of the Empire was concerned.

"I promised her—"

"I'm sure," Vi interrupted, somewhat harshly, "this will not be easy for any of us. But Fiera understands the sacrifices of her position. She always has. And part of why I am doing this now is for the safety of her and the babe. I want the sword gone well before she's vulnerable."

I don't want her to die, Vi stopped herself just short of saying. She wouldn't risk this world's failure for revenge on those who had wronged her family. But she would risk it to save lives.

No matter what Taavin insisted, Vi wanted Fiera to live. Her father needed a mother, the Empire needed its Empress. Her job was to prevent the Crystal Caverns from ever being tampered with, and who was to say—perhaps preventing Fiera's death was the key to all that.

If Fiera lived, the Emperor might remain a more measured man. He might never seek out Vhalla to open the Crystal Caverns. He might even ease some of his brutality in the North.

When Vi looked at everything through that optimistic lens, the future had never seemed brighter.

"We have to do this," Vi said softly, pleading. "We must, at all costs, keep the sword safe. This is greater than you, or me, or even Fiera. More hangs in the balance than I can explain."

Zira approached her silently. Vi felt the weight of her stare and was struggling to keep her knees locked under the pressure it put on her shoulders in addition to all the pressure that was actually there. Zira reached out, resting her hand lightly on Vi's white knuckles. With a reassuring magic only mothers seemed to possess, Vi stopped trembling.

"I will take the sword tonight and go."

"Mother bless you," Vi breathed in relief.

"While I gather my things, go and wrap it in leathers for me. I want it bundled so tightly that you can hardly tell it's a sword at all." Their roles had switched, and now Zira was giving the orders. "Then meet me down in the dungeons."

"The dungeons?"

"You remember the way, I trust?"

"It was the first area of the castle I had the pleasure of touring," Vi said with mock delight. How far she had come from that night. "Let's move quickly, there's no time to waste."

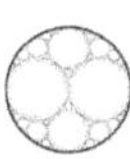

Vi waited in the hallway that led down to the dungeons. It was a singular pathway—easy to block and defend against any kind of breakout. A guard lingered farther on, keeping watch. Though, judging from his heavy snoring, the only thing he was watching were the insides of his eyelids.

"Sounds like Topperen is on duty tonight," Zira murmured as she approached. "I was hoping that would be the case." She passed an iron key to Vi.

"What's this?"

"A key to the cell we need to get to."

"You're not locking me away again, are you?"

Zira snorted. "The time for that has passed. Come along."

They padded down the hall, tiptoeing into the faint glow of the room beyond. Sure enough, an elderly man was sleeping with his head tipped back, mouth open, drool cascading into the stubble of his cheek. He didn't so much as stir as they inched across the room.

Once back into the relative darkness of the first row of cells, they moved faster again. Two men slept with their backs to the bars of the first two cells. Vi recognized the cell she had been thrown into as they passed it.

Zira led them down to the far end of the hall, to a black door nestled into a shadowed alcove. On the other side was a spiral stair, and down that was another hallway of cells that led to another black door.

Down they went—three, four levels of jail cells. Each level became more maze-like, with branches of halls leading off of it. Each level was more rough-hewn, carved into the bedrock that ran underneath the Waste.

Vi stared at the countless empty cells, wondering why there were so many. They seemed to stretch endlessly on into the darkness. All too soon, she answered her own question: the Burning Times. One of the darkest parts of Western history, during the reign of King Jadar, when he rounded up the Windwalkers of the East and used their magic for nefarious purposes.

She looked at the sword she was carrying. How many had died for this sword? Stopping the vicious cycle spiraling around the Crystal Caverns seemed as hopeless as counting every cell in this seemingly never-ending dungeon.

They came to a stop at an unassuming cell. With her thumb, Zira smoothed away the grime and cobwebs that coated the lock.

"Unlock it," she ordered, and Vi did as she was told.

Zira entered the cell and went back to the cot in the corner. The furniture nearly disintegrated when she pushed it to the side and they were both left coughing through clouds of dust. But, as the haze settled, Vi could see a staircase winding down.

"A passage out," Vi said, stating the obvious.

"Not used in over a year now. We might need to get a new cot to hide the entrance."

"When was it last used?"

"During the siege, for scouts."

"Is this the only hidden way out of the castle?"

"Yes."

That explained why they never sent more than scouts. It was a secret too precious to be entrusted to many. And the passage appeared to be too narrow to fit more than a single person at a time—certainly not a way to get the mass amounts of soldiers it would take to launch a surprise attack out of Norin.

"Why didn't King Rocham flee through here?" Vi asked.

"Because he was going to die on and for his land. The idea of flight or surrender never crossed the man's mind. I only learned of it when Fiera entrusted me with that key—to save her siblings if that's what it took."

"Where does it lead?" Vi peered down into the darkness. It was so intense that not even the light of the torch Zira was holding could penetrate more than the first three steps.

"Southwest. It'll let me out of a cliff side."

"Just south of the ridge where all the nobles live?"

Zira paused, staring at Vi for a long moment. "Yes… How did you know?"

"I'm good with maps, and the terrain of the city made it an easy guess." She wondered if this path was anywhere close to the one out of the Le'Dan estate.

Vi handed out the sword to Zira. With it, she felt like she was giving up a part of herself. She had never felt more vulnerable than when she watched Zira's hands closing around the weapon. Doubt fluttered through her mind; the memory of Jayme's betrayal rode on gossamer wings. Instinct told Vi not to trust Zira. But here Vi was, trusting despite every betrayal she had endured.

She was here in this world to bring about the end of cycles. And she'd start with the cycle of people she cared for betraying her.

"I'm putting all my faith in you with this." Vi raised her eyes to Zira's. "Don't let me down," she added softly.

"I wouldn't. Letting you down would be letting Fiera down. If nothing else, trust that I will always do everything in my power to see the wishes of our Empress done. And she wishes the sword to be safe."

It was nearly painful to uncurl her fingers from around the leathers. But Vi did it. "Fiarum evantes," she whispered.

"Kotun un nox," Zira replied, and then disappeared into the darkness.

Vi watched her go, grabbing the watch at her collarbone. The hairs on the back of her neck were on end. Her ears were filled with whispers and the sounds of distant drumming.

This was a moment fate shifted. Vi could feel it.

But had she changed the course of time for the better?

THERE WAS THE SMALL matter of procuring a corpse before dawn.

Vi made her way quickly back through the labyrinth of passageways. She trusted her instincts to lead her back and tried not to question too much. Questioning would make her pause, second-guess, and turn around or change course. Doing so would only waste time and get her lost.

Still, she breathed a sigh of relief when she emerged onto the top level of cells.

"*Durroe sallvas tempre*," Vi whispered to mask her footsteps. She treaded lightly past the elderly guard and through the castle.

Out of the castle and across the drawbridge, Vi glanced at the horizon. The sky was still completely dark. She had a few hours before dawn, and before any suspicions could be raised.

Vi made her way through the city to the Cathedral of the Mother. Detached from the main building and off to the side was the city's morgue, where all bodies were held ahead of Rites of Sunset.

Bracing herself for the smell, Vi walked into the halls of death.

She was pleasantly surprised that it did not reek of decay. Instead, there was a chalky, herbaceous smell in the air. A Crone was stationed at a wide desk set in the center of the mostly empty, rectangular room. Behind her were rows of tables on which bodies were laid out. Over half of the tables were empty, but several had human-shaped figures underneath dark red cloths.

"Fiarum evantes," the Crone murmured sleepily, bringing her milky eyes up to Vi.

"Kotun un nox," Vi replied dutifully. "Crone, I fear my friend might have fallen today… Do you have any bodies here that have yet to be identified?"

The Crone lifted a gnarled finger, running it down the page of the open ledger before her. Vi was impressed her eyes could still see well enough to read at all, especially in the low light of the room. She tapped a few notes.

"Four are unidentified. Was it a man or a woman?"

"A woman."

"Three, then." The Crone pushed herself upward and Vi could hear the bones in her joints popping.

"Crone, please—" Vi rushed around the table, resting a hand lightly on the elderly woman's back and holding out the other for support should she need it. "Could you tell me which they are? No need to trouble yourself."

"If you don't mind, sweet child?" The Crone gave her a smile. "That would be most kind."

"I don't mind at all. Which tables are they?"

"These." The woman tapped the outlines of three tables in her ledger that corresponded with the back three on the right-hand side. The word "unknown" was scribbled by each of them.

"I'll return promptly," Vi said as the woman settled back into her chair.

The night was going well, almost too well. But given how it had started with the Knights of Jadar, Vi could use a few lucky breaks. In the back corner there were the three bodies. Vi peeled back the coverings of the first two—the third was far too short to be Zira.

Of the two remaining bodies, Vi decided on the woman on the right. Their builds were similar, and whatever misfortune had befallen her was gruesome enough to leave cuts over the majority of her face.

"I'm sorry," she whispered softly to the woman. "But this sacrifice is for all of us."

Vi went back to a clerical table and grabbed a knife. As she cut the woman's long hair to vaguely resemble Zira's, Vi wondered who this person had been. Was she someone important? Or was she someone the world had long since overlooked?

Her heart ached. At the very least, this woman would have dozens mourning for her—even if those mourners were misinformed.

"Yargen bless you," Vi murmured as she covered the body in the sheet once more and burned away the chunks of hair in a flash of fire.

She went back to the Crone and informed her that the body was that of Zira Westwind—that the Empress herself would come to mourn for the loss of her friend and chief guard at sunset. The Crone took Vi at her word and scribbled in the ledger dutifully, even adding that the cause of death was an attack by the Knights of Jadar during guard duty. With that settled, Vi returned to the castle.

Fiera wouldn't be up for a few more hours yet, and Vi didn't feel the need to wake her. Nothing would change if Fiera found out her machinations a few hours later. And Vi could use the time to plan her next moves.

Safely back in her room, Vi settled her bed into place before sitting on it heavily. She rubbed her eyes with both her palms. It felt like forever since she'd last had a good night's rest. But it would wait a bit longer.

"Narro hath hoolo."

Taavin appeared before her, and Vi dragged her eyes up from the toe of his boots to the top of his head, eventually landing her attention on his eyes. He stared down at her; whatever he saw softened his expression.

"You were supposed to be sleeping."

"I know." Vi shook her head and closed her eyes. She couldn't handle the guilt of all she'd been hiding from him. Summoning him had been a bad idea.

"What happened?" he asked softly.

"A lot," Vi whispered.

"You don't have to tell me if you don't want to."

Vi looked up at him and let out a bitter laugh. "I thought I had to tell you everything."

"You should… But I hope you do it because you want to—because you want to save the world. And because you want to confide in me. I can do little else for you right now beyond lending an ear."

"You do more than you know and I don't deserve it." Vi took his hand in hers and hung her head. She'd trudged through a long dark night; she felt like the sun would never rise again.

"You do."

"I don't, because I've lied to you. I've deceived you."

"I know."

Of course he did. Two words had never been more heartbreaking. "Because I always lie to you at this point?"

"No, Vi, because I know you." Taavin knelt before her. "Because I can see it in your eyes."

"Taavin, I didn't—I *don't* want to hurt you." She squeezed his hand. "Somehow I had to balance that with doing what I felt was right."

"I'm fine, Vi. I've endured worse." His grim nature about the fact put a stone in her throat. "I'm more worried about you."

"For the future of this world?"

"For your own sanity," he said gently, covering her hand with his. "I love you just as you are and I want you to be open with me about everything."

"My recklessness included?"

"Your damnable recklessness that might just save our world

included." The corner of his mouth quirked up in a smile that was far too endearing for their discussion.

Vi swallowed the lump in her throat and took a slow breath. She wanted to take him into her arms. She wanted him to kiss her until she knew or wanted nothing else.

But she couldn't. Not until he knew everything she had done and still wanted to kiss her after.

"You were right, I wanted to save Fiera. I still do. I want to save her, Zira, everyone else I can, *and* this world. When I saw the vision of my brother… I knew I had to be bolder. If I was to make this the last time for all of us, I had to do something I'd never done before. And I knew you would say no. So I didn't ask…" Vi proceeded to tell him of the past few days. She told him of the long, dull nights watching Twintle's warehouse. She told him of the Knights seeing her, of her fleeing, and giving Zira the sword.

When she finished, Taavin merely continued to stare at her, holding onto her hands tighter than she had clutched the Sword of Jadar before giving it to Zira. But Vi couldn't tell if it was in anger, worry, compassion, or some likely mix of all three.

"Tell me I haven't done the wrong thing," she whispered, her voice hoarse.

"You have never needed my assurance before." He didn't say the words in such a way that would lead her to believe he meant to cause pain. Yet the lack of immediate support cut her deeply all the same.

"But I want it now." Vi took a quivering breath. Perhaps it was the lack of sleep, perhaps it was all the events that had transpired adding up to a tally that was too high. Or perhaps it was his eyes that were making her come undone. "You're correct—I'll continue to do what I feel is right. I will take council, but ultimately make my own decisions. I will not feel regret or guilt for making the best decision I could at any given moment, given all the information available to me but—"

Her throat was thick and gummy, and she choked on her next words. "But…" Vi continued, or she might not have continued at all. "I want someone to say that what I'm doing is all right. Because in this moment I am so tired and unsure. In this moment, Taavin, I do not feel strong and I am laying myself bare before you asking—begging—for you to lend me some strength before morning comes and I have to face the world alone once more."

His thumbs smoothed over the backs of her hands in a motion Vi couldn't be certain was entirely conscious. Taavin listened intently and was silent when she finished. Vi braced herself for his reaction and readied herself to send him away before he could turn his back on her.

"Vi Solaris," he murmured softly. Nothing had ever sounded more delightful than her name gliding across his tongue. A name that she hadn't heard in so long, it made her ache. "You have done nothing wrong. The burden on you is one that no one can understand, not even I. And you handle it with all the grace of your forefathers. You do your parents proud."

She hung her head as her face twisted in pain. Somehow, he'd known exactly what she'd needed to hear. Every last holdout of her strength vanished and she leaned forward.

Her face buried into his shoulder; his arms wrapped around her. Vi dug her fingers into him, grabbing at the tunic he wore, trying to cross through the barrier that coated his skin like oil that she couldn't wash away.

"I wish you were here," she whispered.

"I am here."

"I wish you were real," Vi corrected, pulling away.

Taavin hooked her chin, his thumb pulling lightly on her lower lip. Through lowered lashes he murmured, "Let me show you how real I am."

He pulled at her and she leaned forward. With a soft exhale, his lips brushed hers. She trembled at the barely-there touch. Slowly, he returned his mouth to hers in a toe-curling, tender kiss.

Vi's hand balled into a fist. She wanted to yank him closer. She wanted him to kiss her until her head spun and she was breathless. Yet she couldn't move. She was putty under his shifting hands.

One hand caressed her cheek. His fingertips ran along the edge of her ear—as though he was as fascinated with their differences as she was. His other hand ran up her side, boldly tracing the outline of her breast, but not lingering. It joined the other and he held both sides of her face, kissing her more firmly now.

She leaned back. It was an invitation, one he accepted. Taavin crawled onto the bed and on top of her.

"Say my name again," Vi whispered as their lips parted briefly.

"Vi Solaris," he obliged, husky and deep.

"Tell me you love me," she demanded.

"I love you. I have only ever loved you. I will only ever love you."

Vi pulled him down onto her. She caressed his back and savored what warmth and weight she could feel. Taavin kissed the soft flesh of her neck, a feather-light trail that ran up behind her ear and back down to her collarbone.

"I can't feel you like I once did," she confessed dejectedly. "Now the sword is gone, and I fear I never will again."

He pulled away, propping himself to hover over her. Vi trailed her fingers down his face and chest. She didn't know how much was forced imagination spiced by longing, and how much was truly tactile sensation.

"It's not the same," he admitted, and the admission hurt more than she expected.

"But your words sound as they always have." Vi shifted away, inviting him instead to lie next to her. The space between them made her ache instantly, but even when he curled around her, that distance didn't truly vanish.

She needed him in a way she'd never needed anyone.

In a way she didn't think she'd ever be able to have again. Why hadn't they made the most of their brief moments together in Risen?

"Tell me," she murmured, her eyes sinking closed as she rested her head on his chest. "Have we ever made love?"

"What?" His whole body went tense.

"Before, perhaps?" She didn't have to say, *before I killed you.* "In one of the other worlds?" There could've been another Vi who was bolder than her on Meru. Or a Vi who found his current form to be enough to touch, and kiss, and explore in ways she couldn't bring herself to no matter how much her body burned with want for him. The feeling of him not really being with her was too great a barrier to cross. "Did we embrace as true lovers?"

Vi tilted her head up when he didn't immediately respond. Taavin looked at her with those same lusty eyes. He was seeing something that told her the answer before his lips did.

"Yes."

"Tell me of it?" she breathed. "Tell me how I felt. Tell me how we moved. How you touched me. I want to hear it all." If she couldn't experience it, she would live vicariously through another version of herself.

"Are you certain?" He shifted uncomfortably.

"If you're willing."

"Of course I am. Those are the sweetest memories I have," he murmured, pressing a firm kiss against her mouth to punctuate the sentiment. "The first time was on Meru, in Risen…"

Taavin spoke unhurriedly, and Vi hung on his every sensual word. Each turn of phrase delighted her. Phantom memories ignited within her as though her body remembered what her mind could not. She felt herself burning from the inside out with a fire she'd never known before.

A fire that felt like it could light the whole world.

23

VI DIDN'T GET ANY sleep that night. Come morning, her clothes were rumpled and her skin was flushed from the fire he'd set in her. For the first time, she felt as though she'd lived a hundred lives with him through his endless stories.

And it wasn't enough.

It wouldn't be enough until she could taste him like those other Vis had.

Vi stared at the window. She hadn't shuttered it the night before, but the paper screens were slid closed. The morning's first light was drawing a slow line across the floor and when it hit the bed, Vi knew her exhausting night would officially transition into an exhausting day.

"You never slept," Taavin mumbled from behind her, kissing her neck tenderly. His fingers traced lazy circles around her stomach, pushing up her shirt farther with every pass. It was a game he seemed to be playing—how far he could undress her before he put her clothes back into place.

It was a line they hadn't dared cross all night. If they hadn't crossed it last night… they never would. Not as long as he remained a specter.

"I didn't."

"You should've."

"If I slept, you would've disappeared."

He sighed softly. Vi twisted in his arms and Taavin placed a gentle kiss on her forehead, mumbling, "You have to rest."

"I will tonight, I promise." Her body wouldn't give her a choice. "I wanted to see one morning with you."

"We don't get such luxuries." He smiled sadly.

"I will find a way for us to have them."

"All right, my princess." Taavin let out a chuckle that was part laughter, part scoff, and all disbelief.

"You don't think I can?"

He hummed, a relaxed smirk draped on his face. She wanted to kiss it off. How dare he look so frustratingly handsome first thing in the morning.

"I will pull you into this world if for no other reason than to force you to have morning breath and bags under your eyes and bed head with me," Vi threatened.

"I would give anything in the world for that. Anything to be a normal man, and for you to be a normal woman. But that is not our destiny."

"I'm writing destiny now." She wanted the statement to sound strong and full of conviction. But her voice was tiny and wavering. The more she thought about her task, the more impossible it seemed. Especially now with the sword out of reach. What had she been thinking, sending it away? "And I will find a way to bring you back into this world."

His shining green eyes consumed her focus. Vi was only vaguely aware of his hand lightly running up and down her spine. Taavin took a deep breath and Vi readied herself to combat his obviously forthcoming objection. But instead he kissed her one last, long time.

"You should go," he said.

"I should."

"Do you need me to vanish to make it easier for you?"

Vi laughed lightly and pulled herself from his arms. Their parting hurt, like what she imagined a plant to feel when it was ripped from its roots. "I will summon you again."

"Please do."

At long last, she relaxed the spinning glyph around her wrist and watched him vanish into the air. The parting was familiar, but it hurt more now than she remembered. In a few short weeks on Meru she'd somehow managed to grow accustomed to his physical presence. She'd taken it for granted.

Now, she would do anything to have him back.

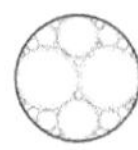

Fiera took breakfasts most often in her chambers now, so Vi headed there. The halls smelled of eggs and freshly cooked rice, but the only servants in sight were those who attended to bathing and dressing.

"Good morning," Vi greeted the handmaid outside Fiera's room. She and the two guards surrounding her all nodded. "I have a matter of grave importance to speak with our Empress about."

"Please wait just a moment." The handmaid held up her hands. "Cleric Joan is in with her now—she should be finished shortly."

No sooner had the girl stopped speaking than the heavy wooden door opened and a black-eyed woman emerged. She was as gnarled as a Crone and her skin had long been leathered by the sun. Her hair had turned to white, but she looked at the world sharply. There was still strength in her steps.

"Tell the kitchens I would like her to have plain rice this morning, one sliced prickly pear, and some more of the barley tea from the East," Joan instructed the handmaid.

"I think Jake said they have run out of the tea."

"Then tell him to pull some out of his arse. Or use these supreme culinary skills he keeps bragging about to make something similar. These are not my demands—they come directly from our Empress."

"Yes ma'am!" The handmaid sprinted down the hall. Joan's attention landed on Vi.

"Fiarum Evantes, I'm—"

"No time for or interest in formalities, I know who you are. This whole city knows who *you* are," Joan said dully. "You have a severe look on your face. Whatever it is you have to say, say it well and don't upset her much. This pregnancy is becoming hard on her and if she keeps her stress and work up, she's headed for a difficult labor."

"Understood." The cleric spoke like an officer, so Vi responded like a soldier.

Without another word, Joan left and Vi allowed herself into the royal chambers.

An entry hall opened up to a large sitting area connected to a wide balcony that stretched the length of the quarters. The Emperor and Empress sat out on the balcony, a table between them. Tiberus had draped his coat over the back of his chair. Fiera wore her hair long and unbound, her simple dress cut generously to accommodate her protruding stomach.

"Is breakfast already—" Fiera turned, her expression dimming when she realized food hadn't arrived, then brightening again when she realized who had arrived instead. "Yullia, what a delightful surprise!"

"It is impossible for newlyweds to have a morning alone," Tiberus grumbled, just barely loud enough for Vi to hear.

"Forgive my interruption, your highnesses. Were this not a matter of supreme importance, I wouldn't have come so early."

"Matters of supreme importance seem to follow you," Tiberus said with a glance at her. He had a stack of papers Vi vaguely recognized. They were nearly identical in format to the trade and grain reports her father used to study.

"Your highness, they follow *you*—I am merely graced by proximity."

"Your flattery is improving." He didn't even look up this time.

"Well, I do seek your indulgence."

"In what?" Fiera asked.

"I would like a word alone with you," Vi responded directly to her.

Fiera looked between Vi and Tiberus. "Anything you say to me, you can say to my husband."

"Very well." Vi couldn't blame her. It was a stretch to separate them at this point. She knew Fiera's primary goal was to keep peace in her growing family for the sake of all of Mhashan. Even with the Emperor's heir growing within her, she still acted cautiously. "It's regarding Zira," Vi started delicately, remembering what Joan had just told her. "I'll say foremost, she's well."

"All right," Fiera said slowly, understandably confused. She turned to Tiberus but the man shrugged slightly to indicate he had no idea either. "Why wouldn't she be?"

"Because this sunset we will go to the Cathedral of the Mother to mourn her death."

"I don't follow."

"The Knights of Jadar are getting bolder, your majesties. Just last night there was an attack down at the docks resulting in Lord Twintle's warehouse being burned." Vi resisted a satisfied smirk.

"Traitorous snakes, I told you to cut them off at the head." His words lacked any real bite. Clearly, this was an argument they'd had too many times for scathing words surrounding the Knights to still cut deeply.

"I told you there were good men among them—men who now fight for Solaris." Fiera gave a sideways look at Tiberus and then turned her attention back to Vi. "So I assume Zira is off taking some kind of action against them?"

"Yes, I've acquired intelligence about their network in the Waste. We hope to cut off their support and force them to the surface. But for our plans to work, they must believe Zira is dead—she must be an unknown factor in play."

"I see." Fiera stroked the bulge of her stomach in thought.

Tiberus glanced up at her and Vi was caught in his ocean blue eyes for a long second. In them, she saw the eyes of her brother.

"You really are a dangerously clever one."

"And I use my cleverness to support Solaris." Vi could read between the lines. She knew what he was really saying.

"Let's hope so, and that Zira is not the latest convert of the Knights. Otherwise we'll have to kill her, too."

"Zira would never betray me," Fiera insisted to Tiberius. Then, she said to Vi, "I will do what must be done this sunset to mourn her. But regarding a body to burn—"

"Fear not, I've already taken care of the logistics," Vi interrupted.

"I'd better not ask for specifics, then, and merely thank you for your continued service to the crown."

Vi gave a low bow. "The honor is mine," she said and dismissed herself.

On the way out, when he no doubt thought she was out of earshot, Vi heard Tiberus say, "You should keep an eye on that one. Someone who is always at the center of trouble is likely the cause."

More than you know, Vi wanted to say. The world was a puppet, and it was her job to pull the strings.

She headed right for Deneya's office, checking her watch along the way. It was still two hours before the council was scheduled to meet. That should be enough time.

"Deneya," Vi said as she entered. Thankfully, the woman was behind her desk. Vi had learned that Deneya gave herself extra time in the mornings to prepare for meetings on account of how the numbers and letters "danced" across the page.

"Whenever you show up with that face, it's rarely good."

"I've never claimed to be a good omen."

"Then you're living up to expectations." Deneya returned her quill to its inkwell and leaned back in her chair. "What do you need me for this time?"

"I need you to adjust the docket for today's meeting."

"That's usually Ophain's responsibility. Take it up with him."

"He likes you better," Vi countered.

"I can't argue that." Deneya stood. "What am I having him adjust?"

"The head of the city guard will need to discuss the Knights of Jadar."

"Why?" Deneya asked cautiously.

"To talk about last night's arson of course. Poor Lord Twintle."

"What did you do?" Deneya almost sounded delighted. "And how dare you for not taking me with you to do it. I would've loved to *juth starys* the man seven ways to the next world."

"Hopefully there is no next world," Vi mumbled.

"What?"

"Change the docket. I have to file a report with the head of the city guard." Vi started for the door. "A murder and arson in one night… The Knights were busy."

"Wait, murder? Tell me—"

"No time." Vi shot the woman a smile over her shoulder and was off down the hall.

Despite getting little to no sleep, she felt great. Control was an intoxicating thing. And Vi was finding she couldn't get enough.

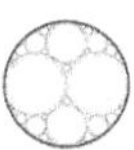

"Forgive me for my tardiness." Twintle arrived for the meeting at the last possible minute. The man had still donned his impeccably tailored and pressed clothing, but there were hairs out of place and stubble was on his chin that wasn't usually there.

He looked like a man who had not slept an hour the night before and Vi delighted in it.

"The man of the hour," Euclan, head of the city guard, said from the end of the table.

"We're all sorry to hear of last night's misfortune," Ophain said with sincerity.

Vi resisted the urge to tell the royal that Twintle was the last one he should feel bad about. Twintle was the one attempting to orchestrate the fall of Ci'Dan and Solaris. Vi kept her mouth shut and a small smile in place.

"Yes, my misfortune…" Twintle said cautiously, looking from person to person. His eyes lingered for a little longer on Vi.

"The Knights of Jadar are getting too bold." Ophain shook his head. "That's why Euclan is here today to discuss what we can do about them."

"The Knights of Jadar?" Twintle repeated, confused.

"Yes, the arson at your warehouse is believed to have been sparked by them," Euclan said.

"That's… not possible." Twintle shuffled back a step.

"I understand how hard it is to see an order that you yourself were a part of fall so far. It guts me to see it." Ophain balled his hand into a fist. "Fiera has pleaded with our Emperor for leniency. But I think the time for such things has long since come to an end."

"Especially given the murder."

"Murder?" Twintle was on repeat and Vi relished his confusion.

"The Knights of Jadar murdered Zira Westwind last night when she was on patrol," Vi said sadly. "She was ambushed and cut down. They acted like a band of thugs to bring down one woman." Twintle narrowed his eyes at her and Vi could see the veins in his neck bulge. She sighed heavily, intentionally mistaking his expression to rub salt in the wound. "I know, it's heartbreaking. There will be a Rite of Sunset for her this evening."

"Then…" Twintle finally ground out, "allow me to suggest we focus on mourning the loss of one of our own, rather than worrying about my warehouse. I'll be able to get it back in order straight away. It was only property, after all. A loss of life is far more severe and our focus should remain there."

"Good of you." Ophain gave Twintle a nod as the lord took his seat.

"That still leaves the matter of defending our fair city from the Knights of Jadar. The murder of one of our Empress's right-hand women should be treated as nothing less than an attack on the crown itself. I would propose…"

Vi tuned out Euclan and instead focused on the quill she was twirling in her fingers. However, the sensation of a pair of eyes on her quickly stilled her hands. Vi slowly lifted her gaze to meet Twintle's. His stare was unwavering. The man was barely controlling his rage.

Without so much as blinking, Vi looked back to Euclan and pretended not to notice Twintle's intense stare for the rest of the meeting. He somehow knew this all circled back to her.

Part of her hated the fact. It meant he'd be watching her every movement. But a part of her was satisfied by his discovery.

Let him hate her.

Let every Knight of Jadar hunt her down. She would find a way to bring about their end, and save this world.

IT HAD BEEN NEARLY three weeks since Zira left with the sword and there hadn't been any word or further issue from the Knights. Vi's days had become almost routine, each starting with her practice with Yargen's magic.

Magic was magic. Taavin had told her so once, long ago, when Vi was first attempting to make sense of her powers. All sorcery was a means to harness the gift of Yargen, everything made possible by words, or feelings, or sparks of power.

Yet, in her, Vi could feel something different and distinct. Something that hadn't been there before. She could feel her own powers of fire and light. They crackled under her skin and sprang forth with a command. But there was also something more.

Something Vi had long since decided was the power of Yargen itself.

Holding out her hand in the early morning light, Vi focused on pooling that magic within her palm. Yargen had entrusted her with the remnants of her power from an old world. So why shouldn't she be able to use it like any other magic?

A hazy blue glow collected around her fingers. Vi narrowed her eyes and took a slow breath. She worked to distance herself from each inhale and exhale. The slightest jostle would disrupt the intense focus it had taken to get this far.

Tiny flashes and motes of light appeared in the thickening haze of magic. It felt as though she held a small microcosm in her fingers. Every muscle was rigid, her joints aching from holding herself in a precise form.

More power. Vi attempted to dredge it up from every nook and cranny. Her hand began to tremble; sweat beaded on her brow. She was going to lose it.

All at once, the power snapped back into place with a *pop* she could feel in the center of her chest. Like the rush of Deneya's spiced liquor, Vi shivered as it flooded her veins and made her head spin. Pulling out Yargen's power at all was nearly impossible. But if she had more…

If she had the sword.

Vi pushed the thought from her mind. Everything was going according to plan. The last thing Vi would do was muck it up by seeking out the sword.

She'd be reunited with it soon enough, anyway. But first, she had to ensure Fiera survived through her childbirth.

Shrugging on a cropped vest over her tailored, sleeveless shirt and tight-fitting pants, Vi departed her room for the day. She ran through the day's obligations in her mind: she would oversee the soldiers' training, get the reports from Euclan on the city guard, then ensure rounds and rotations for the soldiers were in order.

Zira had done a lot more to keep the castle and city guard running than Vi had given her credit for. Since Vi was the one to send her away, it was now her responsibility to oversee those obligations. Luckily, she'd been trained for the majority of her life to delegate, plan, and lead.

"Euclan, tell me what I need to know," Vi demanded as she entered the cramped guard office next to the training field.

A silver pot of steaming kaha was set beside two clay mugs, adjacent to two bowls heaped with steaming rice topped with egg and shallot. She'd begun to form a routine, and fortunately the castle staff had picked it up quickly. It made it easy for Vi to remain efficient in these busy mornings.

"Twenty guards have requested leave."

"Twenty?" Vi asked as she poured kaha for them both. When she was younger, she would've taken it with some kind of cream or sweetener. But much like she'd found a taste for liquor, Vi had discovered she liked the bitter liquid first thing in the morning. It sharpened her senses even after the longest nights. "That seems a little high, doesn't it?"

"Bad timing, but most of the men have never interacted with each other. Thank you." Euclan took his kaha, drinking it slowly. "I thought perhaps it could be something nefarious... but four of them are imminently awaiting children—"

"So many babies," Vi murmured.

"The post-war phenomenon," he chuckled.

Vi ran her nail along the edge of her mug. *Children.* She'd always expected she'd have some of her own for the purpose of heirs at the very least. But now... Vi pushed the thoughts from her mind.

"In any case," Euclan continued. "I thought perhaps it could be the Knights of Jadar infiltrating our men. But that doesn't seem to be the case."

"I appreciate your vigilance." The Knights of Jadar had been quiet. Vi suspected they were off licking their wounds and planning their next attack. "Let's continue to play it safe—take twenty of the best from the castle tonight for the city patrols."

"You don't need them here?"

"I'll figure it out," she said confidently. "Now, what's next on the docket?"

Vi shoveled food into her mouth as Euclan ran through the day's obligations. Her bowl was clean when he finished.

"As usual, thank you for your time."

"It's my job, now." Vi wiped her mouth with the back of her hand.

"You're a natural. We're lucky to have someone like you to replace—" Euclan was interrupted by the training-side door opening.

Vi's eyes met a familiar pair of dark orbs. She'd know that terrible, spiked haircut anywhere.

"Forgive my intrusion." Luke gave a low bow.

"We were just finishing," Vi said before Euclan could get a word in. "Thank you for your hard work, sir. We'll meet again in two days' time as normal."

"Fiarum Evantes."

"Kotun un nox."

Luke stepped to the side, allowing Euclan to pass. The two exchanged a nod, but little other indication of formality. Vi appreciated the fact. She didn't want to see Luke too friendly with anyone who came in and out of the castle.

"You say it well," Luke said.

"Say what well?"

"That colloquialism of Mhashan."

Vi picked up her mug and took a sip. The kaha had gone cold. But she wanted to keep her mouth busy for a moment to think through what to say next. "I am Western."

"No red-blooded Mhashanese would ever call themselves Western," Luke replied with a dangerous edge to his voice.

"What do you want?"

"Where would I find Lord Ophain at this time of day?"

"Lord Ophain?" Vi repeated. "Why?"

"Is it common for guards to question nobles on their business?"

"Only in the interest of castle security," she replied.

"Do you think I'm a threat?" He smiled thinly.

She'd lose either way. If she said no, she passed up the opportunity to question him further. If she said yes, he'd know she had some idea about the role he might be looking to play.

"The son of the illustrious Lord Twintle and a former Knight of Jadar? Of course I don't think you're a threat." Vi set her mug down lightly, resisting the urge to throw it at his smug face. "This way, please."

She led him into the castle and wound upward through the staircases and long hallways to the royal chambers. There was an audience room at the start done entirely in crimson trimmings and bright red lacquered wood. Vi sat Luke down there, stationing a guard at the door to keep an eye on him before she went and got Ophain herself.

"My Lord, forgive me for troubling you so early." Vi dipped into a low bow as Ophain answered his door. "Lord Twintle's son has come calling for you."

"Ah, yes, that is this morning." Ophain looked back into his room where food still sat out amid a mess of papers.

"I've placed him in the sitting room. Do take your time, my lord. He'll be comfortable while he waits."

"Thank you, Yullia." Ophain smiled at her. It was a wide, toothy expression. Whenever he smiled, all similarities with her father vanished.

"You're welcome."

Vi dismissed herself, but rather than heading back to Luke, she trusted the guard to do his job and instead headed for Deneya's office. She didn't like the fact that Luke was here, and if anyone would have a clue as to why, it'd be Deneya.

She knocked on Deneya's door and waited. Then knocked again when there was no reply. Vi checked her watch. It was late for the woman not to have arrived yet. Luke's presence was making her paranoid and Vi's mind ran through every possibility of misfortune that could've befallen Deneya before she showed up.

"You had me worried." The words burst from Vi as she nearly ran the length of the hall to the woman who'd just emerged from the spiral stairwell. Deneya blinked at her, startled.

"Worried? Why?" Deneya glanced around before adding under her breath, "And aren't you usually the worrisome one?"

"Exactly, don't take my title." Vi fell into step beside the woman. "Now, unlock your office, I have something I need to ask you."

"Say please." Deneya stopped at the door, grinning at her.

"Please," Vi said sweetly, batting her eyelashes.

"All right, in with you."

Vi stepped inside, spinning in place to hold out an eager hand. "Do you have today's matters?"

"I grabbed it from Ophain before coming here." Deneya slid a slip of paper from the stack she held and handed it to Vi.

"So you saw Ophain, then. Did you see Luke, too?"

"Luke? Why would I?" Deneya asked, but then immediately followed up with, "*Oh…*"

"Oh? Oh, what?"

Deneya sighed, cursing under her breath in a tongue Vi didn't recognize. She went behind her desk, setting down the satchel. "That explains it, then," she mumbled, rummaging through the bag.

"Explains what? You seem to be having a very good conversation with yourself. Care to share?"

"Yes, sorry." Deneya handed Vi another letter. On the outside was a broken wax seal. The wax was black, imprinted with two swords fesswise—the Twintle family crest.

Vi scanned the papers, reading aloud. She didn't know if Deneya had the chance to read them yet, and the woman seemed to appreciate it when Vi offered another set of eyes.

"Lord Twintle has cast off his fleet for Oparium… seeks to establish a trade route with the South…" Her attention drifted to the docket for the day's council meeting. "Councilor Luke, maritime." Vi returned the papers to Deneya. "So Twintle is gone, and Luke is here in his stead."

Deneya nodded. "Everything happened quickly last night. Though I can't say why."

"What did you find out?" Vi asked. Deneya had continued to case the city at night for information, searching in areas Vi didn't have time for.

"Twintle had business on the seas, so he left." Business by itself wasn't particularly alarming. But when it came to the Knights of Jadar, Vi was suspicious of every movement. "It makes sense Luke is operating in his stead."

Vi sighed. "I suppose it does. But I still don't like it."

"He's likely just trying to move some of those rubies you found."

"I'm worried it's more than that." Vi tapped her knuckles on Deneya's desk in thought.

"How so?"

"In his last meeting with the Knights, he said he was trying to work with Adela to get the sword."

"What? You didn't think to mention the pirate queen's involvement before now?" Deneya rounded the desk. "That seems rather important."

"Things were quiet, the sword is gone and should be on its way to the East by now." Vi shook her head. "I continued to hope that the mention of working with Adela was merely the ravings of a madman seeking to make himself look stronger and more influential than he actually is."

"You're right about Twintle being a madman." Deneya folded her arms. "Mad enough to actually go through with it."

"And if he's gone out to sea, there's a possibility you're right." Vi cursed under her breath. "Keep a close ear on the ground for any indication of Adela's actions."

Deneya nodded. "Though I suspect she won't step foot on this continent herself… She has middle men for that."

"Good." Because if Vi saw her again, she just might kill her this time.

"There's one other thing," Deneya cautioned.

"Tell me it's good news. I could use some."

Deneya shook her head solemnly. "Your name is being whispered among the Knights."

"My name?" Vi wished she could be more surprised. But she'd

toed the line too boldly with Twintle following the warehouse incident.

"Not much else. But they're cautious and suspicious about you. Be careful, and trust no new friends."

Vi gave a bitter laugh. "You don't have to worry about that. I'm skeptical of everyone."

"Even me?" Deneya arched her eyebrows.

"Even you," Vi replied, though the words didn't ring entirely true. Deneya had worked her way underneath Vi's barriers. Just as Fiera and Zira had.

"You're usually better at lying than that." Deneya gave her a sly grin. Vi snorted in reply.

"Don't push your luck." She started for the door. "I'll see you at the council meeting."

"Drinks tomorrow?" Deneya asked, as though they were casual friends and not allies discussing espionage.

"Usual time and place," Vi replied and stepped out of the woman's office, bracing herself for the council meeting.

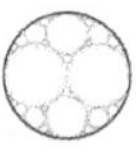

"You have to relax at some point," Taavin scolded. "Being on edge all the time is killing you."

"Being on edge keeps me alive," Vi muttered. She was laid back on her bed, her head in his lap as he rubbed small circles into her temples. Even with the quiver of magic between the pads of his fingers and her skin, his touch could still relax her.

"It's been, what, six weeks since Zira left?"

"Just over five."

"Five, then. No real movements from the Knights of Jadar, Fiera is well, Zira is alive."

"I don't know for sure if Zira is alive." She wished she'd found a way to communicate with the woman. No contact was for the best—it kept both of them and the sword safe.

"I have a feeling you'd know if she wasn't."

"How?" Vi opened her eyes, looking up at the man hovering over her.

He still had the crescent-shaped scar on his cheek—a mark of his old life. All of Vi's scars had vanished when she had been reborn in this new age. Her body was unblemished in its remade form. Some part of her envied the man for retaining his marks. Her scars had been like war medals, showing all she had survived.

"I just do." Taavin shrugged.

"Helpful." Vi allowed her gaze to go unfocused as her eyelids dipped closed once more.

"When are you going to reunite with her and the sword, again?"

"Once I'm confident Fiera is safe. Likely after my father is born." The statement had an odd ring to it, since Vi knew the Aldrik who would be born wasn't really her father—her real father was lost with an old world. Her mind knew the truth, but her emotions were still catching up. "Fiera seems ready to pop any day now. Shortly after she gives birth, there will be a blessing on the child. I've already asked Fiera to start letting it slip around servants that the Sword of Jadar has gone missing and lament over how it won't be present for the blessing."

"You intend to drive the Knights from the city, and away from Fiera, by letting them know the sword is elsewhere."

"That's my hope."

"And you think the servants can get word back to the Knights?"

Vi bobbed her head yes. If Deneya was to be believed, word was getting out of the castle somehow. The most obvious break in the chain would be a servant, someone easily overlooked by most nobles.

"Everything just has to stay according to—" Vi was interrupted by a knock on her door.

"Who's that?" Taavin whispered.

"I don't know," Vi mumbled. "Stay out of sight. I'll release the glyphs if someone's about to come in."

He nodded, stepping into a corner of her bedroom as Vi side-stepped through the sliding screens into her sitting area. She opened the door to find an unfamiliar servant waiting there, a letter rested on a silver tray.

"Apologies for bothering you. A courier arrived with this and said it was of supreme importance."

"What type of courier?" Vi asked, picking up the letter. It was folded into thirds, a wax blob holding it closed. There was no insignia to indicate who it might be from.

"A city courier. I have no other information, m'lady." The young man bowed. "Good evening."

"Good evening," Vi replied before locking the door behind him.

"A letter?" Taavin asked as he emerged.

"Yes, and a strange one at that. It's sealed, but there's no crest." Vi flipped it over. "Yullia" was scribbled on the front with the words "imperial guard" underneath. She pressed on the folds, popping the letter open like an eye. Like this, she could make out the words inside. "Not sealed well." Vi frowned, thinking of Jayme reading her letters.

"'I require you for a matter of grave importance. Meet me at the Hog and Bone Inn, room fourteen. *Fiarum evantes,*'" she read aloud.

"That's it?" Taavin moved to her side, reading over her shoulder, confirming the answer to his question. "Speaking of suspicious things…"

Vi set the letter down on her chair, intentionally leaving it where it could be found by someone looking for her if something went awry. She grabbed a cloak from her closet and strapped a sword onto her hip.

"Wait, you can't be thinking of going." Taavin grabbed her wrist.

"Of course I am."

"What if it's a trap by the Knights?"

"Then I'll kill them all and show them I'm not one to be trifled with. Then they'll know their best course of action is to clear out of this city," Vi said with all the vitriol she felt for the group.

"Think about this logically…"

"I am."

"No, you're acting on emotion and indulging your vendetta. You're reaching for too much, Vi. First saving everyone, now eradicating the Knights of Jadar. *Some things are meant to happen,* and preventing them will be met with failure at best, or at worst…"

"At worst?" Vi prodded when he trailed off.

"At worst you could create a world where you're not born again. Where there is no Vi Solaris."

"If everyone I love lives long and healthy lives in that world, then so be it."

"You don't mean that."

"I do." Ever since her vision at the docks, Vi had come to terms with the idea of not existing herself if it meant the world was safe. If Vhalla, Aldrik, and Romulin lived on, even if they weren't really her family, it would be enough for her.

"And if you fail in this timeline and there is no new Vi—no Champion—they'll all be condemned to death by Raspian's blight."

Vi bit the insides of her cheeks and scowled at the door. "I know all this. I'll be careful, I promise."

"Vi—"

She dismissed him with a wave of her hand. Taavin vanished, though his words lingered. They clung to her like he had, holding her in place.

Was he right? Was she overreaching?

Vi shook her head and started forward, out her door, down the hall, and out of the castle. She had everything under control. She was the one with all the power, pulling the strings.

She had nothing to fear.

VI KEPT HER HOOD up and her head down all the way to the Hog and Bone Inn. The inn wasn't far from the main entrance of the city, a fairly straight shot from the castle. But Vi took a longer route. She wandered down side streets and sprinted through alleyways.

She glanced over her shoulders and remained as alert as possible. But the night was quiet, and she arrived at the quaint inn without issue.

The building was four stories tall, long but not particularly wide. Its storefront was well lit with two iron lanterns and she could hear the sounds of mugs clanking and music from the bar within. Not wanting to raise suspicion by lingering, Vi entered and headed directly for a back hallway.

It looked like rooms one through ten were on the first floor, so Vi proceeded to the second. Sure enough, the first room she crossed had the number eleven painted on the door. Halfway down the hall was fourteen.

Vi stood outside the door, contemplating the latch for a moment. She could mask her face with *durroe*, see who it was first and then come back as Yullia. She could force entry and catch them flat-footed and off-guard.

Balling her hand into a fist, Vi went for the simple and most direct approach—she knocked, and held her breath as the door cracked open.

Her eyes met a familiar dark pair. They were framed by a short-cut fringe and hair that didn't extend past the ears. Even though the woman's clothes were different, Vi recognized her with ease. That meant anyone else could too.

"What in the Mother's name are you doing here?" Vi half-whispered, half-snarled. Then looked around quickly to make sure the hall was still empty. Thankfully, it was.

Zira opened the door slightly wider, and Vi took the invitation, allowing herself in. The swordswoman didn't speak until the door was closed once more and locked. "I had to come and warn you."

"Warn me?" Vi did a quick sweep of the room. A bed against the wall to the right, a chamber pot in the corner to the left, a dresser… the lack of things made the sword's presence all the more noticeable. "You brought the sword back? You even made a stand for it?" Vi balked at the little wooden stand, emblazoned with a silver phoenix.

"It felt right to give it a place of honor, even when I was on the road."

"I told you not to let anyone know you even had it." Vi spun, advancing on the woman. The conspicuous stand was the least of her worries. "Are you mad?"

"I had to bring it with me. I wasn't about to entrust it to anyone else," Zira said, defensive, holding her ground as Vi intruded on her personal space.

"Of course not, because you were supposed to take it East. By now you should've been past the Crossroads, by now it should've been long free of their reach." Vi wanted to scream. She'd never been so angry. She never expected someone to make her feel more vicious than Jayme had.

But here they were.

"I am only here one night," Zira said calmly, levelly, as though speaking to Raylynn during a tantrum. "Only one night to warn you."

"You leave *now*."

"Then let me say what I came to say. I'm here anyway."

"Very well. Speak."

"I did as you said—I went to the Nameless Company and waited. Eventually, word of my 'death' arrived back to me. I left the Nameless Company and traveled on the road through the deep Waste, places where the Knights of Jadar are strong. There, I learned that they're planning an attack on the castle with forces they've gathered from Adela. They say they have powers beyond what we can imagine. Powers of the Pirate Queen and—"

Vi held up a hand for silence. She took several deep breaths, more like panting, to prevent herself from shouting. Her plans… all her careful plans… were coming undone because of one woman's foolish honor and ill-thought decision.

"I know about the plan to work with Adela," Vi said, dangerously composed.

"You do?" Zira seemed honestly surprised. "They were speaking as though it was just coming together, as though—"

"Why do you think I sent you away?" Vi gripped the woman by the collar. Zira's hands flew up, grabbing Vi's wrists so hard the bones popped. But Vi continued to cling through the pain. "What do you think prompted the sudden urgency?"

"Unhand me," Zira commanded, deadly soft.

Vi obliged, but only reluctantly. She spun away before she really did try to throttle the woman. Vi ran a hand over her hair, smoothing away the pieces that had escaped the taut braid she'd woven through and around a knotted bun.

"All right, listen." Vi looked back to Zira. "We can still fix this. You take the sword and go now, tonight. It isn't safe in this city." Especially not with Twintle on the move. "Go back to the Nameless

Company once more, wait just a week or two to make sure no one is following you, then continue on."

"And you'll still meet me in Cyven?"

"Yes. I'll find the sword wherever you are, have no doubt about that." Even now, it called to her. Perhaps it was all the work Vi had been doing to further explore and manipulate Yargen's magic. But she felt it even more keenly than before—even with it wrapped tightly in layers of leather, even without touching it. "I'll leave now. Wait just a little, to let anyone following me do so, then you slip out after."

"All right." Zira nodded curtly. "Yullia, I was only trying to—"

"I know." Vi met her eyes. "I know you were trying to protect our Empress. But you must have faith and believe me when I say that protecting Fiera is my current, sole goal. All of this is for her, and her child."

"Very well. I'll trust you, and meet you in the East."

"Good."

Without another word, Vi stormed out of the room. She barely resisted slamming the door behind her to punctuate the conversation. She knew she'd acted rashly. She understood Zira's motivations. She'd apologize later. Right now, she was seeing red, and sparks were crackling against her hands. Her fingers were clenched so tightly they hurt. But Vi was afraid that if she unraveled them, her spark would get loose and burn the whole place down.

Vi emerged into the cool desert air and gulped it down like a tonic that would soothe the flames raging within her. She walked several paces into the street and stopped. Tilting her head back, Vi looked at the stars above and tried to relax the tension throughout her body.

A familiar voice interrupted her thoughts. "Are you all right?"

She didn't believe for a second that he or his smug grin actually cared about her. Luke strolled out from the inn. *Had he been in the bar when she'd entered?* Vi struggled to remember.

"What do you want?" Vi asked.

"Is that any way to address a lord?" He arched his eyebrows.

"I think not. It's odd to see you in this area of town, at this time of night."

"I didn't notice you paid such close attention to my comings and goings," Vi said flatly.

"I think people notice what you do a lot more than you give them credit for."

"I'm flattered." Vi started back toward the castle. She needed to get Luke away from the inn before Zira left.

"I'm glad I could flatter you. I do hope you have a good night, Yullia. I'll see you at tomorrow's council meeting. I can't wait for Euclan's report. The Knights of Jadar are becoming so infamous, next we'll hear about them killing ghosts."

Vi stopped dead in her tracks. She was so focused on her general annoyance with Luke, so overwhelmed with her hatred, that Vi didn't realize what he had been doing—stalling. She hadn't asked the right questions out the gate. Like, why was he there at this time of night? Or, had he followed her?

Her stomach went sour. Without another second's hesitation, Vi sprinted back into the Hog and Bone.

The bar downstairs was as cheerful as it had been when she'd left. Though three patrons who had been hunched around the corner of the bar were now gone. The hairs on the back of her neck lifted upright.

No, no, no, her mind repeated over and over.

Movement at the very back caught her eye; in the alleyway behind the inn, the flutter of a cloak rippled in the dark before the door snapped shut.

Vi dashed out the back door and into the dingy alley. Darkness clung like grime in all the corners. Two men and one woman were arguing about thirty paces away.

"… payment and then you'll have it."

"Give it to me now," the man on the right snarled.

Vi didn't have to wonder what "it" was, given that the woman was holding the sword.

"Drop it and I'll let you live," Vi lied. She was going to kill them all.

The three turned. Vi's heart dropped though her stomach at the sight of the woman. Across her forehead in place of eyebrows were three faintly glowing dots.

A morphi. There was a morphi in Norin.

"*Juth c—*"

"*Juth mariy.*" The man on the right stopped her magic, shattering it before it could form. He said to the woman, "Go, they know the deal."

The woman holding the sword leapt into the air and the dark wings of a large crow stretched out between the pulses of magic. The Knight of Jadar stared, slack jawed, as she flew away. He blubbered, trying to make sense of what he had just witnessed— until the other man uttered a quick, "*Mysst soto larrk,*" and cut his throat then and there.

"They said a 'strange sorcerer' was here," the pirate said with a smile. "I assume you're one of Lumeria's?"

Vi didn't even dignify him with a response. "*Juth calt.*"

The man crumpled, dead on the spot. Yet another from Meru who hadn't considered all the creative ways Yargen's words could be used. She looked upward, scanning the dark sky. But the morphi was already gone with the sword. And that meant—assuming "they could pay" as the pirate had said—it would be in the Knights' hands before dawn.

Cursing aloud, Vi rushed back inside. She ran past the doors and up to the second floor. The door to Zira's room was slightly ajar. Vi pushed it open to confirm her worst fears.

Zira lay dead on the ground in a pool of her own blood.

Vi was transfixed by the body, bile rising in back of her throat. It wasn't for the gruesome way in which she'd died. But for what it meant.

Yargen will come for her life.

You can't save everyone.

Some things are meant to happen.

Every terrible phrase Taavin had uttered in caution seemed to echo up through Zira's gaping mouth. The woman's wide eyes judged every inch of Vi for not heeding them.

The floorboards slammed into her knees as Vi collapsed. Her shoulders hunched and she dug her nails into the wood, feeling it splinter beneath her nailbeds. She exhaled ragged breaths, somewhere between tears and screams.

SHE HAD TO MOVE.

She had to pry herself off this hard floor and keep moving. The Knights were likely to investigate, especially when the sword was delivered short of one of their own and one of Adela's men. But Vi was still barely managing to breathe. Her thoughts were jumbled.

"*Narro hath hoolo.*" The moment Taavin's shoes blinked into existence, Vi blurted, "I messed up. I should've listened to you, to my father. I messed up."

His knee met the ground before her, his knuckles hooked her chin, and Taavin slowly raised her face to his. "Tell me how this happened."

It was a soft command, but a command nonetheless—as if he somehow knew that she needed his tenderness, but she also needed orders. They might be the only thing that kept her moving through the shakes that were still trying to take control of her limbs.

"Zira, she came back, the Knights, Adela's men—" Vi stopped

herself short, her eyes following Taavin's to the dead body in the room. She restarted, "The letter was from Zira. I came here and met her. She'd learned of the Knights' plot involving Adela and came back to warn me—for Fiera's sake. She brought the sword with her.

"I told her to leave… but I was too late. I don't know if the Knights followed me, or if they'd intercepted the letter and read it. For all I know, one of Adela's men was the courier who delivered it—she seems to be good at using letters to her benefit.

"But by the time I realized, it was too late."

"They killed Zira and took the sword," he finished what she couldn't say.

"Yes… There was a morphi who flew away—a crow. I'm sure they'll bring it back to wherever the Knights are waiting and Adela will have her rubies and they'll have the sword. Assuming she doesn't just take it for herself."

Taavin shook his head. He turned away from Zira, stood, paced to one end of the small room and back. He shook his head again, and again before grabbing it and letting out a groan as if he were in pain. "I thought… I really thought this was it. I let myself believe."

"I can get it back," Vi said, stronger than she'd felt in the past hour. Something about seeing him hurting, in pain, and doubting her brought her strength and conviction rushing back. He needed her to be strong and keep herself together. She was the one who could act and change fate. Vi stood. "I *will* get it back. I know their plan and I know where they're going. I heard them talking about taking the sword to the Crystal Caverns at their meeting. Do you think Adela will help them further?"

Taavin, unresponsive, stared at Zira's cooling body. Vi knelt down and gently pressed the woman's eyelids closed. His gaze didn't waver, and Vi wrapped one arm around his waist, guiding his eyes to her.

"I cannot imagine what you've seen. I know this is likely one more body on the pile," Vi whispered. "But I need your help now. I need you to stay with me and help me fix this." He finally nodded, clarity returning to his eyes. They were both on the cusp of falling apart, barely held together by each other. "In any of my past times, did Adela help the Knights of Jadar after they got the sword?"

Taavin pulled away and held out his hands. He mumbled words of Yargen and power flowed from her watch. Vi waited as he finished culling through all of his memories.

"They maintain a relationship with her, but they've usually only had one transaction at a time, then a longer stretch of time before the next."

"She's no doubt too expensive for them." Vi thought about how hard Twintle had to work to salvage enough rubies to buy just a few of Adela's crew. She looked at the blood-soaked floor again and hated that working with Adela had been a good investment for them. "It's just the Knights and me. I'll ride off and intercept them before they get to the Caverns."

"If you can find them."

"Good point." The Waste was large and it seemed unlikely she'd know the exact path they'd be traveling. "Then I'll go on ahead, and meet them at the Caverns. I'll stop them from turning Yargen's magic against itself."

She started for the door, but was stopped by two arms wrapping around her waist. Taavin squeezed her tightly from behind. Always at her back, always defending and supporting.

"You know just when my bones are rattling," she whispered. "And right when I need you to make sure none pop out of place."

"I know you," Taavin whispered back. "Good luck protecting our world."

The well wishes weren't enough. But nothing he could've said would've been enough. Perhaps he knew it too, because Taavin vanished without another word.

Vi swallowed hard, strode down the hall, and left out the back door of the inn, alone.

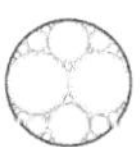

The castle was in chaos the moment she arrived. Servants sprinted from room to room. Some carried flowers, others were clerical assistants hauling towels and blankets; most carried food, to the nobles gathering in the main hall, or to the royals waiting in an antechamber not far from the Imperial quarters.

Vi didn't have to ask anyone what was happening. It was obvious enough to her, even without future knowledge.

She trudged up the main, grand stairway of the castle. She ignored the inquiring looks of nobleman and servant alike, as if she'd somehow become someone who knew things the rest of them didn't.

She'd thought that, hadn't she? A bitter smile crossed her mouth. She'd thought she had the upper hand on all of them. Humility was a necessary elixir for her now.

"It's only clerics beyond this point." A young man stopped Vi in the hallway. He wore the usual pale blue of the Southern clerics. The same robes Ginger had worn. "There's a place you can wait right down the hall."

She'd seen the place. She'd ignored it. But Vi didn't point that out. Instead, she smiled and said, "Thank you."

Turning on her heel, Vi walked down the now familiar hallway, realizing this would likely be her last time. She ached all over, but it was hard to put her finger on the exact reason why. Was it because she'd warmed up to this place and its people? Or was it because it was another familial home she was walking away from?

Side-stepping into an alcove, Vi uttered a quick, "*Durroe watt ivin*," and stepped into the skin of the young cleric she'd met outside of Fiera's door weeks ago.

This time, when Vi passed by the man in the hallway, he merely gave a friendly nod and let her pass.

It was quiet in the Imperial chambers. Ginger had explained the birthing process well to Vi and she'd made it out to be a painful affair and understandably noisy as a result. But there was an almost serene stillness to the air. At least until Fiera's snappish comments broke the silence.

"Out. Out with all of you, I've had enough of your prodding! I will summon you when the pains come with any kind of regularity. Now leave me be to what peace I can manage."

Vi hastily stepped off to the side, positioning herself in a doorway at the end of a bookshelf. From this position, she was mostly concealed from the flow of clerics that streamed out of the room. Vi waited several moments to ensure there were no stragglers before she continued on to the bedroom.

The Imperial bedroom was as lush as Vi would've expected it to be. A bed large enough to fit four grown men was framed by a headboard that stretched halfway up the tall wall. A circular canopy was hung from the ceiling, the gold metal railing mirroring a crown, and supporting bolts of fine white silk fanned out behind the headboard. Pillows were piled high and would've dwarfed any other woman.

But Fiera remained imposing. Even amid all the excess, she somehow commanded the sole focus of anyone who entered the space.

Now, her angry eyes were turned to Vi.

"I told you all to get out. I understand what is happening to my body and will summon you when it is time or I am in actual pain. I have been stabbed through in war; I can handle a few contractions. Now, leave—"

Vi released her magic, allowing the illusion to dissipate like fog on the wind. Fiera, to her credit, didn't shout or cry out. Her eyes narrowed slightly and her head tilted, as though she was trying to figure out what she had just seen.

"Come closer." Fiera lifted a hand off her stomach and motioned to the bed. "Sit." Vi did as she was bid and eased herself onto the edge of the bed. "Who are you, really?"

Vi gave the woman who would be the grandmother of a new Vi a sad smile. "That's a difficult question, because sometimes I'm not sure anymore."

She looked to Fiera's stomach protruding like a massive hill underneath the thin sheet. In there was the man who would be her father. *No*, the man who would be the father to a new Vi. A new family she'd never known.

She still loved that man. And she always would. Just as she already loved the Romulin and Vhalla of her vision, and the Fiera that lay before her. Even though they were different people, they wore the faces of her family. They fit into the person-shaped voids left behind by the past world exactly.

"I've come from a time very far away… but one that looks very much like this one," Vi said softly, bringing her eyes back to Fiera. Taavin had cautioned her against sharing who and what she was—and she never had in any time before. If there were ever a time, this was it. She was already deep in a mess of her own making; how much could being honest with Fiera hurt? "I'm not the same person I was, then. And tomorrow I won't be the same person I am today."

"Time is relentless."

"In ways you can't imagine."

"That magic…" Fiera trailed off and winced. Her hands smoothed over her stomach and the pain seemed to have vanished as quickly as it came. She didn't seem worried, so Vi wasn't either. "Are you from the Crescent Continent?"

"What?" Vi whispered. This was shaping up to be a night of surprises.

"Tiberus told me about it not long after the wedding. Naturally, I didn't believe him until I began rummaging through my father's old records—the ones he'd always kept hidden. There's little written, but there's more than we think there. Tiberus thinks there are powers worth fighting for. Tell me, if he does fight for them, would he be successful?"

"Tiberus's fate is decided," Vi said as gently as possible. "He's long since chosen his path."

She couldn't bring herself to say that Tiberus would eventually fall to another as thirsty for power and conquest as himself. He'd fall before he ever had the chance to attempt attacking Meru. Though, knowing what she did of Meru, that fact was likely for the best.

"I know." Fiera's eyes were sad enough that they said everything her lips did not. She knew the man she'd married. "And my son?"

"What?"

"You can see the future, can you not? Or was it all a lie?"

"I can."

"Then tell me: what is my son's fate?"

Vi took Fiera's hand, wrapping her fingers around the Empress's. "Your son will live a hard life. But he will grow to be a good man. He will be the kind of man who loves his family and his people fiercely. He will defend them at all costs. He will be the kind of man who will board a ship and sail into pirate-infested waters for the woman he loves."

Her voice cracked toward the end. Sorrow flooded her and the only lifeline Vi had was Fiera's hand. She clutched it tightly.

"Good." Fiera's eyes closed as an expression of relief overtook her. She seemed to sit easier on her pillows.

"You didn't ask about your fate."

Fiera looked at her once more, a small smile playing on her lips. "I don't have to."

"Have you seen it?"

"Yes—in your eyes, right now." Fiera squeezed her hand. Vi felt herself unraveling.

"I wanted to save you," she whispered. "I've tried so hard. I've tried everything to save you."

"The Mother has a plan for us all. I'm glad I could protect my people when Tiberus came. That I could honor my family and see the Ci'Dan bloodline live on… it is enough." Fiera gently stroked her stomach.

Vi hung her head, shaking it from side to side. "Her plan for you ends in death. It always does. I've tried more times than you or I can fathom to save you. To give your son the mother he deserves."

"Perhaps there are things my son cannot learn if I am there." Fiera wriggled her hand free, cupping Vi's cheek. "I am not afraid of my future."

Her expression was open and honest. Vi studied those brave eyes, memorizing them, imprinting them on herself. Everyone told her she had Fiera's face. Perhaps, through all this, she could gain her bravery, too.

"I have to go now. I can't stay and try to protect you further from the vicious fate that wants you dead," Vi said, though she didn't move. Fiera was stable, warm, and confident even in the face of overwhelming odds. Part of Vi was trying to steal it through osmosis.

"Where will you go?"

"I tried to protect the sword. I spoke true when I told you that it was my sole duty to defend it and this world… Because of me, Zira gave her life to that end. But the Knights of Jadar have the sword now. And if they go to the Caverns, they will seek to—"

"Use the sword to unlock the power there," Fiera finished. Another wince and another massage of her stomach.

"How did you know?"

"The sword was locked away for a long time… But when the war with Solaris began, my father told me where it was hidden. It was my duty to use the sword to keep our people safe. So I read as much as I could on the old records from the Burning Times." Fiera grimaced at the last two words. It had nothing to do with her body and everything to do with the dark aura cast by mentioning the long-ago period during which the West captured and murdered Windwalkers in the East. "The records held information on the sword—not much, but enough."

"What kind of information?"

Windwalkers were the one affinity on the Dark Isle that was said to be immune to crystal taint. Knowing what she knew now, Vi would postulate it was because of what aspects of Yargen's magic they inherited from the scythe. Or perhaps it was because the scythe had long been removed from the continent. Either way, she made a connection that she never had before: The Burning Times were Jadar's first attempt at unlocking the power of the Crystal Caverns.

"Mostly how the sword could be used to free the deeper power in the Caverns. But the writings had enough on the power within the sword itself that I was able to fortify the barrier that helped protect Norin for so long."

"You… you formed a barrier," Vi whispered. That night of the surrender, she had seen Fiera and the sword—how the wall around Norin had held against all odds. It was more than just the magic of Groundbreakers. Fiera had imbued the wall with the power of Yargen. It explained why the sword had felt weaker than the scythe. "I-I should've spoken to you much sooner," Vi blurted. Guilt swelled like summer heat. If she'd only spoken with Fiera rather than keeping everything a secret, she would've had an ally in figuring out the power of the crystals rather than struggling on her own. "What can you tell me about this barrier? How do I form it?"

"I don't think I could teach you—" another hiss of pain and a deep breath "—at this exact moment."

For the first time in her life, Vi cursed her father.

"Tell me what you can," she implored. "There isn't much time. The Knights have only just taken the sword and if I go after them now—"

"I would if I could." Fiera squeezed her hand. "But it took me years of study to learn and gain even the smallest mastery of that magic. However…"

"However?" Vi asked cautiously. Fiera had a glint in her eye that Vi wasn't entirely certain she liked. It was the sort of spark Vi usually associated with a bad idea. She knew it well, because she'd seen it in the mirror many times.

"I could do it."

"What?"

"After my son is born, I could go with you."

"You— you'll— I haven't given birth before but I know enough to know you shouldn't be riding hard across half the Empire immediately after," Vi said bluntly.

"Weren't you the one to tell me my life is forfeit?"

"I didn't mean—"

"If it is the Mother's will that I die, regardless of what actions you or I take, then allow me this. Allow my death to mean something as my life has meant something."

"I cannot allow this," Vi insisted. "It's suicide. What you're suggesting is suicide."

"If you have magic that allows you to wield flames and take the faces of others, do you not also possess healing abilities beyond those of our clerics here on the Main Continent?"

"I do…" Vi said hesitantly. Well, she didn't. Her use of *halleth* still hadn't progressed very far. But Vi suspected she knew someone who had a much better handle on it.

"Then heal me, relieve my pain, and let me go with you. Perhaps then it won't be suicide like you say. Give me the chance to surprise you and fate itself. Perhaps your error has been trying to save me, when I need to save myself." Fiera settled back on the pillows, wincing once more. "This is my choice. Honor it."

It was a demand Vi finally obliged. She would do her best to see Fiera's will done, and keep her alive as long as possible. Her plans might have been ruined, but she had stayed this long to be by her grandmother's side—no, her friend's side. She would stay longer.

"Very well."

"Good. You know, you're nearly as stubborn as I am." The grin Fiera wore made Vi wonder if she suspected more than she let on. "Now, fetch me a quill and parchment while I still have a clear head and can focus enough to hold a quill. I wish to leave a letter for my sisters."

VI HOVERED IN THE alcove she'd hidden in before, wearing the face of the young cleric, this time with Fiera's letter in hand. She watched as Fiera called for the clerics and they bounded through the door, no doubt having been waiting outside the entire time.

Demands flew from Fiera's mouth and the healers began to flit in and out, bustling to meet her orders. Her contractions were coming closer together. She was demanding a draught to speed them further, to "get the child out" of her at all costs.

In the chaos, Vi slipped out unnoticed.

She walked through the halls, waiting until she was alone to release her illusion. Down a narrow wooden stair with handrails so worn by time that they were oiled to a shine, and through a side hallway, Vi let herself into Fiera's old room.

The smell of cinders overwhelmed her. Every heavy velvet chair and curtain was coated in the scent of incense—an aroma too potent to have faded since Fiera moved into what were now the

Imperial quarters.

Vi headed for the bedroom, remembering what Fiera had said.

My sisters and I used to leave notes for each other…

They had a system, she'd explained. Fiera seemed to think that once it was known that she was missing, her sisters would execute a covert search. If either of them entered the bedroom, they'd head straight for the ornately carved headboard.

Kneeling on the mattress, Vi pushed on one of the carved suns and it slid to the side, revealing a tiny, hollow space. She placed the folded-up note inside, careful not to break Fiera's seal, then slid it back closed. Vi didn't know what the woman had written. But she trusted Fiera wouldn't betray Vi's true nature. Trusted her enough not to give into curiosity and temptation.

After, Vi headed down to the council. They were all gathered in the chambers and, from the sounds of it, Deneya had brought in her spiced liquor for everyone to enjoy. The fact complimented her plans nicely. If everyone was slightly sauced, they'd notice oddities on a delay.

"You there." Vi stopped a servant as he was about to carry a carafe into the room. "Tell Councilor Denja to step out, please?"

The boy gave a nod. After a few seconds, Deneya emerged as requested. The moment her eyes met Vi's she strolled over, her pace quickening when she was out of sight of the rest of those gathered.

"I'm not going to like this, am I?"

"You didn't like anything about me from the first moment—admit it."

"Sounds about right." Deneya put her hands into the pockets of her trousers, a motion that reminded Vi painfully of Zira. "What do you need, Champion?"

"How committed are you to this post?"

It was likely the Knights would pin the bodies in the alley and inn on Vi or Deneya as repayment for Vi's earlier movements against them. When Fiera vanished, there would be suspicion around that, too—especially since Vi and Deneya would vanish alongside her.

At best, Vi hoped Fiera's letter would absolve them both.

Perhaps the royal family would strive to save face by keeping Fiera's disappearance a secret, claiming she died on the birthing bed as they had in Vi's time.

But by now, Vi knew better than to hope for the best.

She had to plan for the worst.

"Lumeria instructed that I was to keep an eye on the events of the Dark Isle, specifically surrounding the Crystal Caverns," Deneya said somewhat cautiously. "Though how I do that, specifically, is up to me."

"Excellent. The Crystal Caverns are just where we're going."

"Excuse me?" Deneya balked.

"I don't have time to explain in detail."

"When do you ever?" She sighed heavily.

"But we're going tonight. How good are you with *halleth ruta*?"

"Quite excellent, if I do say so myself." Deneya puffed her chest slightly.

"Superb. You'll be the one to heal Fiera, then."

"Excuse me?"

"I can stop her from feeling pain with *halleth maph*, but my flesh mending needs work. You'll need to go up there as soon as the room quiets following the birth, masquerade as one of her servants or clerics, heal her, then sneak her out. Meanwhile, I'll be readying us to go. I'll take the Empress's warstrider and—"

Deneya grabbed her shoulder, shoving her against the wall. Vi blinked, seeing stars for a moment. The world came back into focus with Deneya's face right before hers, their noses almost touching. The woman was much stronger than Vi had given her credit for.

"Stop, and explain this to me properly if you want my help."

"The Knights of Jadar got help from Adela's pirates. I underestimated them." Accepting fault was a bitter pill, but the more she did it the easier it became, and the faster Vi moved on from it. "There was a morphi and a Lightspinner. The morphi got off with the blade before I could stop her. The Lightspinner is dead."

"Bloody pirate queen," Deneya snarled, though not at Vi.

"If we don't go after them tonight, we might not get to the Caverns before they do. We can get a head start because the Knights need to detour to get the sword from Adela. If they get to the Caverns before we do, Raspian is free. It's over."

Deneya looked at her with her brilliant, purple-ringed eyes. Vi could almost feel her prodding, poking into her brain for the slightest hint of a lie. She must've found none, because Deneya released her.

Vi eased away from the wall, rolling her shoulders. "Help me?"

"What did you say I told you once? The other me in that other world of yours… Seek me out, and my sword is yours."

"Well, is it?"

"Yes." Deneya nodded. "Lumeria put me here to watch over the Caverns. I've been here for decades and you, in a few months, have accomplished more than I could toward that end. I'm aligned with you, Vi, before all others."

"Good. Then pack lightly, but make sure you have all you need. We won't be coming back. After, get to Fiera. She knows of Lightspinning and about Meru. You won't surprise her."

"She does?"

Vi ignored the woman's shock. "She does. When you get her stable, meet me at the entrance to the dungeons."

"Very well." Deneya was clearly still skeptical about the whole plan—which Vi hardly blamed her for—but she didn't question further.

They parted ways and Vi returned to her room, rummaging through it for a pack and two bags. She loaded the pack with basic clothes and supplies. On the way through the castle, she ran to the guards' storerooms for a few salves and potions, then the kitchens for rations, filling the other two bags with as much as they could carry.

Vi headed for the dungeons next. She cursed her luck that the same elderly man as before wasn't stationed at the entrance. It was a young guard whose name Vi couldn't remember. She stashed the bags behind a sculpture two hallways up and then sprinted back down, gulping air to catch her breath so she wasn't winded.

"Report," Vi commanded as she strode into the room.

"Captain!" The man jumped, stuttering over his words. "Nothing new to report. All is quiet."

"How many do we have jailed?"

"Currently, just three here."

"Their crimes?"

"Unruliness… a servant charged with castle theft… one of them is suspected of being a Knight of Jadar." He read off a list.

"No issues from them?" The guard shook his head. Vi forced a gentle smile. "Then I think you should go upstairs and enjoy the festivities."

"Pardon?"

"It's not every night an heir is born. Go, celebrate with the rest for three hours." She hoped it'd be enough time to get Fiera through. If not, Vi would figure out something else when the time came. "I'll take care of things here." Vi punctuated the sentiment with a conspiratorial wink.

"Are you sure?" The man was already headed for the door.

"Absolutely. Go on, have fun, time's ticking." Vi glanced at her watch for emphasis, and when she looked up, he was gone. She counted down a minute before following behind him, backtracking to her supplies, and then returning to the dungeons.

Down into the darkness, Vi wound through the mazes of cells. Even though she'd only been down this way once, Vi walked with confidence. Her mind had instinctively made a map of the area.

With the key Zira had entrusted her with, Vi opened the cell door and pushed the cot aside. She summoned a mote of flame, and her courage with it, before stepping down into the inky blackness of the underground tunnel.

The rapid beating of her heart slowed as Vi ventured further down the path. The tunnel was rough-hewn—cut out from the rock in some places and mortared with stone in others. Every now and then she had to duck underneath a rotting support beam, or sidestep so her and the bags could fit through. But the pitch black of the tunnel's entrance was far more intimidating than the tunnel itself.

There was only one path and it felt like forever. Eventually, much as it had with Erion's escape route, Vi saw the first traces of pale moonlight on the rock. She extinguished her flame and stepped out onto a wide ledge that overlooked a small ravine with the ocean on the other side.

To her right, the cliff stretched upward, peaking at the rich area of town. To her left, the path continued down and away from Norin—out of sight, thanks to the large wall that still bordered the sea on this side. The walkway would be wide enough for a horse, Vi decided as she made her way quickly along it.

She went down far enough that she could see how the path wound through the rocky outcroppings of the cliff, hidden by archways and overhangs, twisting around large boulders, before the path finally blended into the open Waste at the far southern edge of the city.

Armed with this information, Vi sandwiched her bags between two large rocks and sprinted back the way she came.

By the time she arrived at the stables, her side ached and her lungs were burning. Even having worked to keep up her stamina by training with the soldiers, Vi could tell the past few months had been relatively easy on her. She felt soft in places she hadn't in what seemed like years.

"How to get the horses…" Vi murmured, hovering in the shadows near a side door to the castle.

People streamed in and out of the main hall. There were guards everywhere. She could go into the city and steal a random horse. That would certainly be easier.

But Vi didn't want any horse. She needed a warstrider—no, *two* warstriders. The beasts were bred for long, hard rides through the Waste's sands. They had the size and stamina to support two people and supplies with ease. They were her best chance of getting ahead of the Knights.

Vi had a black and white warstrider mare named Midsummer

she'd inherited from Zira. The woman wasn't able take the horse with her, given the circumstances of how she'd left the castle. The creature had been a gift from Fiera and was almost as impressive as the Empress's all-black stallion, Prism.

"All right," Vi said with conviction. If she couldn't convince herself this half-baked lie would work, then how could she expect anyone else to believe it? "Let's do this."

During the next lull in the flow of people, Vi strode out into the stables focusing on one boy who was busy keeping up the tack room.

"You there." He turned to her, looking exhausted. "I need my mount saddled, as well as the Empress's, and taken out. Plain leathers, please. Nothing ceremonial."

For a brief second it seemed like he was going to inquire further. But either he was too tired, or Vi's rank was too high for him to question. The boy nodded and began going about the request.

Vi glanced down the stables. The stable master was hunched over his ledgers, intermittently barking orders at the others. Word must have spread like wildfire of Fiera's labor and some of the nobles who had longer rides were coming into town.

"All set," the boy said, before dragging his feet toward the stable master for his next task.

Sure enough, both horses were ready. Either he'd done quick work or she'd been distracted for longer than she thought. Vi mounted Midsummer, grabbed Prism's reins, and calmly started toward the drawbridge.

A couple nobles and stable hands glanced at her. But Vi kept her pace unhurried, natural. She kept her shoulders back and eyes focused ahead with intensity. She employed everything she'd ever been taught to make herself appear like she was meant to be there, doing what she was meant to be doing.

"Woah there, hold up, just where are you going?" The stable master ran out, stopping her just when she was about to cross onto the drawbridge. Vi didn't have to feign her annoyance.

"I'm taking the Empress's horse to where he'll be boarded for the next few months."

"Excuse me? Boarded?" The man put his hands on his hips and sighed with a shake of his head. "Why does no one tell me anything?" he mumbled.

"Things have been a little hectic," Vi said apologetically. "I only found out last-minute that the Empress has arranged for him to be boarded with a master of horse outside the city. Since she won't be able to ride for a few months, given her condition, she wants to see Prism exercised and trained around young ones. That way he'll be in prime condition when she's ready to ride again with the young prince."

Was training horses to be around babies and children a thing? Vi knew it was for noru.

"Right, right, to Ronaldo I'd bet?" Vi nodded, not having the slightest clue who Ronaldo was. "Makes sense, given he bred the bastard." Despite insulting the mount, the man patted Prism's neck fondly. When he spoke next, it was to the horse, "You be good now. None of that biting, you big oaf."

The man wandered away, and Vi left the castle and city without issue. Once in the Waste, she rode along the outer edge of Norin and back to the rocky area where the path met the sands. Vi tied off the horses and loaded their saddlebags with her supplies. For the second time, she wandered back through the tunnel, up into the dungeons, and back to the jailer's room.

Now, she had nothing to do but wait.

She paced the floor. She poured out a glass of some suspect liquor to take a sip and then abandoned it. She sat for a few minutes, only to find herself unable to be still. She jumped back to her feet.

Every minute that passed felt like a red-hot poker stabbing her palms or feet, making her fingers twitch and her steps hasten.

She couldn't speed up the process of Fiera's labor. She'd risk getting in the way, or not being here when they arrived, if she left. She had to trust Deneya and Fiera... and Yargen, that this would all work out.

Footsteps echoed down the hall and Vi sprinted to the door,

sliding to a stop. The young guard she'd dismissed earlier looked at her, startled.

"S-Sorry to keep you waiting." He clearly mistook her eagerness.

"It's no trouble," Vi said sweetly. Likely too sweet. Her voice was bordering on once-I-stop-being-kind-you-might-end-up-dead. "Merely eager to hear of the status of our Empress."

"That's what I came down to tell you." He beamed from ear to ear. "A Ci'Dan is now the crown prince of the Empire."

Vi tried to stop a bubble of emotion from shooting up her throat, but she couldn't, and it burst forth as an oddly suppressed sound of joy. The man who would become the father to a new Vi had been born. Relief flooded her. It engulfed her in a feeling of rightness that she had finally, finally seen something come to pass according to plan.

"That is truly good news." Vi beamed. Now, Fiera would be sending the clerics away so she could get much needed rest. Deneya would be swiftly healing her. "I can only imagine the party going on up there."

"It's one for the books, that's for sure!" He laughed, quickly sobering when he added, "How about you go and enjoy it?"

"I think you'll have a far better time than I. Take the rest of the night off. There's no issues here."

"Truly?"

"Truly."

The young guard didn't waste another second before sprinting back the way he'd come. Vi continued to hover at the entrance, waiting. She waited there until her foot began to tap, until she had to begin pacing again.

Her watch read just shy of six when Vi heard a single set of footsteps again. She'd have to send him away once more. What excuse would she use this time? Vi was racking her brain when she emerged from the jailer's room.

Unnaturally blue eyes met Vi's own. Nestled in Deneya's arms with sweat-slicked hair and deep circles under her half-open eyes was Fiera. The woman who could always command a room with her mere existence had never looked so small.

They stared at each other long enough that Fiera lifted her head off Deneya's shoulder. Softly, she said, "We should go now. They'll be searching for me soon, and we have important work to do."

WITH THE SUN RISING at their left, they rode hard through the blood-red sands of the Waste.

Fiera was situated in front of Deneya on Prism. The saddle the horse had been initially strapped with was now attached to Vi's mount. Apparently, it was easier to ride double on a horse without a saddle—things Vi had never learned growing up in the North with noru and stable masters always attending her.

The Empress was mostly limp, her head tilted back against Deneya's shoulder. Luckily, the elfin woman was significantly bigger, so she seemed to be having no trouble holding Fiera astride as she drifted in and out of consciousness. Around both of Deneya's forearms near the elbow were brightly shining glyphs that mirrored the one around Vi's wrist.

Halleth maph. Stint pain. Vi focused on Fiera's body overall. Deneya focused one spell on her body as a whole as well. And then one specifically on her nether-regions. Layered as such, Fiera should feel nothing. If she did, she was doing an excellent job hiding it. Not even the bounding of the horse seemed to bother her.

Vi twisted in her saddle, looking behind them. Norin was already a dot far on the horizon. She lifted her free hand and uttered, "*Kot Sorre.*"

Kot was a new word Vi was learning on the go, thanks to Deneya's instruction. She remembered it mentioned in Sehra's book long ago, but there wasn't much on it other than it was a word that covered movement. *Sorre* was to push and *sidee* was pull.

The words burst from her with a surprising amount of force, enough that it had nearly startled her out of her saddle the first time she'd used them. A glyph shone in the distance where Vi directed it, pushing across the dunes. The sand slid over their tracks, covering them.

They continued throughout most of the day. In her time, the Crystal Caverns had long been struck from the maps. But it hadn't been hard for her as a child to suss out where they had been based on various stories, accounts, and poorly modified cartographer's notes. Due south-southeast of Norin was a long stretch of Waste, small, nameless villages dotting the vast sands until they reached the pine forests of the South. Then there would be the town of Mossant. Further south from there were the Caverns.

It was a general idea, but if Vi's instincts proved correct they would be on a more direct path than the Knights of Jadar. They would get to the Caverns first. They had to.

"We need to stop," Deneya said, calling over wind and sand. "The sun is getting high, and we need to give ourselves and the horses a break."

Vi knew that the only person among them who truly needed to rest was Fiera. Deneya's phrasing was merely kindness.

"You're right," Vi reluctantly agreed. She wanted to push onward until the horses' legs gave out and collapsed at the opening of the Caverns. But the journey was going to take at least two days, likely three, even at their aggressive pace. They had to rest eventually. But so would the Knights. No one could make the trek in one burst.

There was nowhere to seek shelter from the sun, so they arbitrarily came to a stop. Vi dismounted first and helped Fiera down; Deneya followed. Fiera had about as much life in her as a limp rag. While Deneya set up a desert tent she'd brilliantly thought to bring, Vi gave Fiera some water from one of the two bladders she'd packed.

"So much blood," Vi murmured.

"You'd be surprised how much blood a woman's body can hold," Fiera said between sips. "Though this is natural for after birth—so the clerics would have me believe."

"How do you feel?" That was the most important thing in Vi's mind.

"I don't feel much of anything," Fiera said lightly, resting her fingertips on the back of Vi's hand and drawing their attention to the glyph around her wrist. "Likely because of these. Are they difficult to make and maintain?"

"Not really, not when you get used to them. I imagine it's much like the wall of flame you kept to protect the sword." The mere mention of the sword soured and silenced her. If only she'd done something more. She should've taken it herself and left Fiera to fate. Her staying had done no one good.

As Vi silently admonished herself, the tent went up and the three huddled in the shade.

"You should rest," Deneya said to Fiera.

"We all should." Fiera laid back, trying to make room. Neither Vi nor Deneya moved to take it. Within moments, she was out.

"Relax your *halleth*," Deneya instructed Vi. "You should recover some of your magic as well."

"So should you."

"Once I know she's deeply asleep, I will."

Vi did as she was told and they both watched Fiera. The woman didn't even stir. Deneya relaxed one of her glyphs as well. Fiera groaned slightly in her sleep, but otherwise, no change.

"I can keep this one." Deneya held up her arm. "Let her get some good rest. I healed most of her tissue… so what's taxing her should only be the physical and mental exhaustion."

Vi looked at Fiera for a long moment and then turned back to Deneya. She didn't want to see the once strong woman so frail. "Thanks for healing her. I'm apparently shite with mending skin."

Deneya chuckled. "It's more of an art, that's for sure."

Vi drew her knees up to her chest, pulling them close and resting her chin on them. She stared out at the desert. In the middle of the day, the Waste was blindingly bright.

"I shouldn't have let her come," Vi murmured, thinking back to her conversation with Fiera on the birthing bed.

"Why did you? I didn't question before, but now I'd like to know."

"She's studied the crystals, more than I have, with books I didn't even think to search for." *If there was a next time…* She dared think the words. She would be sure to tell Taavin to tell the next Champion to seek out tomes from the Burning Times. Perhaps her instincts to manipulate the crystals were right. She just needed to go in a different direction. "She can make a barrier that I'm hoping will be enough to keep the Knights of Jadar and anyone else out of the Caverns. If no one gets into Raspian's tomb, no one meddles with it and he's never set free."

"She doesn't look like she's in a position to do much of anything." Deneya sighed. "I hope she'll make it."

"Me too." Vi still couldn't look back at the woman and mother she still felt like she'd condemned to death. Raylynn would grow up without a mother because of her. Now… if Vi wasn't careful, this world's Aldrik would as well. Her hand had struck the chords of fate and there was dissonance all around.

"I'll take first watch and give the horses some water." Deneya stood. "You should get some sleep."

Vi didn't object. She laid back, wiggling as close as she could to Fiera in the small tent without disturbing the woman. They were face to face, and Vi reached out. With just the side of her pinky, she touched Fiera's open palm. The woman slept on.

I'm sorry, Vi mouthed the words, not daring to say them aloud.

She was sorry for so much that Fiera had and would endure. Sorry for what, regardless of what Taavin said was fated, she felt like she was taking from the world—taking from Aldrik.

But if this worked… Perhaps it would all be worth it.

Perhaps Fiera could yet be right.

Before the dawn of the second day, they crossed into the South. Shrub trees grew up from the Waste. Stubborn grasses became pine-carpeted forests as the canopy stretched higher and higher above them.

Vi still felt a rush tingling through her as the first blustery wind caught her cape, sending it flapping behind her.

"Lyndum," she whispered.

"Pardon?" Deneya asked quietly so as not to disturb the sleeping woman leaned against her. The horses were moving slower now, due to exhaustion and the new terrain. Snowbanks were in the distance, their vast, blinding whiteness as fascinating as it was unnerving to Vi.

They were out of the harshness of the desert, but stepping into a frosty world Vi had never known.

"This was supposed to be my home in another world," Vi confessed. "But I've never come here before."

"Just who were you in this other world?"

Vi looked to Fiera. The woman's head was tipped back and her jaw hung open. She slept more than she was awake. But every time she woke she seemed stronger than the last.

"Her granddaughter," Vi admitted. "Well, the granddaughter of a woman very much like her. I know that's likely impossible to believe but—"

"I don't really think so," Deneya interrupted. "You have the same face."

Vi chuckled softly. "Everyone told me so. Now I got to see it for myself and… I don't know, we seem different enough. She's stronger than I am."

"Self-doubt doesn't suit you."

"Maybe it's not so much doubt as it is finally being honest with myself about my own limitations?"

Deneya clicked her tongue. "Humility, reasonableness, they're good traits. Can't argue, won't argue. But… I've seen a shift in you these past few days. You were so self-assured. Now you seem like you're doubting each step you take."

"Failure has a high price, and I'm paying it." She had some hesitations now, what was the harm in it? "Taavin was right this whole time and I didn't listen. I might not be able to make up for it now… nonetheless, I'm trying to be more careful."

"Take care in deciding where to step, so when you do, you're certain of your path," Deneya advised. "You keep looking back. Those decisions have been made and the ink in the history books is already dry. Keep your eyes forward."

Vi nodded, twisting the reins in her fingers. Deneya was right: forward was the only path for them now. Forward into the snowdrifts that stretched across the forest floors from the last vestiges of winter. Forward to the place where every line of fate collided.

"Now, how much longer until we're at this town you mentioned?"

"Mossant? If we push, we might get there before the day is done."

"Good, I'd like a bed."

There wasn't much conversation for the rest of the day. Each of them was dead tired. The inside of Vi's thighs ached and her fingers had gone numb. They'd prepared for the Waste, but Vi hadn't packed appropriately for snow and cold.

In Mossant they restocked and slept at an inn for a night. The horses had time to rest and be fed properly. They were warm and safe. It was the best possible thing for them right before their final push to the Caverns.

The main road in and out of Mossant lead to the Great Imperial

Way. That was the road they had come in from. But the road they left on was far less maintained.

It was more of a hunting path. Branches reached out for them, trying to snag on their packs and clothes. The overgrowth was annoying and, to Vi, oddly comforting. Had a group of Knights come trudging through, they would've left their mark on the frail branches. The absence of any such tracks meant they were still ahead of the Knights—for now.

That night, they laid eyes on the entrance to the Crystal Caverns. They came to a stop at the edge of a ridge. Switchbacks led down to a valley where Vi could see they curved up and around once more to a narrow cliff.

"So, that's it, then," Deneya spoke first. Her breath appeared as a cloud in the fading light of day.

"That's been the cause of my family's shame…" Fiera murmured. The birth hadn't been too hard on her—or Lightspinning was far superior to Waterrunners and clerics of the Dark Isle—and the Empress was far more alert after staying at the inn than she had been in days.

Set into the mountain face was a large, pointed archway carved directly into the stone. It was a gaping hole that Vi suspected was positively massive up close. Carvings of wyrms and men surrounded the archway.

Raspian.

A shiver ripped through her. She could almost feel his presence curdling in her stomach like cream mixed with vinegar. She felt the edge of his magic in the air like red electricity right before it collected into a bolt of lightning.

"How could anyone see this as something to tamper with?" Vi mused aloud.

"Men are ambitious fools," Fiera said dryly.

"Judging from the snow, we're still ahead of them," Deneya observed. She sounded as uncomfortable as Vi. "Let's get this over with."

THE MOON HAD JUST risen when they arrived at the entrance on foot. Their horses were tied off down the mountain, behind some large rocks and out of sight. Vi used *kot* to hide their footprints once more.

Deneya went in first, followed by Fiera. Vi approached the entrance but stopped, hovering where the snowdrift met the stone pathway within. An invisible force pushed outward like the dying sigh of a dragon. She stared up at the icicles that lined the top of the archway, imagining they were teeth. Imagining they might come crashing down on her at any moment.

"Yullia?" Deneya called back. "Is everything all right?"

Nothing was right about this place. "I'm fine."

Vi crossed the threshold. The moment her boot met the crystal-dusted floor of the Caverns, turquoise magic pulsed outward like a ripple in water. She felt magic ebb and flow from her as ripples reverberated all over the stones, bouncing off each other, reaching every corner. They illuminated the magical veins in the walls, columns of crystal becoming sources of light.

"What did you do?" Deneya asked.

"I don't know." Vi shook her head and took another step forward. This time, there were no other pulses of magic.

"Well, now we have some light, at least." Fiera gave a slow turn. "It's large enough to fit a palace in here…"

Now that she could see properly, Vi assessed the Caverns. A pathway had been cut through the center—perhaps it had been made that way from the beginning—leading to another smaller archway. The ceiling was so high above them that it was merely a hazy blue, motes of Yargen's magic falling toward them like snowflakes.

"A palace of death," Deneya muttered.

"What?"

"Don't you feel it?" Deneya asked Fiera. Vi could. "This place… it's *wrong*."

"Wrong or right… let's set up this barrier." Vi turned to Fiera. The faster they could get out of here, the better. Perhaps, if they moved quickly enough, they could get out of sight before the Knights arrived and there would be time yet to return Fiera to the West. Vi's heart skipped a beat, nearly tripping her on hope.

"Let's go farther in." Fiera pointed to the inner archway. "I need a smaller opening to attach the barrier to. I can't just make it in the air and the main entrance is too large."

"All right," Vi agreed, solely to buy herself time to think. She needed to protect the Caverns—to prevent people from entering entirely. If Fiera needed something to attach the barrier to, then perhaps she could use *juth calt* to collapse the archway? If she did that, then—

"What's that?" Deneya asked, taking a few hasty steps forward.

They'd crossed into another antechamber, smaller, but the crystals were larger here. They felt older. Their power ran even deeper below the earth, to a realm beyond Vi's perceptions.

Deneya squeezed through the center of two massive stone doors, barely pulled open.

"What's in there?" Vi called.

"I don't know," Deneya's voice echoed back.

Vi and Fiera shared a look before they proceeded up a few stone stairs and into the final chamber of the Crystal Caverns.

Here, crystals spiraled outward from a center point. They were embedded into the stone and glowed faintly, a dull thrum of power brightening and dulling with every step Vi took around the perimeter. The stones at the edge of the area were three times the size of her, brought to wickedly sharp tips.

She walked to the center of the room, crouching down and running her fingertips over the ground where all the magic seemed to pool together. Deep below the stone, encased in a place that was only partly anchored in this world, was an evil she knew by name. Vi slowly stood, backing away from that deep and rumbling pulse that made her tremble.

"The doors will do," she declared. "This is the source of it all. This is where the true power lies." She looked to Deneya. "This is where Raspian is trapped and where no man must reach."

"Raspian?" Fiera repeated, understandably confused.

"A dark god," Vi answered, starting for the doors once more. She didn't want to linger longer than necessary. It felt as if any moment the ground would crack and Raspian would reach through the mantle of the earth to consume her and all of Yargen's power whole. "The one thing we must ensure is never set free."

Fiera narrowed her eyes slightly at her. Out of everything, this was what made her skeptical. Vi finally found the limits of what Fiera's mind was willing to accept.

"Let's close the doors to this room and seal them." Vi wondered if the doors had been sealed once before. Perhaps King Jadar had been the one to find a way to open them with his captive Windwalkers. "Denja, help me?"

"What about the other crystals? Those out here?"

"I think… the Crystal Caverns were originally just this room and, over time, the magic spread to take over the whole cave," Vi mused. "The crystals are older and older the further we go back.

But the crux of it all is here. This is what we have to protect."

Back in the second antechamber, Vi and Deneya faced the doors.

"*Kot*, at the same time, then?" Deneya asked.

Vi nodded.

Together, they uttered, "*Kot sidee*." It felt as though someone pulled a rope through her chest as the magic came toward her. Vi took a step backward, watching her glyph crash against the other side of the door in tandem with Deneya's. The heavy stone groaned loudly, and closed with a heavy *thud*.

"Will this work for your barrier?" Vi asked Fiera.

The woman was in a daze, staring blankly at the room they'd just been in. She took a step forward and, for one second, Vi thought she was about to ask them to open it once more. Vi saw the same hunger in her eyes that she'd seen in Tiberus: hunger for power.

"Can you make a barrier over the doors?" Vi asked again, gently resting her hand on Fiera's shoulder.

"Wh—*oh*, yes, I think I can." Fiera blinked several times, as though the world was coming back into focus.

"Show me how to do it."

"I usually have the sword for it…" Fiera started uncertainly. After they'd sprinted across half of the continent, now was not the time to hesitate.

"There are a lot of crystals here. Perhaps you can show me the motions using the magic of those instead." Vi encouraged her to continue.

"With the sword, I imagined the power imbuing the stone the Groundbreakers had built. It knotted with their magic and reinforced it. As though the sword was the pin holding every magical chain together."

Vi could imagine it. But imagining something and putting it to practice were two very different things. And there were obvious gaps in Fiera's summary.

"How did you do it?" Vi pressed.

"It's hard to explain. Magic… *appeared* in my mind. Something

I can't make sense of—like a Crone speaking in tongues. But the sword was what helped me make sense of it all."

Crossing over, Vi took the woman's hand in hers, giving it a squeeze.

"The sword isn't here now. But I am, and I will help you," Vi vowed. "I know this magic, too. In a different way from you. But together, we can do this."

Fiera opened her mouth in hesitation, then gave a small nod, abandoning any protest.

Together, they strode up to the door, standing at its right side. Fiera timidly rested her hand on one of the large crystals. Vi mirrored the motion, closing her eyes, and allowing herself to feel the magic within.

"Come to me," Fiera whispered, her voice thin and almost afraid. "Mother, come to me."

Vi tried to feel the magic seeping up from her marrow as she'd practiced, meeting the crystal under her palm. She drew on the crystal, allowing it to fill her, allowing it to be a catalyst. Yargen was within her. If Fiera had faith in the goddess, then so would Vi. She would entrust her mind and her actions into Yargen's hands.

The stone drew her closer and Vi breathed, "*Thrumsana*," her lips nearly touching the smooth crystal as though she had been subconsciously about to kiss it.

Magic flooded her. It swelled up from the crystal and ripped through her. Vi was helpless to the currents and allowed herself to be pulled along them. There was sound, but not of the same sort the first time she'd used the word. This was not the chaos that had assaulted Taavin.

A thrumming disturbed her thoughts. Vi opened her eyes once more to find Fiera drawing lines of flame along the door. But rather than burning orange, they burned blue.

"Fiera…" Vi whispered in awe.

The woman held out her left pinkie, swirling it through the air, as though she were a spinner drawing magic onto the spool. With the index finger of her right hand, she drew across the door. Lines and circles, interconnecting. The flames burned low and bright, lingering long after she finished them.

Vi quickly stepped around to Fiera's other side. She grabbed one crystal with her left hand and took Fiera's magic spinning hand with her right. Fiera looked at her a moment, her trance-like state startled.

"Keep going," Vi encouraged. "Let me be a catalyst for you."

Fiera nodded and then turned back to the door as though she was facing off against a great opponent. She took a deep breath, and threw herself back into her countless lines of flame. Vi drew out the crystal's powers just as she had practiced all those nights with the sword. But when Vi had extracted the crystal's magic before, she hadn't known what to do with it. Fiera did. So she funneled the magic through her and into Fiera.

The woman's flames began to harden, condensing into crystal. Fiera worked faster—every motion more decisive, every line wrought with fierce determination.

She slumped, nearly falling back. Vi caught her only because she'd already been holding the woman's hand.

"I'm fine," Fiera said before Vi could ask. "I must finish this… I must."

Fiera continued with her determined fervor. Blue fire illuminated the room as much as crystals did. But every wild motion of Fiera's hand seemed to throw her off-balance. Her cheeks were gaunt, her eyes dull.

"Fiera, stop this," Vi whispered.

"What you said… it told me, I have to finish this. I heard it. I heard what must be done."

Thrumsana… Taavin had told her never to use a word of power unless she fully understood what it did. This was the second time she'd used it on instinct. Just like the first, someone was suffering for her carelessness, trapped by the magic *thrumsana* unleashed.

"Fiera—"

"It's nearly finished."

"Vi," Deneya gasped. Her shock was so apparent that she didn't even think to use the name Yullia in front of Fiera. "It's a glyph. It's a word of Yargen."

Fiera pressed her palm into the center of the flames. Everything erupted at once. Fiera was thrown back, Vi with her. They tumbled and Deneya rushed forward, catching them both on an arm and easing their fall.

Vi looked from Fiera, slumped in Deneya's arm, body limp and eyes closed, to the symbol on the door.

Just like with Sehra's book, sounds filled her ears. The fire crystalized, cementing itself as fragile crystals on the door. In it, Vi saw a glyph of Yargen. A word that Vi had never heard or seen before.

"*Rohko*," Vi breathed.

The chorus in her mind snapped into harmony. Everything came together at once as the thin crystal lines Fiera had made spiderwebbed out, growing as though time was progressing at twice its normal speed.

In less than a minute, the doors were covered by faintly glowing stone. And the innermost chamber of the Crystal Caverns—Raspian's tomb—was sealed.

"Fiera, Fiera," Vi said, shaking the woman. Deneya had laid her down carefully on the walkway, murmuring *halleth* over her again and again.

"There's something strange about her." Deneya's head jerked up, her eyes worried. "I can't describe it. Her magic—Yargen's magic… There's something *in* her now, something that wasn't there before."

"Crystal taint," Vi whispered in knowing horror. "Because their powers are fractured, the affinities on this continent can be tainted by Yargen's magic. She'd avoided it with the sword now and I dared to think…" Vi cursed under her breath. She'd been the one to pump Fiera's body with power from the crystals. "I don't have time to explain it properly—we just have to get her out of here. She'll be fine if we can get her away from the crystals."

"Then let's go." Deneya shifted and slid her arms underneath Fiera, lifting the woman with ease.

"Are all elfin so unnaturally strong?" Vi asked. She'd seen

Deneya carry Fiera like that to leave the castle. The woman didn't even grunt with the exertion. And Fiera was no small woman.

"I make it a point to train regularly." Deneya gave her a smug grin, then turned her head further, looking back at the door that was now sealed. "What happened? And that word you used, it made her create the glyph in flame…"

"It's one Yargen gave me," Vi affirmed.

"What does it do?"

"Excellent question…" Vi reflected once more on the past two times she'd used it as they walked through the archway and back into the main chamber of the Crystal Caverns. "I think it awakens some kind of knowledge or awareness in someone?"

"Like *samasha* to a Lightspinner just beginning?"

"Perhaps something like that." It felt like a lifetime ago that Vi had *samasha* used on her and she had to work to remember what Taavin had said the word meant. "But for more than just the words of Yargen. I think to some greater truth or purpose."

"I'm surprised Taavin hasn't told you not to use words until you're certain of what they mean. In this time, that's a standard warning from the Voice."

"Oh, he did… But perhaps Yargen gave me that one because of my recklessness." Vi wondered what Taavin would think when she told him of how the word had been used again. After all she'd done, Vi doubted he'd be surprised.

Movement at the entrance of the cave caught Vi's eye. In the time it took for her to look, the archer had already loosed his arrow. She opened her mouth, but no sound came. The projectile moved faster than thought, faster than she could react.

For those brief moments, they'd felt victorious. The world had been hopeful. And Vi had almost dared to feel safe.

The arrow lodged itself through Fiera's neck and into Deneya's shoulder. Deneya dropped to her knees with a shout. Vi stared at the crimson tide pouring from them both.

So much blood. How did Fiera still have blood left to bleed? The macabre thought was the only one Vi could wrap her head around.

"Vi!" Deneya snarled, snapping off the fletching of the arrow and sliding Fiera off of it. The woman was limp on the ground, as dead as Zira had been.

Halleth. Her mind placed the word on her tongue. But Vi was silent. There was no word to bring back the dead.

Vi slowly lifted her gaze. The world was fuzzy. The haze of the crystals had never been so bright or thick. She felt drunk, and everything seemed to have a nauseating tilt. Her motions and thoughts had a sluggish delay.

She saw the men running toward them. The archer nocking another arrow.

"*Juth calt*," the words slipped through someone else's lips. They couldn't be hers. Everything had gone numb. The archer seized and fell. Vi wrought her wrath next on the man running through the opening of the cave. Again, she repeated, "*juth calt*."

Kill them all.

Clearly that was the simplest solution. She should've done it from the start. Holding back was a fool's decision.

She was the agent of the goddess, a traveler between worlds. What good was humanity to her now?

The Knights of Jadar had been an enemy of her family. In every world, they rallied against Solaris. In every world, they resulted in the death of Vi's grandmother and left her father motherless. It had been her vision to break that cycle.

A vision that was now tunneled.

"*Juth calt*." Another body fell, and fire exploded in front of her face.

Vi was tackled off to the side, a heavy body on top of her. "*Wein*," she heard Deneya say in her ear. Magic engulfed them and another burst of flame charred the woman's barrier but left her unharmed.

"Get off of me," Vi demanded. "Get off of me!" she roared. "I'll kill them. I'll kill them all!"

Vi pushed on the stump of the arrow, still in Deneya's shoulder.

The woman howled and reared back. Vi launched to her feet.

"Keep her at bay!" Twintle shouted and more flames erupted around Vi.

"Do you think you can hurt me with your fractured magic?" Vi asked as she stepped through the fire, emerging on the other side. "I am part goddess. What do you think your flames will do?"

A Waterrunner was the response to her question as ice formed around her feet. Vi tugged against it, allowing her spark to roar, echoing the chaos in her mind. The ice turned to vapor as Vi glared at Twintle.

"I should've done this months ago," she snarled. "*Juth calt.*"

His body limply meeting the floor was the sweetest sound she'd heard in ages.

"Watch out! *Wein!*" Deneya shouted, stepping in front of Vi, her body acting as a shield. An arrow bounced harmlessly off of the protective barrier her word of power formed over Deneya's skin. "There's too many of them, we have to get out of here."

"We can take them." Vi motioned to the bodies on the ground. With two words, she'd killed four men. "They're nothing compared to us."

"I will not twist Yargen's words in that way." Deneya grabbed her wrist. "How you are using *juth* is the work of elfin'ra."

"It's the work of the Champion," Vi countered.

"What sorcery is this?" a voice echoed from within the antechamber, distracting them both. He very clearly wasn't talking about their magic. "It won't open." Vi rushed toward the center aisle once more, looking back at the Knights who fought against the barrier of crystal that covered the doors.

They slammed the sword of Jadar against it again and again. But the barrier held. Vi reached out for one of the pointed crystals protruding from the floor at her side. She forced her power into the stone, exerting her will and feeling it rush from crystal to crystal, maintaining the barrier at the door. The sword wasn't even chipping it. The fools had no idea how to wield the power of Yargen.

"What have you done?" the nameless Knight shouted at her.

Vi merely smiled. She smiled like a madman, baring her teeth, even as an arrow punctured her arm that was grabbing the crystal.

"Flee," Deneya yelled at them, her voice echoing off the high rooftop of the Caverns. "Run, as quickly as you can. Hide back under the rock you crawled from and never show your face again. Fiera's blood lives on and will guard these Caverns until the end of time."

The men began to run back toward them and Vi watched them sprint past. They regarded her with wary eyes, as though she was the blood of which Deneya spoke. The three were almost at the entrance to the Caverns when she rapid-fired, "*Juth calt. Juth calt. Juth calt.*"

One by one, they fell. The crystal sword clattered to the ground at the entrance, skittering away from the last man's lifeless hands. The rest of the Knights had already fled down the mountainside and Vi doubted they would dare return for the sword. Especially not if she killed them first.

Vi took a step forward, ready to give chase.

"Enough." Two strong arms wrapped around her like the thick ropes of a ship. Vi writhed against them and Deneya hoisted her upward. The pain in Vi's arm seared in a way that almost felt delightful. "Enough!"

"I should've killed them ages ago when I had the chance." Vi kicked her feet, trying to break free of Deneya's hold. The woman was a rock behind her.

"But you didn't because it's not you," Deneya shouted in her ear over Vi's grunts and snarls. "You didn't because you aren't a cold-blooded murderer."

"Clearly I am!" The darkness had finally overwhelmed her. Vi felt completely charred. Just when hope had begun to take root again, she burnt it away. Giving in was easier. "I am worse than them; I can be worse than all of them."

"But you're not. And you should never try to be."

"This is what the world needs me to be."

"The world needs compassion from its Champion, not killing.

You can kill a thousand men, Vi, but their blood won't quench that fire burning within you."

Vi went still and pressed her eyes closed. Her head dipped and her chin nearly touched her chest as she hung limply. Deneya set her back down gingerly. When it was clear Vi wouldn't fight any longer, she unraveled her arms.

"I don't know what pain fuels your flames, but I can see you're burning alive."

Her head jerked upward and Vi stared, slack-jawed at the woman. She felt seen. For the first time in a long time, someone other than Taavin could see her. Really see her. It was terrifying and vulnerable, but in an oddly welcome way. Vi gave in to the sensation, leaning forward and pressing her forehead against Deneya's uninjured shoulder.

"I wanted to save her," Vi choked out. "I wanted to save her, and Zira, and I wanted to stop the Knights."

"I know." Deneya stroked her hair like a child. Like they weren't awash in blood and surrounded by bodies. "But you protected the Caverns."

"No…" Vi pulled away and looked to Fiera. "*She* did. Even though I was the Champion, she was the one who sealed the Caverns." Vi staggered over and knelt down next to Fiera's body. She tucked a stray strand of hair away from the woman's face, thinking back to Zira. She hadn't even given the woman a proper Rite of Sunset. "Help me?"

Deneya nodded and walked over. She first healed her shoulder and Vi's arm, murmuring, "*halleth ruta sot*," twice. Then she scooped up Fiera and brought the body out onto the cliff. The snow was churned up, rocks jutting out where footsteps had crunched through to the ground below.

"Set her there." Vi pointed to a mostly clear area. "We'll send her off at sunset."

"What about the rest of them?" Deneya and Vi both turned back, looking at the carnage still littering the Caverns. "You can't leave them be."

"I could. They're traitors and murderers." Vi thought back to how Fiera had handled the traitors in the streets. What had been mere months ago now felt like years.

"All men deserve a proper sendoff. Even the worst among them," Deneya insisted. Out of everything Vi had expected the woman to be for her, a moral compass wasn't one of them.

Vi barely stopped herself from disagreeing. She wanted to. But the sentiment struck a chord with her—it sounded like something her mother would've said.

Vhalla Yarl, the woman Vi knew, was gone now. But every act she took was still a testament to her memory. That world was gone, save for what lived on in her. Was she becoming a woman her mother would be proud of?

"Pile them up off to the side. I'll burn them all at once." *It was better than they deserved,* a nagging voice told her in the back of her mind. But treating them like men, rather than meat, quieted the darkness that had consumed her and reminded Vi of her humanity. If only slightly.

Deneya carried the bodies from the deepest part of the Caverns. Vi couldn't quite lift the men at the opening, but she could push them along with the careful use of *kot sorre.* By the afternoon, the bodies were all lined up in the snow, waiting to be burned.

Vi finally went over to where the sword had fallen. She stared at it for a long moment, as though all the blood that had fallen had been wrought by this singular blade. Finally, she hoisted it for the first time in what felt like an eternity.

The weapon shone brightly with power. The whole of the Crystal Caverns seemed to glow brighter for a moment as the hilt met her fingers.

This was the magic she had been expecting all along. The sword no longer felt thin and weak, but recharged with the essence of Yargen. The more pieces of Yargen's power Vi drew together, the stronger they all became.

"Well, you have it and the Caverns are sealed... what now?" Deneya asked, sitting with her back propped against the archway.

"That's an excellent question." Vi twisted the sword in the light before setting it down carefully on a bed of crystals. "*Narro hath hoolo.*"

The magic spun out from her watch as it always had. But instead of being the usual orange-yellow glyph, this time it was a pale blue. Vi watched as Taavin was cut out from the empty air, color seeping into his outline before the magic vanished entirely. She watched as he blinked, focus coming to his eyes before he turned to her.

"Vi—" Taavin stopped himself mid-turn, frozen.

"Taavin?" Vi asked cautiously, taking a small step forward. The wind tousled his hair and Taavin shivered, as though he could feel the cold. As though he were—her hand closed around his. "Are you?"

"It's the magic of the Caverns," he murmured, pulling his eyes from the crystals surrounding them and looking to her. "It heightens everything."

It makes you real, Vi wanted to say. She could feel the puffs of cool air that curled by her cheek. Vi searched his eyes, wanting to touch him all over. Wanting to savor this moment. But knowing it was not the time or place.

"You made it," he continued, as if he wasn't feeling the same ache she was. "And the sword?"

"Here." Vi took a hasty step away and grabbed the sword. "And Raspian's tomb has been sealed once more."

"Sealed?"

"We can show you," Vi offered.

As they walked back through the Caverns, Vi and Deneya gave him the quick run-down of everything that had transpired. Vi filled Taavin in on the conversation she'd had with Fiera. Deneya told him of her healing Fiera, and the woman's determination to come and defend the Caverns—to right the wrongs of her forefathers.

The short walk to the sealed door wasn't nearly enough time to cover everything. But they got through the broad strokes before Taavin's focus was drawn elsewhere. He let out a gasp the moment he laid eyes on the door.

"What… what is this?" His confusion had never delighted her more.

"*Rohko*," Vi said aloud. The word was as strong as a cornerstone, able to support the immense weight of a building without cracking. "Is this barrier… this word from the goddess, is it new?"

She hoped against hope, and Vi nearly let out an involuntary noise of relief when Taavin gave a small nod. He was still trying to consume the doorway with his eyes. It wasn't enough; he slowly approached the doors, resting his fingertips lightly on the crystal barrier that seemed to have already grown thicker.

"You have the sword. The Knights didn't get in. There's a barrier," he murmured, as if trying to keep it straight in his own head.

"I'm no expert at all this. But we did well, I think." Deneya folded her arms over her chest.

"Only one thing will tell—" Taavin turned, looking down at Vi. "Have you peered forward yet?"

"Not yet." She didn't know if she was ready to. She didn't know if her heart could take what she might see. If she saw a future of light, what did that mean for the rest of her time as a traveler in this world without a home of her own? If she saw a future of darkness… Did that mean the sacrifices made to get here had been for nothing?

"You have to," Taavin said, as if he, too, was riding the tumultuous currents of her thoughts.

Neither of them wanted to hope. Ignorance would be kinder.

But the goddess hadn't been kind to either of them when she'd given them this duty.

Vi held out the sword between two open palms and took a deep breath. She drew power from the Caverns—in through her feet, leeching it from the air like moisture to a plant. A blue flame erupted over the flat of the blade before her and Vi stared directly at it, her heart racing.

She wasn't ready. But that didn't matter. The world washed in white.

And all Vi could do was brace herself for the future.

31

T HE LIGHT FADED INTO darkness.

Vi blinked several times, looking around. Slowly, shapes came into focus. A thin, bright line of crimson circled the horizon perfectly. It continued in all directions. But Vi couldn't tell if it was from an early dawn, about to break, or the last light of sunset vanishing from the world.

The color bled upward, casting the clouded depths of the sky in a bloody ombre. At the top, the clouds parted, the heavens had opened, and stars stretched to infinity. It was as though she stood on the top of the world. Everything stretched outward from this place where the earth and sky met.

A crack of red lightning struck from sky to ground. There, on the steaming rock, was the hulking, godly form of death and darkness incarnate. Raspian's skin was red and shining, like a blood-filled ruby. From his skeletal visage to his writhing hair, Vi knew the face of death. He turned his eyes to her, snarling and baring his razor-sharp teeth.

Oddly, she wasn't afraid.

She stood in a well of calm and strength. There was a prevailing sense of rightness with the world. Rightness at facing off against this wretched creature.

Once and for all.

Vi took a step forward without thinking. More like, the body she was in stepped forward. Most of her visions had Vi as an outside observer, but this time she was rooted in another form. A form that sprang wildflowers from barren earth with a single step.

A hand appeared in her field of vision—her hand, or the hand of the person she was in. Every color of the rainbow splashed across the woman's body, brilliantly bright, deep and rich. The colors were so vibrant, Vi thought they'd sear into her eyes forever and make everything else seem dull.

Clutched in the woman's hand was a blue staff.

The staff of the Champion.

Raspian tilted his head up to the sky and let out a cry that seemed to shake the earth itself. The woman braced herself, guarding against a shock-wave of magic that radiated out from the man. Vi tipped her head back and gaze skyward to see the moon had appeared in the center of the clouds. It was cracked, like an egg, a dark red yolk pouring at Raspian's feet and collecting in the shape of a great dragon.

Still, the person Vi occupied didn't panic. Though Vi certainly felt like she should.

As the dragon took its shape, cut from primordial essence, Raspian lifted his hand, pointing at the staff the woman still held outright.

"Let it be done," he said without moving his jaw. The words seemed to resonate as thoughts, grating sharply in Vi's mind. She wanted to wince, but she was subject to the vision before her.

She couldn't turn away, even if she'd wanted to, as Raspian lunged for her. Lunged for the woman whom Vi knew at her core was Yargen herself.

Vi returned to the world with a sudden jolt, right as Raspian launched his first attack. The sword clattered to the ground as it slipped from her limp hands. Her arms swung at her sides and Vi staggered, forward and back. She gripped her head with one hand, her stomach with the other. The unnatural calm of Yargen had left her, and now Vi was filled with a panic that tasted like sickness.

"Vi." Two hands on her shoulders. Stable, sturdy, warm, all the things she'd been missing for months. "What did you see?" Taavin asked softly.

She shook her head, leaning forward and pressing her face into his shoulder. Taking a deep breath, Vi inhaled the scent of him. Somehow, he still smelled faintly of the incense that burned in Risen a world away, and sunlight on a warm summer's day. She missed those scents a painful amount.

"Vi, you need to—"

"Give her a moment, she's been through enough," Deneya snapped.

A soft huff of amusement slipped through Vi's lips and Taavin's arms closed around her. She let out a sigh. *Let this embrace never end*, Vi wished.

She did not pray. Because she knew what gods would be out there to hear her prayers. Vi didn't want to leave her delicate wishes in either of their warring hands.

"Raspian is set free," she finally whispered.

Taavin released her, almost pushing her back as though her words had burned him. He held her at arm's length. As though with her, he could hold away her vision and prevent it from coming to pass.

"What?"

"Raspian is set free," she repeated, louder. "He gains a physical form, I saw it."

"I don't understand." Deneya took a step forward, physically inserting herself into their conversation. "We sealed the Caverns. You have the sword. How do they manipulate the tomb?"

"There are other crystal weapons. The crystals will never be safe," Taavin muttered. His arms dropped to his sides and he slumped, swayed, righted himself, and then swayed again.

"No, they'll never be safe on this land," Vi agreed easily. Perhaps there was some of Yargen's unnatural calm still in her. Or perhaps feeling Taavin there had given her a peace she'd long since given up on.

No matter what, they were opened. They couldn't stop the Crystal Caverns from being destroyed, not even after ninety-three times. Not even after what had seemed like their best showing yet, despite all Vi's shortcomings.

Vi slowly ascended the steps to the crystal-coated doors. She ran her hands along the stone. Feeling the deeply rooted magic within.

Destruction always reaped destruction.

"Maybe that's it."

"What is?" Deneya asked. Even Taavin stopped his murmuring.

Vi turned to face Taavin, bracing herself for what she already knew his reaction would be. "Maybe that's been our error all along."

"What has?" Taavin lowered his hand to look at her with his piercing green eyes.

"All these times, we've been trying to stop the Caverns from being opened, stop Raspian from being set free."

"That is your job—to change the fate of the world and prevent that."

"But what if there's another way?" Vi asked. The words felt like blasphemy ignited by a spark of red lightning in the darkness. "I'm supposed to change fate, but keep enough the same that I'm reborn. I have to alter the outcome of events, but accept that some things will always happen. Don't you think it sounds rather impossible?"

"If it were easy—"

"—we would've already done it, I know," Vi finished hastily. "Think about it," she implored him. "What was the problem in our world? What were we trying to stop?"

"The Crystal Caverns were destroyed and Raspian was set free." Taavin played along.

"Now, think about it in a different way. Why was Raspian being set free a problem?" She'd talk him through it so he'd understand. So she could vet this mad idea that had overtaken her.

"Because he's evil and darkness incarnate."

"Because Yargen *couldn't stop him*, because her power was fractured by the crystal weapons being destroyed across time," Vi corrected. "If Raspian was set free, but Yargen had all of her power, she could face him once more. It would be like every other war of light and dark through the ages."

"Stop." Taavin held up both his hands. "You're thinking about *letting* Raspian be set free?"

"Yes. And I know how it sounds," Vi added hastily. "But no matter what we've done, throughout the history of the Dark Isle, men have sought out the Crystal Caverns. They will continue to. Even if we're successful, Yargen's magic and Raspian's tomb will never be safe as long as they're within the reach of power-hungry people—here on the Dark Isle or anywhere else.

"What if, rather than stopping the Caverns from being opened, we focus instead on merely preserving Yargen's power? We store it in the Caverns. We allow the crystal weapons to be brought here as time dictates so a new Champion can be reborn, just in case I'm wrong."

Taavin nodded approvingly at that sentiment.

"We preserve the events that must happen to see a new Champion born. We allow the crystal weapons to come here, and allow the people of this world to *think* they've been destroyed. On the surface, it will all look the same—or same enough. But we'll hold the ace. We'll transfer the power from the crystal weapons into the Caverns, rather than allow them to be destroyed."

"Can you do that?" Deneya asked skeptically.

"With enough time to practice." Vi lifted her hand off the crystals, feeling the way the magic clung to her. She'd seen Fiera work to manipulate the crystals. She'd already begun exploring the notion herself before that.

"So we allow time to progress, ensure that all the stones in the river and Apexes of Fate are attended to, to see a new Champion reborn," Taavin started, somewhat hesitantly. "But when the weapons are brought here, throughout time, you'll transfer their power to the Caverns?"

"Yes." Vi knew what she was about to say next would be the hardest for them to swallow. "Then, when all of her power is here, we will be the ones to open the Caverns, properly."

"Wait…" Deneya tilted her head to the side, processing. "Tell me I can't be following this right. You want to be the one who sets Raspian free?"

"If I do it, I'll make sure all of Yargen's power is collected beforehand so she can do battle." *And she will win*, that quiet calmness from her vision assured Vi. "Once she is victorious, she will seal him away somewhere new—somewhere far from this place and far from the knowledge of men who would try to tap into power they don't understand for nefarious purposes. It'll not only ensure success in this time, but the safety of the world for eons to come."

Taavin turned away from her, as if he couldn't even bear looking at her when she presented him with this theory. He ran his hands through his dark, plum colored hair, short waves curling around his fingers.

"He can only be set free by destroying the seal on the Crystal Caverns, which means turning the part of Yargen's magic that's contained within the crystal weapons against the portion of her magic that's here in the Caverns. Which results in the Caverns weakening and ultimate destruction."

"But does it have to?" Vi asked, an honest question. She let it hover in the air, waiting to see his response. When there was none, she repeated, "Does it have to? Or… do you not know?"

"I can't claim to know all the details of her power. I have the benefit of experience, but that still only comes from trial and error."

"And have we tried this?"

"No."

"What happens if we fail?" Vi dared to ask, though she already suspected the answer.

"Everything repeats again." He turned back to look at her with his dread-filled eyes.

"Then I think it's worth trying," Vi said definitively. "Maybe, with a few years' time here, I could learn how to use the crystals for purposes beyond just transferring their power. With all of Yargen's power collected here, I have to believe we can break the seal without destroying her magic." *Rohko* was in her mind—to seal. If the word could make a seal, perhaps it could also be used to break one. "And if I'm wrong in that assumption… then the new Vi, the new Champion, will face whatever happens then."

"Your plan works, assuming Yargen is able to return to the world and—"

"She does," Vi interrupted Taavin. "She was in my vision, facing off against Raspian. What if that vision wasn't of failure, but of success? What if that's what she wanted us to work to all along?"

Vi descended the stairs hastily, crossed over to him, and stopped short as she was pinned in place by his wary eyes.

"Is she always this insane?" Deneya asked Taavin. Even in his state, he managed a nod. Vi ignored it.

"If we're working to see a Vi born in this age, we know when the crystal weapons will come. Their fate is linked with Solaris. They'll all return here, in the end, in the hands of my family… And I'll be ready to meet them when they do.

"Thanks to your memories, I'll know where they'll come from. I know how they'll get here. I can shepherd time along. Rather than trying to completely alter fate, I'll just nudge it in the right direction."

Vi had no idea if her plan would work. But she was ready to defend it and continue defending it. She no longer just wanted to keep Raspian sealed away. She wanted to see Yargen usher in a new age of light. She wanted the one thing she'd always wanted: To keep her family safe.

And Solaris would never be safe as long as the crystal weapons and Caverns existed on the continent.

Deneya folded and unfolded her arms, as though she was

uncomfortable in her own body. Taavin paced several times. The silence grew heavy.

"You know what you're suggesting, right?" he finally said. "You know what it means for the people you love?"

"I do," Vi whispered softly.

"This idea of guiding time, guiding events that happened before…"

"Means people will be hurt as they have always been," she finished for him, for once reading his mind. "People will die," she corrected herself, not wanting to mince words. "They'll die like Fiera did. They'll suffer under the blight of the crystals on this land."

Vi swallowed hard, looking at the crystals that surrounded her. This was the physical essence of Yargen's power—the power of life, light, and creation. But it had only ever spelled death for those she loved. It was a stain on her family's history. One that Vi would take up the torch from Fiera to burn away.

"But those deaths will mean something, this time. We're on the right path. This time, it ends."

Don't miss the epic conclusion of Vi's story in...

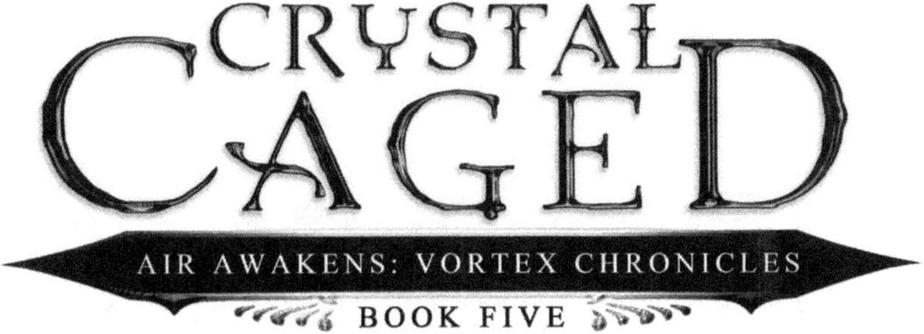

Learn more about CRYSTAL CAGED (Air Awakens: Vortex
Chonicles, #5) and grab your copy at:
http://viewbook.at/CrystalCaged

Want to make sure you never miss a giveaway, cover reveal, or
release day?

Sign up for Elise Kova's Mailing List:
http://elisekova.com/subscribe

ABOUT THE AUTHOR

ELISE KOVA has always had a profound love of fantastical worlds. Somehow, she managed to focus on the real world long enough to graduate with a Master's in Business Administration before crawling back under her favorite writing blanket to conceptualize her next magic system. She currently lives in St. Petersburg, Florida, and when she is not writing can be found playing video games, watching anime, or talking with readers on social media.

She invites readers to get first looks, giveaways, and more by subscribing to her newsletter at: http://elisekova.com/subscribe

Visit her on the web at:
http://elisekova.com/
https://twitter.com/EliseKova
https://www.facebook.com/AuthorEliseKova/
https://www.instagram.com/elise.kova/
See all of Elise's titles on her Amazon page:
http://author.to/EliseKova

www.ingramcontent.com/pod-product-compliance
Lightning Source LLC
Chambersburg PA
CBHW071129180726
48291CB00007B/2103